ALFRED OF WESSEX

Book Two:

VENGEANCE

MICHAEL CARDEN

Also by the author:

Alfred of Wessex, Book One: Inheritance

The Bike Ride Books series by Mike Carden:

The Full English: Pedalling through England, Mid-Life Crisis and Truly Rampant Man-Flu

A Bit Scott-ish: Pedalling through Scotland in Search of Adventure, Nature and Lemon Drizzle Cake

A Lake District Grand Tour. Pedalling through Lakeland: The Challenge, The History, The Wildlife, The Scones

ACKNOWLEDGEMENTS

This is a work of historical fiction
and so any names, actions or characters
resembling modern persons are entirely coincidental.

My thanks go to those who have helped me along the way,
including Jenny Ashby at the English Companions and
Peter Bone.

The cover photo is of a fabulous replica of an Anglo-
Saxon sword unearthed at Abingdon; the replica was made
by Patrick Barta, photographed by Tomas Man, and I am
grateful to them.

The cover design is by Amelia Blantern.

This is a novel
rather than a history book,
but for the historical background,
please see the notes
at the end of the book.

You will also find there
a list of the major characters.

You can find a bibliography online
at https://mikecarden.co.uk/

Wessex, 875 AD

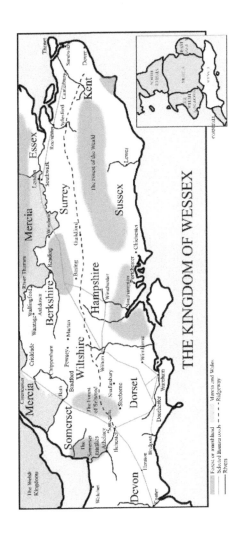

THE KINGDOM OF WESSEX

ALFRED OF WESSEX

CHAPTER 1

Wareham's great hall was silent.

From small windows high in the walls, with the shutters pulled to the side, beams of a bright morning sun picked out his friends in half-light, half-shade.

Alfred stood at one end of the long table. To his right sat Elswith. A shaft of sunlight reflected back from his wife's gorse-flower yellow over-dress, the white sleeves of the under-dress and the white veil covering her hair. He was aware of the serious expression on her pale face as she watched him.

They were all here, his closest friends from the battles and raids of four years before. All here, he thought, except for those who did not survive those battles. His brother above all. His brother who he had not been able to save. His brother who had nominated him as his heir to the Kingdom of Wessex, which was why he was here now.

Had he wanted to be King? Even now he sometimes wasn't sure. But King he was. And for four years.

He felt like he was a different man. Stronger. More confident, perhaps. Decisions came to him more easily, though he wasn't sure if they were always the right ones. He felt ready. Ready for whatever would come. Usually, anyway.

Noth was sitting to his left, closest friend since they were boys, when Alfred's father and brothers had been Kings of Wessex. The sunlight gleamed on the golden embroidered thread at the neck of Noth's tunic and played across his face. From within his beard he had a half-smile of encouragement for Alfred.

Then there was young Wulfred. He was no longer the boy who had defied his uncle, the Ealdorman of Hampshire, to fight alongside Alfred, but still had a young face under a mop of fair hair. He also had his usual keen expression, as he too waited for Alfred to speak.

Further along the table sat Osric, captain of the King of Wessex's warriors. Alfred's warriors. Osric pushed dark hair from his forehead, his face serious, his eyes intense as he watched Alfred scanning those seated at the table.

Next to Elswith was Ethelwulf, her half-brother and Alfred's Ealdorman of Wiltshire. As so many times before, Alfred thought how alike they were with their dark hair and brown eyes.

Then there was Odda, Ealdorman of Devon, and Garrulf, Ealdorman of Dorset, his closest allies amongst the Ealdormen on the Council. A balance, along with Ethelwulf, against those who continually opposed him, the Ealdormen of Hampshire and Somerset, who even now maintained that Alfred's nephew should be King of Wessex.

Opposite Osric was Athelheah, the Bishop of Sherborne appointed by Alfred, and the Bishop of Winchester, purple capes over their long white robes. They were a contrast with the Ealdormen in their long tunics belted at the waist with loops for scabbards for a sword and a long-knife.

By them sat Forthred, his brother's Secretary and now Alfred's, a loyal, quiet man, seemingly always ready with a quill and vellum.

Alfred leaned forwards, hands flat on the table.

"We're almost exactly four years," he said, "into the agreement I made with the Danes following our defeat at

Wilton. King Guthrum gave us five years in return for thousands of pounds of silver and we've made more payments since to keep the eastern shires safe. Well, fairly safe." He frowned, looking around the table. "We had hoped we had one year left."

No one spoke and he went on, "When my sister and King Burgred of Mercia fled a year ago, we thought the Danes might sweep on down into Wessex following the collapse of Mercia. They didn't, of course. Not then. But, Osric, would you repeat for us all what you have heard from Kent?"

He sat, while Osric stirred. "Yes, Alfred. Guthrum clearly feels that his hold on Mercia through King Ceolwulf is secure and is now back in East Anglia, his own 'kingdom'. He has taken large numbers of warriors with him and has been sending out messages for more to join him."

There was murmuring around the table, serious faces digesting the information.

"And there's more. Halfdan, who had joined forces with Guthrum to attack Mercia, is apparently confident in his own position in Northumbria. We know he has been fighting for lands in Ireland but now he has also sent word to gather longships in Northumbria. He's been inviting other vikings to join him there."

"Spell it out for us, Osric."

"There's no firm word of their target, but with the Kingdoms of Mercia, East Anglia and Northumbria already under their thumbs, I believe they're preparing for their next invasion. Wessex. Alfred, I believe the Danes are coming."

There was silence as the words sank in. All there knew how close Wessex had been to extinction when last the Danes had invaded the Kingdom.

Alfred pulled a map towards himself across the table. Made for Alfred and Noth by a tutor when they had been young, the map's vellum was old and torn. Just as viking raids on churches had brought the writing of new scriptures to a halt, there had been little map-making and other scholarship for some time. This was the best they had.

Those around Alfred leaned across the table to see as well as they could.

In its rough way, the map showed the heartland of Wessex - Wiltshire, Somerset, Dorset, Devon and Hampshire, plus the Cornish peninsula beyond Exeter. It also showed the eastern shires, Berkshire, Kent, Sussex and Surrey, only more recently part of the King of Wessex's domains.

The map sketched in the Kingdom of Mercia north of the River Thames and, further east, the Kingdom of East Anglia. Further north again was written 'the Kingdom of Northumbria', though none of those present had been that far north. Nor were they likely to, with Halfdan's Danes settling there.

"What about our western neighbours? Ealdorman Odda?"

The Ealdorman of Devon shifted his big frame on the wooden bench. He was only a little older than Alfred, but looked more than that. He had a great, bushy black beard, long hair part way down his back, but with either side of his head shaved. Big-chested, combative, he was a good man to have at your side.

"The Cornish are restive. There are even rumours that Halfdan's brother, Ubba, has been in Cornwall seeing King Hywel at Launceston, stirring up trouble. Hywel's father has died and he may want to show he is in control. I keep plenty of warriors in Exeter, and we range through Cornwall every so often to remind them where power lies. But if the Danes looked like they were going to win, I have no doubt the Cornish would join them in attacking Wessex."

"And Ireland?"

Odda went on in his loud, deep voice, "The Irish and the Norse in Dublin are keeping each other occupied at present. No, our main threat is from elsewhere, although there are enough pirates a-viking in the west who would fall on Wessex to take advantage of any weakness."

"What about immediately north of us?" Noth asked Osric. "If Guthrum has taken warriors to East Anglia, how does that leave Mercia?"

"The east of Mercia is firmly theirs – not all the men left with Guthrum by any means. Leicester, Lincoln, Tamworth and so on, are now effectively Danish towns. And the Danes are lording it over all those English who decided to stay rather than flee."

"What about the west?"

"When the Danes set up this Ceolwulf as their puppet king of western Mercia, most of the Ealdormen and thanes acknowledged him. Those few who didn't are now in Wessex." Osric nodded at Ethelwulf. "And of course their lands have been parcelled out to Ceolwulf's friends."

"Have any of them joined Guthrum in East Anglia?"

"We don't know. There will always be some who go over to the enemy completely, looking only for the best for themselves."

"But Cirencester, Hereford, Worcester and so on, they are still in English hands?" Alfred asked.

"Yes, not Gloucester though. Guthrum has left a large contingent there. And of course Ceolwulf has sworn a solemn oath before God to hand over the Kingdom to the Danes at any time they demand it. Guthrum still has hostages to that effect. Times are hard in the English-ruled lands, with grain and meat and horses sent east to the Danes as tribute."

"Horses," the Bishop of Winchester said. "Always horses. It's the same in our eastern shires – Kent, Surrey and Sussex. The tribute is always to include horses."

Osric spoke. "It makes the Danes so hard to fight. We only have horses for a proportion of our own men."

Alfred ran his hand through his beard. "And Guthrum still holds sway in London?"

"There's little change," Osric replied. "The moneyers and traders of London apparently get along just as well with Guthrum as they did with Mercia when London was a

Mercian town."

"So," Alfred said, "Guthrum and Halfdan have a free hand to gather warriors, horses and longships for an assault against Wessex. And meanwhile, Wessex is still divided. Speaking of which, when are the Ealdormen of Somerset and Hampshire due?"

"In about two hours."

A commotion in the doorway of the great hall interrupted the friendly talk amongst Alfred's friends. All eyes turned to find the Ealdormen of Somerset and Hampshire making their way across the great hall, several other men behind them.

"Ealdorman Eadwulf," Alfred said, "and Ealdorman Wulfhere."

Ealdorman Eadwulf was a tall man, with a long nose and a thin-lipped smile. He seemed even slighter than when Alfred had seen him last, and thinner in the face, but the expression had not changed, the expression which suggested that nothing and nobody quite came up to his standards.

"Ah, Alfred. Thank you for the invitation to the Council."

Alfred paused. Both Ealdormen had been invited to all the major Councils of the past four years, but had attended few of them.

"I'm glad that you can be here, Ealdorman Eadwulf – when you've been unable to attend recent Council meetings."

"I have not, I'm afraid, been well. Otherwise, of course..."

As they looked at each other, Alfred assumed this was nonsense.

"And Ealdorman Wulfhere, we've not seen you at a Council for some time. I'm glad that you were also able to come today."

Where Odda of Devon had been thick-set and cheerful, Wulfhere of Hampshire was much heavier, and grim. His jutting jaw and thick, greying moustache and his shaved head were just part of an aggressive posture that Alfred had not missed these past four years.

"There are things to discuss, Alfred. I've brought my sons as well."

He gestured towards two young men with him, who Alfred remembered all too well. Wulfstan and Wulfhard. They were both a little older than Alfred, Wulfstan was becoming a copy of his father, with a sulky, belligerent face only part disguised by a thick brown beard and long brown hair over his ears. The other, Wulfhard, was the younger of the two. He was clean-shaven, taller and bigger-shouldered. He still carried something of his father in him, but maybe not quite the same anger.

The Ealdorman of Hampshire lumbered over to the table, with no further word to his King. The sons, Alfred found, were both eyeing him. He really did not like these two, no more than he liked their father.

Another young man hung back. He was not at all familiar to Alfred. The stranger stepped forward. He was young, not much more than a boy perhaps, short, slightly pinch-faced, with thin dark hair.

"You... er... will not remember me, Lord King. But I am here with my cousin, Ealdorman Eadwulf," and he gestured towards the Ealdorman of Somerset, who had been quietly observing the meeting of Alfred with the Ealdorman of Hampshire.

"Ah, yes. Alfred," Eadwulf said, "this is my cousin, Eadred."

"Welcome, Eadred."

The young man sat by his cousin and Alfred waited until all were seated.

"This," he said, "is an important meeting of the Council. There are big decisions to make."

He paused, and gradually received nods of assent, then

gestured them to take their places at the great table.

"Thank you all for coming," Alfred said to them. "Now," he began, his voice loud enough to quieten the murmurs. "I've proposals to make to the Council. I'm sorry that all the Ealdormen aren't able to be present. The Ealdorman of Berkshire is ill. I propose to meet the Ealdormen of the eastern shires separately at Canterbury."

He looked around the table. This would have been easier had all his Ealdormen been present and more amenable, but he would have to work with what he had here.

"Guthrum and Halfdan are gathering their forces. The Danes are coming. We don't know when or where, but they will come. And we must be ready for an invasion of Wessex."

"So what do you have in mind?" the Ealdorman of Hampshire's over-loud voice said.

"I have three main proposals. Firstly, I intend that Wessex should build many more longships than we have now. And build all these new ones in the viking style, as fighting vessels not as merchant ships that can fight. While we are doing that, I have arranged to hire Frisian longships and their crews."

"And where," Wulfhere said, "do you intend to find the coin to do that? When we're still paying off Guthrum. Perhaps you've held back something?"

Alfred breathed deep. It was so important to stay in control.

"I've held nothing back, Ealdorman Wulfhere, as you well know. The payments to Guthrum have been arduous for all of us. But if we don't take these steps now, then we may just end up paying the Danes off all over again. We must all finance a fleet of longships capable of beating off an attack."

"A fleet? Responsible to you, but paid for by the shires. Oh, I don't think so."

Eadwulf's nasal voice then added, "I'm afraid the shire of Somerset has nothing further to spare by way of coin. It's all being used on our own defensive measures."

Odda was obviously becoming more and more agitated. "Ealdormen, this won't do. King Alfred is proposing a means by which he can defend the Kingdom of Wessex, while you're intent on saving coin for your own shires. The King's plans are more important than that."

"Odda," the Ealdorman of Somerset said to him, "we're merely pointing out the realities. Now, I think Alfred had two other proposals. And I would like to hear those as well."

Alfred looked from one to the other of them, then said, "Very well. My second proposal is that we build up a much larger force of warriors. As many of them with horses as possible, so that they'll be available to react to attack on any part of the Kingdom."

"And who will control this force?" Wulfhere asked.

"They'll be under the control of Lord Osric on behalf of the whole Kingdom."

"King's men then. Not shire men."

"They'll be available to defend all the shires of Wessex."

Wulfhere brooded a moment, then said, "And your third proposal?"

Alfred scratched at his chin through his beard. This was not going well, though that was not unexpected. "I propose that we fortify as many towns as possible. Ramparts and walls, with strong gates. Much like the Danes do when they take over an English town. I intend that we learn from them."

"So how will that be paid for?"

"I propose that each Ealdorman find the coin for the fortifications within his shire."

"Ah, I thought so."

"Wulfhere, Eadwulf," Alfred said, exasperated. "You oppose all my plans. Do you have alternatives?"

"Oh, I think we should have more longships and more warriors, but under the control of the Ealdormen, where they can be most useful. I think there might be a temptation for you to use the threat of the Danes to extend your own power at the expense of the Ealdormen."

Osric's deep voice interrupted. "Some might say that the opposite had happened."

"Meaning?"

"Meaning that in Alfred's grandfather's time, Ealdormen of the shires did not seek to control the King. They supported him. There seem to have been some Ealdormen who have turned away from that."

The Ealdorman of Hampshire brooded, but said nothing, while Eadwulf placed both hands together finger-tip to finger-tip, and pursed his lips.

"I," Osric went on, "have been patrolling the northern border constantly these last four years. I need more men. I must have more men. You will not send the men of Hampshire or Somerset, so it is the King who must control extra warriors. The same applies to longships. They must be under the control of the King or the Danes will pick off one shire after another and the whole Kingdom will be lost."

"Lord Osric, I'm sure we all appreciate the invaluable work you're doing on the border," Eadwulf said, "but you will not sway Wulfhere or myself. We will not be persuaded that it is in our shires' interests for us to cede any of our powers. I am sure that will also apply to our heirs going forwards. And that, Lord King, should be an end to that discussion."

"So of the five Ealdormen here," Odda's bullish voice came in, "only Garrulf, Ethelwulf and I are in favour?"

There was a silence. The answer was clear to all.

Odda shook his head in frustration, and then a thought seemed to occur to him. "And what did you imply by 'heirs', Eadwulf? Heirs to what? Your own lands or as Ealdormen of Somerset and Hampshire?"

Alfred jerked his head up. Ealdormen could nominate heirs to their own private lands, but not to the shire and the lands pertaining to the shire. That was not the way in Wessex. An Ealdorman did not, could not, have an heir. Those were decisions for the King.

He had been examining his hands while Odda and Eadwulf had been speaking, trying to think how to bring the Ealdormen of Somerset and Hampshire into an agreement. Instead, suddenly, Odda might have ended any chance of reconciliation.

Wulfhere got quickly to his feet. "He means heir to everything, Odda. Everything. Lands and shire. Hampshire will go to my sons. Somerset will go to Eadwulf's cousin. The Ealdorman of Hampshire and I believe that if Alfred was nominated as heir by his father and brother, then we can nominate our own heirs. I for one will not allow my sons' inheritance to be given away."

Odda was also on his feet now, standing opposite Wulfhere, as was Osric at the other end of the table. Alfred glanced at his other friends. All of them showed different degrees of anger.

"Your own lands," Odda said, "are yours to give. Your shire is not. In Wessex, Kings appoint Ealdormen."

"They might do in Devon, but they don't in Hampshire or Somerset. And I think you may find that there are Ealdormen in eastern Wessex who feel the same."

"You see, Alfred," Eadwulf's voice came from between the two as they stared at each other, "this is where we disagree." Eadwulf went on, "So we would be a little chary of giving more power away in the form of more warriors and longships, if a King of Wessex might use them to deprive us of our rights."

"Ealdormen!" Alfred had remained seated through all this, and raised his voice for the first time. "Please sit. And control yourselves. We can debate this, but not here and now."

There was a silence as Wulfhere looked from the Ealdorman of Devon to Osric, antipathy on all three faces. "Well, debate then, if you wish, but the Ealdorman of Hampshire remains the power in Hampshire and you would all do well to remember that. I will not countenance interference in my own running of the shire."

"So will you do nothing to help Wessex build up its defences against the Danes?" Alfred said to him.

"On the contrary, I will build up Hampshire's defences, so as to protect her from any attack." He paused, looking at Alfred. "Any attack at all."

He sat down, followed by Odda and Osric, and there was a silence as all took in the implication of his words.

"What Ealdorman Wulfhere means," Eadwulf broke the silence, "I'm sure, is attacks by Danes or Norse. And I would like to say that the shire of Somerset plans to take its place in the fight against the Danes. To do that, we do need consistency, and I'd like this Council today to endorse the choice of my cousin Eadred as my heir to the shire of Somerset, so that I can train him properly in the ways of the shire."

All eyes turned to Alfred, who rubbed at his chin through his beard.

It was Osric who spoke. "This Council cannot bind the King on his choice of Ealdorman. Nor can it properly suggest who might be a suitable Ealdorman when your time should come, Ealdorman Eadwulf."

"I think both are possible, Lord Osric. Perhaps the King will want to ensure the shire of Somerset's full participation in his plans by allowing this concession. Lord King?"

Alfred sucked at his lip, then raised his eyes to the Ealdorman of Somerset. "I'm sorry, Eadwulf. I'm not prepared to commit myself now. Should your cousin prove that he'd be a suitable Ealdorman, that would be a different matter. But he has not done so yet."

"He is my choice, Alfred, and that should be good enough for you. Unless, of course, you have other plans for the shire of Somerset." His eyes strayed to Noth, sitting quietly but attentively at the other end of the table. "Or why else would my sister's daughter, Ealhburh, have been married to my cousin, Lord Ethelnoth?"

"I've made no decisions about the shire of Somerset in the event of your death, my Lord." He was conscious that he had raised his voice, and he calmed himself. "And nor do I intend to."

"Not even to bind my shire into your plans for dealing with the Danes?"

"I'd hope that you would take your part in that, even without my agreeing to appointing Eadred as heir to Somerset."

"Well, we shall see," he said.

CHAPTER 2

"Archbishop," Alfred said, bending to kiss the ring on the outstretched hand.

"Lord King."

The words had not been said with great pleasure and Alfred looked up to find the elderly cleric's face hard and unfriendly.

They were in the Archbishop's private rooms in Canterbury, Alfred having arrived with Noth, Wulfred and Forthred that morning.

The room was sparsely furnished, with two high-sided wooden chairs facing each other across a small table.

The Archbishop was clothed in his usual purple robe, his staff of office leaning against a table bearing a large bible.

"Archbishop, you probably know why I am here. I have had a letter from the Pope. No doubt you know about it."

"Yes, Alfred."

Alfred waited, but nothing more was forthcoming.

"He's admonishing me for taking payment from the Church to help with payments to the Danes."

"And not only that, I think."

"I had no choice, Archbishop. The Church lands I have taken over were owed in debts or in lieu so that Wessex can make those payments."

"That is not how the Church sees it. The Pope and I insist that you return them."

"With the threat of excommunication."

"I have not asked for that."

"An excommunicated King would be difficult for all concerned. You included, Archbishop. And without the payments to the Danes, Wessex and your Church would no longer exist. That silver has to come from somewhere."

"Alfred, I went along with your crowning as King, although I was not consulted at the time. There were and are other candidates."

Alfred thought of his nephews, Helm and Wold, his older brother's sons, his sister-in-law Winifred's sons. These two legitimate, unlike his other nephew, Oswald. Helm had been the choice of both the Ealdormen of Hampshire and Somerset and both Helm and Wold were under the care of Winifred and Wulfhere in Hampshire. Who knew what trouble they might stir. Especially if they had the support of the Archbishop.

"Is that too a threat, Archbishop?"

"I am a man of God, Alfred. I do not make threats. Nor does the Pope. However-"

"Yes, 'However'. Archbishop, when the time comes I will freely endow churches, abbeys and nunneries and I will rebuild what the Danes have destroyed. But first, Wessex must survive. Will you support me in that?"

There was a pause.

"For now, Alfred. For now."

The Ealdormen, thanes and clerics of Kent, Sussex and Surrey were crowded into the royal hall in Canterbury. The atmosphere was ripe and the noise level high.

On Alfred's left sat the Ealdormen of Sussex and of

Surrey together with the new Ealdorman of Kent, each of whom now held considerably more royal land than he had the day before.

To Alfred's right at the high table, the Archbishop rose to his feet and some of the noise abated.

Raising both arms wide, the Archbishop closed his eyes and began the opening prayer in Latin. Within seconds, there was silence apart from the old man's voice intoning.

When he had finished and sat down, Alfred waited. He had hoped for more. Some words to show a measure of support.

Alfred stood. "Archbishop, Ealdormen, thanes, Abbots, Bishops. Thank you for coming to my Council."

There was a rumble from those present.

"First, I would like to hear from our new Ealdorman of Kent his views of the position here."

The Ealdorman of Kent rose, all eyes on him. He was bearded, tall, well-built, with one hand on the hilt of the sword in its scabbard on his belt. He was a fighting man, and this was the reason Alfred had appointed him.

The Ealdorman described raids by longships around the coasts, but no significant inroads made by armies. These were vikings - pirates - under no leadership but their own.

Then Alfred told of his own hopes and plans for when the time came - the longships, the ramparts around towns, the larger fighting force of warriors.

"But there may be no time," he said. He told them what he knew of the Danes in East Anglia and in Northumbria. None of it was news to the Ealdormen.

"For now," he went on, "we must be united and prepared to fight wherever they may land. And as part of that unity, I have given you gifts of land. In return, I ask your loyalty and your fighting men, whenever I call for them."

The answering noises from those around were, he thought, not entirely enthusiastic.

***

"It sticks in my throat how much you had to give them to keep their loyalty."

Alfred and Noth were talking quietly in the guest room following the Council.

"No choice, Noth. The Archbishop told me that a good number feel they have been bled dry by the payments I have needed for the Danes. He says that if and when there is another Danish invasion, some may decide to take their chances with the Danes. I'm hoping my gifts tie them to me at least as much as the oaths they swore to me."

"Did it help your father when he gave away a tenth of all his lands when he went to Rome?"

"You know it didn't. But tell me what else I can do. The Danes are coming, Noth."

"It doesn't help with the Ealdormen of Somerset and Hampshire either. And the Archbishop is not exactly an ardent supporter."

"No, though I wanted to speak to you about Somerset. Keep this to yourself, but I plan to make you Ealdorman instead of young Eadred."

"What?"

"You are a cousin of his as well, more distant admittedly. You have manors there already and I've given you more."

"A good bit more distant a cousin, Alfred."

"And you're married to Ealhburh, his niece. She brings her own lands."

"But Eadwulf probably hates me. Why would he accept me as heir?"

"He won't know. I'll not accept any nominated heir from him. But should Eadwulf die any time soon, you will be the next Ealdorman of Somerset. In the meantime, I will give you more land there and you should spend time in the shire. Meet up with old friends and distant relatives. Spend time with Ealhburh."

"But Alfred-"

"I need Somerset on our side, Noth. And I can't think of a better way."

"Eadwulf will realise, surely. And then what?"

"Then, I don't know."

"You could alienate Eadwulf and probably Wulfhere just when you say the Danes are coming. You realise that?"

Alfred frowned. "It's a risk, I know. But between these Ealdormen, the Archbishop and the likelihood of another Danish invasion, what isn't a risk? Noth, every decision I make is a risk."

"Time we were back in the west then."

"Yes, let's leave tomorrow. Elswith was going to meet me in Wareham. Will you go to Somerset? To Ealhburh?"

"If you want me to."

Alfred smiled. "I do. And Elswith would definitely want you to."

"Alright. And then I'll meet up with you in Wareham. You didn't tell the Council here in Kent that you already have four longships underway."

"No. No, I didn't. They can know soon enough."

Elswith's arm was linked through Alfred's as they walked through Wareham's market.

The town was busy with traders and farming folk looking to sell their wares to the King's household, his warriors and the shipwrights brought in to work on the longships at the boatyard.

Alfred tried to ignore their calls, though Elswith smiled acknowledgements, and they made their way towards the river.

"So you haven't been excommunicated?"

Alfred smiled. "Not yet."

"The church wouldn't really, would they? You're fighting pagans."

"I don't honestly think so, Elswith. But I could do with

more support from the Archbishop."

"Is he undermining you?"

"I think you can say we have a truce just now."

"Is that enough?"

"I hope so."

They walked on in silence, passing through the gate and heading towards the river, then Alfred said, "I was going to bring Ethelflaed with us to the boatyard."

"She's helping Bennath with the little ones." She stopped walking and turned to face Alfred, talking quietly. "I've heard that people are unhappy that we have a Cornish nurse for them. They say you can't trust someone Cornish."

"Bennath? She's been with the family since she was young."

"I know that. And I don't mean that I don't trust her. It's just what people are saying - where her loyalties would lie if the Cornish allied with the Danes again."

Alfred pondered. "No," he said. "Bennath would be fine."

They walked on, though Alfred was still wondering about the Cornish within Wessex as they reached the boatyard teeming with craftsmen and labourers. There was shouting and swearing in a number of languages, especially Frisian.

In the centre of all the activity stood two part complete longships, each held in place on the riverbank by a network wooden beams.

While one longship was mostly still skeletal, the other had low, planked sides running in smooth curves which rose to meet high up at prow and stern.

"They look beautiful, Alfred," Elswith was saying. "So sleek."

"We're building them a little bigger than most of the viking longships. The Danes want to be able to row up rivers as well as cross seas. We need to battle them at sea and keep them away from our rivers. So a larger longship should have an advantage."

One of the Frisians looked up, smiling. He had broad shoulders from years at the oars of a viking longship, before his escape to Wessex, though it was clear that he was not so lean in the body as he had been.

"Radmer," Alfred said. "They look wonderful."

"Lord King, Lady Elswith," Radmer said, "they should, with my friends here to build them for you."

"We're grateful."

"Thank you, Lord King."

Alfred said, "So this one is nearly ready. The second one?"

"A few weeks."

"And you have one almost complete at Exeter?"

"Yes."

"What about the one at Southampton?"

"Not quite finished, Lord King. And, well, it is more difficult there than here."

"Tell me."

Radmer moved closer, his voice lowering. "The Ealdorman of Hampshire keeps warriors close by. I think when the longship is complete, unless you hurry it away, you may find that it is an Ealdorman's longship, not a King's."

Alfred frowned. It was easier building longships in Dorset and Devon where Garrulf and Odda were his friends and supporters, than in Hampshire. But Southampton had shipwrights already, who only needed some Frisian guidance. It had been a calculated risk. One that now he was beginning to regret.

"Thanks for telling me, Radmer. When can it be ready? And can it be rowed out at night?"

"Soon. And yes. The Ealdorman won't like it."

"No, he won't. Do it though."

"I am sorry for you, King Alfred."

"For me?"

"You have this threat from the Danes. Invasions. Raids along the coast. And behind you there are those who oppose you in every way they can. Who want to be little kings in their own lands or perhaps the power behind a different King of Wessex. Almost at any cost. You should be very careful, King Alfred."

Alfred felt Elswith's hand tighten on his arm.

"Careful, Radmer? Or take the fight to the enemy?"

"Which enemy, Lord King?"

CHAPTER 3

The pain in his stomach had come on during the night. Alfred had lain awake trying to find a comfortable position. Finally he had drifted off, only to wake violently in the darkness as the door from their sleeping quarters to the great hall was hammered from the outside.

"Alfred! Lord King!" It was Wulfred's voice.

Shrieks and cries leapt in the darkness from three suddenly roused and frightened children. Elswith's voice tried to calm them.

Alfred jerked upright and pain shot up from deep inside his stomach. He gritted his teeth, but a moan came out even so. Gradually he made himself breathe, trying to master the pain, then spoke toward the closed door, still being hammered from the outside.

"Alfred!"

"I'm coming, Wulfred." Another breath, and he pulled the blanket off himself. He stood, teeth clenched, as another flash of pain ran deep inside his stomach.

"What is it, Wulfred?" he spoke toward the door, although by no means loud enough to be heard over the hammering from outside and the crying inside.

He pushed himself off from the bed toward the door,

aware that Wulfred was shouting something, but unable to hear the words, only the panic in his voice.

"Shush, Edward, I can't hear your uncle Wulfred."

With care, and holding his stomach with one hand, Alfred unlatched the door and pulled it open. The hammering stopped, and he became aware of more distant noises, somewhere beyond the Ealdorman of Dorset's hall here in Wareham.

Wulfred stood in the doorway, part lit by a candle he was holding up in one hand, the other sheltering the flame from the draught of the opening door. He looked dishevelled, fair hair awry, but – significantly – he was wearing his mail-coat, belted at the waist, with a sword in its scabbard.

"Danes, Alfred! Down by the longships. They're attacking the longships."

Alfred cursed under his breath and turned back into the darkness of the room.

"I am so sorry, Lady Elswith," Wulfred said across the gloomy room as he stepped over the threshold to hold up the candle and give Alfred light to see by.

Elswith had baby Gifu crying at her shoulder and a scared Edward huddled on to her lap. Of the children, only Ethelflaed was calm, standing by her mother by the edge of the bed, her eyes reflecting the candlelight as she watched him.

He bent to open the wooden chest by the door, stiffly pulling out his mail-coat.

Taking a deep breath, he began to raise the heavy mail to pull on over his head, but stopped in mid-movement, as pain stabbed upwards and a wave of nausea took him.

Alfred felt a hand on his arm and found Wulfred staring at him, face full of fear and worry.

The young man's eyes moved rapidly to find where to set down the candle-holder, when a small hand lifted it away from him.

"I've got it, Uncle Wulfred," the little girl said, and Wulfred was able to turn and take the mail-coat from Alfred.

Alfred stood, breathing deeply, eyes closed, leaning on the door-frame. He waited, standing still, for the worst to pass. As the pain subsided, he became aware that his younger children were now quiet, watching him, with Elswith soothing them. Outside he could hear a commotion – shouting in the distance and the clashing of weapons.

He stood upright carefully, half raising his arms for Wulfred to pass the mail-coat over his head. The heavy weight bore down on his shoulders, and he opened his eyes to see that Wulfred had reached into the chest to find the belt. Wulfred passed it around him and, as he waited for the belt to tighten, he held his breath. But Wulfred was pulling in the slack with great care and, once the belt was fixed with part of the weight of the mail-coat taken by it, some of the tension went out of Alfred.

"Thank you," he said. "My sword..."

Wulfred was already fitting the scabbard and its sword into the loops on the belt.

"I have your shield, Alfred. Can you walk?"

With a frustration born of pain, Alfred said angrily, "Yes, of course. I'm not-"

Wulfred flinched in the dim light of the candle and Elswith's voice came softly across the room, her children quiet now. "Alfred, Wulfred is concerned for you. And so am I. You're no help like that. Thank the Lord that Noth is back from Somerset. Let Wulfred and him deal with the raiders."

"No. Look, I'm sorry, Wulfred. But I'll be fine as soon as I start moving." He turned back to Elswith and the children. "Elswith, keep the door bar in place, just in case, and I'll make sure there are men stationed outside."

His voice felt tight with the tension and pain, but as he looked down at little Ethelflaed standing there with her candle, big eyes watching him, he said, "I won't be long, sweetheart. Shut the door behind me and push the bar across, if you can manage."

Wulfred held out his helmet, the candle reflecting from

the polished black of the dome and from the brass rims around the outside. Alfred lifted the helmet onto his head, feeling the familiar snug fit of the calf-leather inside and of the nose-piece and cheek-flaps against his face.

Carefully, he moved forward, out of the room and into the great hall where the younger warriors would sleep. The embers of the fire in the centre were glowing and there were the usual night-time aromas of smoke and sweat. There was just enough light to take in the empty benches around the outside of the hall, with blankets and sheepskins abandoned by his warriors. They would be already gone at the first sound of alarm.

Trying to contain the ache and pain from his stomach, he glanced back towards the door to the sleeping quarters. There she was, his little girl in her linen night-dress, standing the candle on the floor and pushing the door closed. He waited a moment until he heard the door bar slide into place.

"Good. Wulfred, we should go."

Following a pace behind Wulfred, Alfred walked gingerly across the darkened great hall toward the outer door. His mind starting to clear, he began to take stock of their defences.

Wareham had a low rampart with palings on top, built recently by Garrulf as Ealdorman of Dorset. But Garrulf and most of his men were away at his hall in Dorchester. And in any case, the rampart didn't cover the riverbank, where Alfred was overseeing the building of two longships.

The main part of Alfred's warriors were on the northern border with Mercia under cousin Osric. At least Noth was here along with some of their warriors, perhaps one hundred altogether. Few enough to defend the ramparts from an attack.

Just two dozen warriors would have been on guard overnight. They would have been spread around the fences on top of the low rampart with some immediately outside the great hall. More would have been at the boatyard by the river just outside the south eastern ramparts watching over two almost complete longships.

None of Alfred's seaworthy longships, with their oarsmen and warriors, were here. They were spread along the coastline of Wessex, with the aim of giving advance warning of viking raids. It seemed that had failed.

As they stepped out into the night air, Alfred saw that the sky was beginning to lighten in the east.

Wulfred had paused outside the oak door, where two warriors stood on guard, mailed and helmeted, swords in hands, looking southwards towards the river, the source of the commotion.

"You two," Alfred said. "Under no circumstances will you stray from this door. You will guard my family with your lives if Danes appear. I'll send other warriors to you as well."

They had both turned to face him in the semi-darkness.

"Yes, Lord King," one said.

Wulfred laid a hand on Alfred's arm. "My shield is here. Can you take yours, my Lord?"

As Wulfred held the shield up, Alfred passed his left arm through the straps on its back and his hand into the iron boss. It was heavy and the strain pulled at his stomach, but he put the pain into a box inside his head and said, "Yes. Now, tell me what you know."

Wulfred reached down and rose with his own shield on his arm.

"Where's your helmet?" Alfred said.

"It's back in the hall."

"Get it first. But be quick."

Wulfred disappeared back into the black of the hall, but in seconds was back, pulling a helmet on to his head.

"Now, what's happening?" Alfred said, already walking towards the noise down the dark lanes.

"The raid seems to have targeted the longships. Noth was first to be raised by the guards and he sent me off to find you." Alfred's pace was starting to quicken now and

Wulfred was slightly breathless. "He's taken most of the men to counter the raid at the boatyard, but also ordered others to make for the ramparts and the town quay."

"Good."

Alfred paused in his stride and listened again to the noises from the riverbank. Behind and to west and east all was quiet and he prayed it would remain what it appeared to be – a raid at the riverside, not a full-scale attack on the town.

He was about to continue when they both heard the noise of booted feet and armed men approaching through the half-darkness. He laid his right hand on the hilt of his sword and slid it free from the scabbard. Wulfred, next to him, did likewise and they stood a step apart, swords held lightly, ready.

He could see a body of men coming fast toward them.

"Stop," Alfred said, his voice surer now than earlier. "English or Dane?"

A voice came from the group. "English, Lord King. We're your men."

"Good. Where are you going?"

"To the north gate on Lord Ethelnoth's orders. Others are making for the west and east gates to reinforce them as well."

"Where is Lord Ethelnoth?"

"At the river by the south east corner. Between the rampart and the nunnery."

"On you go then. Keep careful watch."

Alfred and Wulfred sheathed their swords and stepped aside to allow the men, a dozen of them, to pass.

"He'll be this way, Alfred," Wulfred said, leading Alfred down an alleyway, small houses crammed together on either side. To their right they heard singing, chanting. Women's voices from behind wooden fencing.

Past the last of the houses, on the slope where the rampart and its palisade ran down into the river, Alfred saw men's shapes silhouetted against the flowing water.

With the singing from the nunnery as a background, Alfred heard Noth giving orders in a quiet but commanding voice.

"... and you dozen remain here. Now, when the horn blows..."

Noth tailed off as he saw Alfred and Wulfred make their way through the warriors. There were around fifty there, all armed and many with mail-coat and helmet.

"Alfred," Noth said across their heads, and Alfred made his way through the warriors.

In the darkness, with voices kept low, Alfred was aware of the smell of sweat and ale, and of fear and excitement as the men formed a passage for them.

Alfred said, "Tell me what's happening."

"The Danes have attacked downriver. We only have reports of one longship, but my guess is there are more. They came first to the boatyard beyond the palisade there and they've hacked about the two part-built longships. They seem to have pulled away for the moment and I don't know why. Maybe they've decided we're too many for them, or maybe they're about to launch a raid on the town via the quayside."

"Your plans?"

"I'm about to lead a raid out of the eastern gate. We'll try to get around the back of the Danes if they're still there. If I blow two blasts on this horn, that'll mean that there aren't too many for us and that we're attacking. A further group from here will sally out after us. I'll leave some warriors here on the riverbank to guard the nunnery and more to hold the gate. I plan to lead the raid. Will you join me?"

Alfred had barely opened his mouth to respond, when Wulfred took Noth's arm and spoke softly in his ear. Noth looked up at Alfred and his expression changed. He glanced at the men waiting around them and listening to the talk of their Lords.

"Lord King, on second thoughts, you'd be best placed to take charge of the whole town if you remain at the gate."

Alfred frowned. He understood all too well that Wulfred had whispered to Noth of his condition tonight, but that no word of that should get to the ears of these warriors. He should go on this night raid with Noth, but in truth he was not sure if he was capable of it. Not yet.

Angry with himself, with his body, he said loudly so that all around would hear, "Very well, Lord Ethelnoth. I'll take charge here. You lead the raid."

He felt more than saw Noth nod his head, then his friend was saying, "Where are Elswith and the children? Are they safe?"

"There are just two guards on the door."

Noth spoke to some of the men at his side. "You four, go to the great hall. You're to make sure that no Danes reach the King's family. Does one of you have a horn? Yes? Then blow that if there's any sign of Danes inside the town. One long blast."

Alfred took Noth's arm and in an undertone said, "Noth, I really want to be with you on the raid-..."

"No, absolutely not." Noth's voice was very quiet, but determined. "The men can't know of how the pain takes you, but you must never hide it from your friends. Now, we're going – if you agree my plan, that is?"

"Of course. I'll be at the gate."

"Good." Noth turned to Wulfred again. "Will you take charge of the second party? Two blasts of the horn and out you come. Otherwise, stay here."

The sky was turning bluer in the moments before the sun would climb above the eastern horizon and Wulfred's nod was just about visible.

Noth lifted his head to the warriors around him. "You know your positions. Lord Wulfred will lead the second party from the gate. Those with me, we go now."

He gave a small bow of his head to Alfred. "If you would follow on as far as the gate?"

"Yes, go. Before the sun appears."

***

It felt an age waiting by the gate. The sun was already above the rim of the world, casting its yellow light across the land.

He frowned. He should be out there.

Easing his shoulders backward and lifting his shield on his arm, he tested for more pain, but now there was an ache, not the stabbing pains, and he could abide that. Surely.

A horn blew in the distance. One blast at first, and Alfred looked back over his shoulder in the direction of the great hall, where he hoped warriors would be standing guard, but a second blast came, and this time it was clear that it was from outside the gate. Then there came the sound of fighting. Shouts. Screams. Blade on shield. Blade on blade.

"Men," Alfred said to the warriors at the gate with him, "we divide, one part head right, straight for the river and then cut across along the riverbank to the boatyard. You should take the Danes from behind. The other group will head straight across through those trees."

Wulfred, next to him, said, "We? Alfred, you said you'd stay here."

"No, you lead the party to the riverbank, as fast as possible. I'll bring the remainder on but hold back. It's just in case any Danes plan on coming towards the town through those bushes and trees. And if we're needed in the fight. In reserve."

He lifted his voice to the men standing by the gate. "Open up," he shouted. "The first dozen men through the gate, follow Lord Wulfred. The rest with me."

Wulfred frowned at him, but there was no time to argue, as, with clanks and bangs, the wooden bar was lifted from the inside of the gate and men streamed through.

Alfred stepped through the gate behind the last of the men. Wulfred's group were already heading down toward the river, the low sun glinting on the left side of their helmets and on swords, drawn and ready.

He looked around at the dozen men behind him.

"Is one of you more senior?"

A veteran warrior stepped forward, the grey in his beard matching the iron of his helmet. "I am, Lord King."

"You'll be in charge at the gate here. The gate stays barred, you understand. You know that a horn from behind you means Danes are at the great hall." Alfred motioned to the man's own horn tied at his belt. "Repeat that call towards us, if you should hear it."

The man nodded and Alfred set off grimly towards where the noise of battle was growing. He heard the gate bang closed behind him and the locking-bar clunk into place. He drew his sword, feeling the leather-bound hilt, which balanced the iron blade and its steel cutting edges.

Slowly, he began leading the men towards the sound of fighting ahead.

The sun was climbing above the horizon but it was dark when they plunged into a stand of trees, the noise of fighting growing all the time.

His men had fanned out around and in front of him and, in all honesty, he was grateful. He didn't know if he could really swing a sword at the moment, or if the movement would leave him throwing up on the ground. It had happened before.

Light grew ahead of them and then they were out into the sunlight, the trees behind them, a scene of confusion ahead. Two part-built longships stood side by side. Further downstream, their backs to a longship at the river behind them, some fifty Danes were fighting on two fronts. Noth and his men had come on them from the far side and now Wulfred's men were attacking along the riverbank.

The two sides were evenly matched in numbers. Alfred's men might make a difference.

"Straight in at them!" he shouted.

His men burst past him, directly at the Danes, voices

raised.

Alfred followed them. There was one-on-one fighting. Swords, long-knives, spears, shields clashing, men shouting and swearing.

"Work together," he shouted. Frustrated, he caught the men up.

There ahead of him was a giant of a man, a Dane, sword in one hand, shield in the other, swinging both. Two men of his men fell, the one knocked to the floor by the Dane's shield, the other on the ground clutching at a bloodied arm.

No one stood between Alfred and the Dane.

The man wore a mail-coat and a helmet, the eyes invisible through the two eye holes above the nose guard. But his mouth was clear and he seemed to smile and took a step forward.

Alfred stood side on and raised his shield arm, his right hand holding his sword clear.

Another step from the Dane and the man's great sword was thundering towards Alfred's body. Alfred pulled his shield left. There was a crash as his left hand and arm took the shock of the blow. His own sword arm swung over but the Dane caught the sword on his own shield and took a step back, readying himself for the next attack.

Then there was a horn blown. And blown again. From where the Danes' longship was pulled up.

A commanding voice shouted.

The giant Dane hesitated. Another step back. And another.

And then all the Danes were easing backwards, shields held in a makeshift shield-wall as best they could, making for their longship and holding off the attacking English warriors.

Alfred followed his men down, then stood, sliding his sword back into its scabbard, watching the Danes.

There was no panic there, he could see. The Danes must have practised and practised this movement, the retreat to the longship while under attack.

He shook his head slightly as the front group of Danes used shields, swords and spears to hold off the English attackers while behind them, men pushed the longship into the river.

A shout and there was a surge forward from the Danes that took the men of Wessex by surprise. Suddenly there was a gap between the two sides and the shield-wall broke. The Danes ran back into the water, their shields and swords held high, with men on board pulling them over the gunwale, while the flow of the river drifted the longship away and downstream.

Some of Alfred's men followed into the river, but the movement was so fast that there was nothing that could be done.

Oars appeared, river water splashing up into the dawn sunlight, and the Danes were suddenly moving at speed.

On the riverbank, the English warriors watched them go. Alfred felt their mixture of elation and disappointment. They had won the skirmish here, but the Danes had gone, withdrawing their men confidently, and – judging by just two bodies lying on the riverbank – with few casualties.

Perhaps they had done what they had intended to do? What state were the two longships in at the boatyard, he wondered?

Alfred became aware of Noth and Wulfred walking up the slope toward him. They had sheathed their swords and were carrying helmets in their right hands, shields on their left arms. Both had set faces. It was Noth who spoke.

"Alfred, why are you here?" He sounded angry. "You look like death now that there's light to see by. Why didn't you stay by the gate?"

Alfred bent to lay his shield in the long grass and a twinge made him grimace. He stood upright again carefully.

He looked at his friends and tried to smile, but in truth, now that the Danes were gone, now that the fight was over, he felt like death.

"Noth, I, er..."

He broke off, raising his hands to lift off his helmet. And then it came. The wave of nausea and pain flew out from its box in his head and he doubled over and threw up, narrowly missing discarded helmet and shield.

He felt Noth's hands take his arms, holding him as the pain welled through him and then all went black.

He woke to find Elswith and Ethelflaed sitting by him. He was in bed. A blanket was over him, his mail-coat gone.

There was an ache from his stomach, but not the searing pain.

A dim light came through the open door.

He was in their sleeping quarters.

"Lie still." Elswith.

Ethelflaed's small hand took his.

Behind Elswith, framed against the light from the door, a young woman was holding baby Gifu on her shoulder.

Little Edward, just three years old, was clinging to her legs, his big eyes watching Alfred.

There was a movement to one side and he caught sight of Noth and Wulfred.

"What happened?" His voice sounded strange. Rough. "The Danes?"

Elswith's voice was quiet but firm. "Gone. Wulfred and Noth can tell you later, when you're up to it."

"The longships? Our longships?"

"They can be replaced. Built again."

"Built again," Alfred repeated.

Noth's voice. "And better news, Alfred. You missed puking on me."

Alfred smiled and closed his eyes.

"Sleep now, Alfred," Elswith said.

Yes. Yes, he could sleep now.

CHAPTER 4

It was midsummer's day before the two English longships at Wareham were ready. Meanwhile, Radmer had rowed the new longship away from Southampton at dead of night.

From Wulfhere at Winchester there was just silence.

But now there were four brand new English longships, sleek and shallow of draft, and yet higher and longer than their viking counterparts to hopefully give an advantage at sea.

They were needed. Since Alfred's visit to Canterbury, Dover had been raided, then Hastings and more recently, as far west as Chichester. This was not the fleet of longships said to be gathering in Northumbria. It was not even Guthrum's men, still in East Anglia. These were pirates. Raiders. Vikings.

Berthed around Poole Bay were another five older longships of English make – more traditional in pattern, more like a merchant vessel, but certainly capable of carrying warriors. And for the moment, that was the requirement.

When the three further longships hired from Frisia arrived, the flotilla would be ready. Then they would go in search of the raiders.

Word had it that there were seven viking longships. The combined English and Frisian flotilla would be twelve, but first they had to find the enemy and that might not be easy.

"When do you expect Radmer back with the Frisian longships, Alfred?" Ethelwulf asked.

"Any day now."

Alfred, Noth, Ethelwulf and Wulfred were talking in the great hall at Wareham. The day was windy and wet and the fire on the hearthstone before them flickered in the draughts from the windows high in the wooden walls.

"And then we move east?" Ethelwulf's finger moved along the coastline drawn roughly on the map lying on the table in front of them.

"Yes, I think all we can do is patrol along the coast and just hope that they show themselves."

"More than show themselves, Alfred," Ethelwulf said. "We need them somewhere we can contain them. Otherwise they'll see twelve longships bearing down on them and they'll be off."

"They've been working their way down the coast," Wulfred said. "Coming westwards. Maybe getting bolder? Do you think they might head for Portchester or even Southampton next time?"

"That's a thought." Alfred stroked his beard. "And if they did, we'd have a reasonable chance of blocking off an escape. Suppose we base ourselves at Portchester within the estuary and send patrols out into the Solent, north of the Isle of Wight, to try to sight them?"

"That seems about right," Ethelwulf said, nodding.

Noth placed a finger on the map, "Portchester is in Hampshire. I wonder what Wulfhere will say."

"We'll be defending Hampshire's shores. He'd better not say anything."

***

The Roman walls of Portchester were high, more than the height of three men, and Alfred marvelled at them. He had been here before of course, but each time he came, the power of the place caught at him. The stone-built fortifications were almost square, with each side about two hundred paces long. There were rounded turrets at the corners, along the walls and at the gates.

Many of the uneducated called the walls and buildings magical, built by giants long ago. He knew better, of course. But how could the Romans have assembled the men and the stone to build this structure, so strong that it still stood so many generations later? When his own people... Not yet, he thought, not yet. He surveyed the great stretch of the walls again. Walls like these would certainly keep out a small army of Danes.

"Lord King," the look-out standing by him said. "A sail."

Alfred turned to look southwards, shading his eyes with his hand, and, yes, a longship was coming into the estuary, making for Portchester and the row of longships tied up to the bank below the walls.

"Do you see any banners?" he asked.

The look-out was also shading his eyes against the sun, staring intently. "No, I don't think-... Yes, Lord King, two. I can see the wyvern of Wessex at the mast."

"Good. One of ours."

"And a red banner."

"Red. The Danes have been spotted then. Good. Tell my captains to meet me down by the longships."

"Yes, Lord King."

"And have the call-out sounded."

He looked out again and saw that the longship was making good time towards them. The wind and tide was helping it in under sail, but that meant that it would be the rowers that took them out of the estuary, unless the wind dropped.

A horn blowing below him brought him back to himself and he turned to follow the look-out down the stone steps. He made his way quickly alongside the inner wall towards the gate and then out to where the longships were straining against ropes.

The crews were already assembling, English and Frisian voices calling out and shouting orders. Swords, shields and knives were made ready. Thick leather jerkins and caps were put on. With ten longships here – the other two being out on patrol, there were some three hundred men milling around, readying the longships and preparing them for a fast row down the estuary.

All the men would know that they had twelve craft to the Danes' seven. Surely good odds.

And yet... and yet. These were Danes. Raiders. Pirates. Vikings. They lived for fighting. For raiding. They must train and prepare for exactly this.

Radmer had warned him. No matter the odds, in fact almost because of the odds, these men would fight and fight and kill.

And his men? What would they do?

He waited on the bank looking south at the slim hull of Radmer's vessel slipping through the water towards him under its pale square sail. The sun sparkled off the water.

"Lord King!" Radmer was shouting as men dropped the sail. A rope was thrown and tied to a wooden post in the riverbank. "The Danes are in the Solent. One of my other longships is keeping them within sight," he called, his Frisian accent strong.

"Come ashore, Radmer. Let's talk."

A narrow plank was thrown across the gap from the longship to the shore, and the Frisian came easily across, a life-time's confidence in his step.

"Where are they, Radmer?" Noth asked.

"Heading north-west. Probably for Southampton, or one of the harbours short of there if Southampton is too big a target."

Ethelwulf, standing by Alfred, said, "How many?"

"It is the seven we were hoping for."

"Good," Alfred said. "Let's get going. We mustn't let the faster longships get too far ahead of the older slower ones. But once we can see the enemy, we'll try to enclose them somewhere. It'll do no good just to chase them off. One way or another, we have to give them a bloody nose."

Radmer said, "Lord King, my guess is that they will try to find a quiet bay to rest up in overnight, then hit a town at first light."

"Yes, you're probably right."

"I have told the other longship to keep a watch on where they go, but to stay well back. We should be able to catch them somewhere. Either tonight or early tomorrow."

"You go ahead of the rest of us then and locate your other longship. Then come back for us."

"I-"

"Yes, Radmer."

"I was going to say that perhaps you should allow your men to do this. Your men and my men. The Danes at sea... That is their home. We, you, would be going into their home. Longship against longship. What if... what if you are killed?"

"Perhaps you should stay here," Ethelwulf said. "Who knows what can happen in a battle at sea?"

"No. No, I need to be there. And to be seen to be there."

Ethelwulf frowned. "Please then, take care. What would happen to Wessex if something happened to its King?"

"Alright. I'll take care."

The look in Ethelwulf's eyes suggested he didn't entirely believe Alfred.

"I will," Alfred said.

The oarsmen kept a steady pace as they rowed through the sheltered estuary from Portchester. The vessel flexed slightly in a gentle swell, with the smallest of creaks from the planking, while the oarsmen kept a rhythm, blade in, blade out.

Standing with Noth by the sternpost, Alfred felt the salt wind on his face. He looked around at his flotilla keeping pace so far, the voices of helmsmen drifting across the water.

At the entrance to the estuary, villages and harbours on either side, the waves grew higher. Now the longship was crackling as it rode over waves and down the far side. To Alfred, the waves seemed large and he began to feel queasy. This, he thought, was not his element.

Some of the extra warriors in the longship, trying to keep clear of the oarsmen, seemed to feel like Alfred, one retching over the gunwale.

Next to Alfred, the helmsman had a half-smile on his face. "A calm day at least, Lord King."

Alfred nodded, not trusting himself to speak.

The helmsman gave orders to the oarsmen and they turned westwards and then north-west into the Solent, the Isle of Wight to their left and mainland Hampshire to their right.

The wind was from over Alfred's left shoulder. More orders and the sail was raised, the oarsmen pulling hemp ropes and chattering, the sail snapping as it emptied and filled with gusts of wind.

The land to their right was slipping by faster, the sail pulling them on, the helmsman leaning on the tiller to make constant adjustments, the wake behind gurgling and swooshing. The motion in the water had changed though and Alfred, with relief, realised his stomach had settled.

He had given orders for the flotilla to split once they reached open sea. The older English longships would follow on under sail as fast as they were able.

With two Frisian longships somewhere ahead, if they could locate them, Alfred had seven vessels. He searched the sea behind and could make out the five longships following. He frowned and bit at his lip and hoped he had made a sensible decision. For now, it was more important that they should make contact with Radmer before darkness fell.

Even now, the sun was sinking toward the horizon at the end of a golden trail across the Solent. He looked at Noth and the helmsman and saw that they were screwing up their eyes as they scanned the sea ahead.

"There, Alfred! Radmer, I think." Noth was pointing just to the right of the sinking sun, and Alfred's eyes fixed on a longship powering toward them, oars flashing water into the air. "Yes, he still has the red banner at the mast."

The longship was quite close before a call went up to Alfred's right, which took away the beginnings of a smile of greeting for Radmer.

"Look there! More longships! Look!"

Alfred's eyes moved leftwards and he shaded them from the sun, squinting, before he too could see them. Suddenly it was clear that Radmer was not sprinting back to tell Alfred where he could find the Danish flotilla. He was fleeing.

There were longships coming out of the sinking sun at them. Alfred was uncertain how many of the enemy there were, but he would lay a wager that the group of longships on Radmer's tail amounted to seven. And he had just five here, six with Radmer. Not at all the odds he had intended, against what could be an experienced band of viking raiders in their sea-borne element. This could be a disaster.

"Make a gap!" he shouted, arms waving to the longships around and behind. "Let Radmer through!"

There were shouted orders all around the flotilla, sails quickly lowered, oarsmen manoeuvring their craft with urgency and warriors readying themselves.

Radmer's longship flew through the gap and Alfred watched it start to slew around behind them, before he turned back to squint into the sun.

"They've stopped, Alfred." Noth too was shading his eyes. "They thought they were hunting one English longship. Now they're not sure if they're the hunters or the hunted. Shall I have the horn blown for attack?"

Alfred looked right and left, finding that the other longships, including Radmer's now, were roughly in line. If the Danes would just delay long enough, the slower English longships would have time to catch up. Or, maybe...

"Alfred?" Noth was saying. "Shall I-..."

"No. Turn. Turn and flee. Now."

"But-"

"Helmsman. Turn! And signal the others. Turn, and row straight back down the route we came."

The helmsman grimaced, but he did as he was bid and soon the helmsmen of all six longships were turning their longships.

"Turn and row!" Alfred shouted again. "But keep the line across! No gaps!"

Seeing Noth's expression he said, "If we keep the longships together, the Danes will have less chance of seeing the five longships behind us. And our six longships might suddenly become eleven."

Light dawned in Noth's eyes and, as the order to keep the line across was repeated from longship to longship, realisation came to all those there. Once positioned, Alfred shouted again.

"Forward now! Go!" He waved his arm forwards and his call was repeated down the English line.

Oars bit with venom and the speed built, with Alfred holding on to the gunwale and watching carefully behind. Soon it was clear. The Danes were following and picking up speed. They were quicker, but were they quick enough? Alfred turned to look forward again and Noth was pointing to the south-east, where he could make out the sails of craft low in the water, coming straight for them.

"Helmsman. I don't want the Danes behind us to know that we're about to have another five longships join us. Can you make sure we stay exactly between them?"

"I can do more, Lord King, if you wish. The wind has

been swinging around. We can fill the sails of all our longships and make it less likely that they'll see past."

"Excellent. Do it, and pass the order along."

Cream-coloured sails were soon raised and billowing in the wind, the ropes cracking and straining, but relieving the oarsmen of their work. Alfred looked back to find the Danes had done the same and were definitely closing, their sails glowing in the red light of the sun in its last moments of the day.

He turned his gaze to the front again. The five slower English longships were rapidly growing in size on the darkening water, each having lowered its sail, with oars visible and pulling back and forwards.

"Helmsman. Pass on the following. We keep together until I order a horn-blast, then those longships to our right peel away right and those on our left peel away left. We'll join those going left."

"Lord King, that's better accomplished with oarsmen rather than sails."

"I'll leave it to you. But you can see what we want to do. Those five will come at the Danes head on, while our six turn to come in on them from the sides."

"Yes, Lord King. That's clear. I'll issue the orders."

Soon, shouted orders in Frisian and English were passed down the line either side.

With his head swivelling forwards and backwards, judging distances, Alfred said to the helmsman, "About now, I think?"

"Leave it to me, Lord King. And stay here, please. Our men have trained for this and you have not."

Alfred nodded. "Very well, helmsman. Do it."

A horn blew and sails were being furled. Oarsmen had been ready in place and in a few heartbeats, Alfred's longship was swinging left. Then they were finishing the tight circle and arrowing in towards the Danish longships.

A rhythm resounded in Alfred's ears, oars slicing into water, sword hilts pounding on shields or boat-rails, Frisians chanting 'rah, rah, rah, rah'.

The Danes must have realised they were flying into a trap. They had five longships facing them, another three coming in from their left and three from their right. In the last moments before the English and Frisian longships sliced into the Danish flotilla, Alfred saw individual faces of his enemy, bearded and clean-shaven, helmeted and bald. He saw uncertainty as oarsmen hesitated. In some faces he saw fear, in others, what, anger, bravado?

As the sun sank towards the horizon, a red, bloody glow was cast on the whole scene, even before a weapon had been drawn.

Oars were pulled in. Danes, Frisians and Saxons were standing in their longships and drawing swords and knives, hefting shields.

As Alfred drew his own sword there was a crash, the longship lurching, and he clutched at the gunwale.

Warriors were throwing hooks over the side of a Danish longship. Men from both longships were leaping up and over, red light catching them from the orb half-way sunk into the sea. Swords reflected the fire of the dying sunlight and crashed onto shields and into flesh. Shouts and screams rang across the water, all around.

Alfred waited by the sternpost, Noth next to him, away from the fighting. He felt the weight of the sword in his hand, leaned down and lifted his shield, then watched as his warriors parried and struck. These were men – his men – who had trained for this moment, pitting their lives against raiders who had spent their lives fighting, rowing, sailing. Tough men, who would not give in. He saw his own men go down, as well as broad-shouldered Danes.

Raising his eyes, he saw the same scenes repeated in other longships and it was with relief that Alfred felt another English longship crash into the far side, with warriors from that vessel leaping over to face the Danes in the well of their longship. Now there would be two of his men for each Dane. At last, he felt himself breathe.

The direct light suddenly slid away and, in the gathering dark, the noise of battle and the smell of spilled blood and guts was intense, beating on the senses. But then with some finality – at least on this longship, there was a long, terrible scream, abruptly stopped as something heavy hit the water just beyond Alfred.

The helmsman was shouting orders. "Unhook us! To our right, look. Over there."

It was too late. A Danish longship had found a gap and their oarsmen were pulling hard to escape the blood and destruction on the Solent. Another followed it, leaving an English longship drifting behind, its oarsmen and warriors cut down.

Alfred shouted, "Let those ones go, but make sure the Danes still here are finished."

The helmsman grunted and the longship was pushed away from its floundering enemy, towards another already under attack. An English longship was attempting to tie on to the viking craft and was closest to Alfred's longship. The helmsman was swinging around, when there was a great shout.

Alfred looked up. A huge man had leapt on to the gunwale of the Danish ship, arms stretched to the sky, screaming in anger. He held an enormous sword in two hands as if it were a child's toy. The man was absolutely naked, with tattoos over much of his body, and long, fair hair tied behind him. His chest, shoulders and arms were massive – an oarsman's body. The man's eyes were round and staring, his mouth open and yelling at the warriors below him.

There seemed to be a pause in fighting elsewhere, as all stared up at the Dane, the man's shout going on and on and piercing their heads.

The yell suddenly ceased and the Dane looked down into the English vessel tied on to his own and leapt down into it, his great sword already swinging.

The sword was being wielded two-handed in a figure-ofeight, over and across, left and right. Wherever it hit flesh or bone, it bit through with hardly a pause. Men were screaming and dying or scrambling to escape.

Behind the man, the Danish longship had been cut free from its entanglement with the English craft and shouts called the warrior back. But still the sword swung and he was moving down the centre of the longship, inflicting pain and death as he went.

Alfred's longship was still moving in towards the scene and now ran up against the other English vessel. The collision made the Dane stumble, but then he was up again, leaping onto the gunwale rammed by Alfred's longship.

Above the fighting, his eyes seemed to lock with Alfred's. He jumped, missing abandoned oars and gaining his feet, flailing back and forth with his sword as men backed off.

He screamed and lunged in the direction of Alfred. Noth stepped in front, shield high. Two more of Alfred's men next to him.

Suddenly everything changed. Another crash of longship on longship made the Dane stumble again and the sword's swing went wide of its human mark, hit the mast and stopped.

There was a moment of weakness now, of vulnerability, and it was an oarsman lying as if dead at the man's feet, who made him pay. A long-knife flashed up into the Dane's thigh, and one hand left the sword. More men recognised the moment and they were on him with knives, swords and spears, and he was down, and dead.

In the sudden silence that followed, Alfred raised his eyes. The sky was a mid-blue and darkness was drifting over the scene. The Danish longship had moved off, oars biting into the sea. He could make out other longships drifting now in the breeze, English, Frisian and one Danish, all fighting ended.

Then Noth, next to him, was sliding his sword back into its scabbard. "We did it," he said softly. Noth's arm came around his shoulders. "We've captured a longship and run the others off. Alfred, we did it."

Alfred paused, listening to the moaning and crying from warriors and oarsmen nursing wounds or fallen friends. "Yes," he said. "Yes, I suppose we did."

CHAPTER 5

The land sloped gently down to the river Frome through the lanes of Wareham, where the thatched wooden houses had their doors and windows open to the July sun.

There was some noise ahead of Alfred, Elswith, Garrulf and Odda as they left the great hall and a crowd appeared before them when they passed the last of the houses. The crowd were intent on the action in front of them on the riverbank.

There was going to be a sea trial - the captured Danish longship, a Frisian longship and one of the new Wessex-made longships, each of them tied up against the riverbank.

The sea trial was clearly going to be popular, and there was a great deal of calling and shouting – advice, encouragement and derision, depending on how bets had been placed.

By the time Alfred and his friends had made their way through to the riverbank, Radmer was standing at the sternpost of the Frisian longship, the furthest downstream of the three vessels. Like the Danish longships, this one was sleek and low. At prow and stern the sides rose to high points topped by carved dolphins riding above the waves. This would be a fast vessel in the sea trial.

With brief commands in Radmer's own language, ropes were cast off and the oarsmen rowed a reverse stroke so as to keep the longship in place on the water gently flowing eastwards towards the great inlet of the sea – Poole Bay.

"Lord King!" Radmer called across. "We're ready to show that we can beat that viking longship and the English longship."

"Rubbish!" Noth shouted at him. "Now clear out the way, so that we can get this good English longship into open water."

Radmer smiled and waved and, with a brief word to his oarsmen, the oars suddenly bit into the water. With the strength of arm and stream, the Frisian longship sprang forward and in moments was gone. The crew had been selected from the best of the Frisian oarsmen. They would be good.

"Right," Noth shouted, "let's get going, and show these Frisians what a good solid English longship can do."

Noth, Ethelwulf and Wulfred made their way across the plank from the riverbank to the longboat, where the oarsmen were already in place and preparing themselves.

"Alfred!" Noth called across. "I'll wager we can see off those other two!"

Alfred cast his eyes over the longship. It was a sleek-looking vessel, not one of the old-fashioned solid English longships, capable of carrying men or goods, and which were wider and built to sit deeper in the water than the Frisian or the viking longships. But good as it looked, it was new, relatively untried, and crewed by Garrulf's men of Dorset.

Alfred knew, as did Noth despite his bluster, that in a straight sea trial this longship should stand no chance at all.

The real competition, Alfred thought, ought to be between Radmer's Frisian longship and the captured Danish longship, both crewed by Frisian oarsmen. But not all thought the same as Alfred and the betting was still taking place, Noth's longship gaining almost as much of the support as the other two.

"It's too soon for that longship, Noth," Alfred called across. "Another few weeks and you may be right. For the moment, my wager is on the longship that will be under my feet." He gestured at the captured Danish longship tied up to his right.

"Ha. Come on then. Let's go!"

As he said that, ropes were let go and oars bit, and Noth was suddenly thrown down into the boat. Laughter rocked around the riverbank, but the longship did not stop and was soon out of sight down the river.

Alfred turned to the man next to him. Garrulf was a wiry man, somewhat older than Alfred but with a young man's smile through his trimmed beard. His hair, in contrast was long and unkempt, brown streaked with gold from time spent in the sun in his native Dorset.

"Ealdorman Garrulf," Alfred said. "Would you like to join us?"

"I think I'll watch from a distance, Lord King. I prefer soil under my feet," he replied. With a slight bow of his head he made his way towards one of the smaller craft tied up along the riverbank.

"Odda?"

"I wouldn't miss it."

Alfred looked at Elswith. "And you'll be the judge?"

"Oh yes."

Alfred examined the Danish vessel tied up at the riverbank.

It rested low in the water. Its overlapping planks, alternately painted blue and gold and red, narrowed as they rose to the bow and stern posts. Each of these was topped with a golden dragon's head facing forwards and backwards.

The mast in the centre of the longship was bare, its cross beam and sail lying along the vessel's length to be clear of the rowers. Each of these oarsmen sat with the base of their oars resting on the deck, the blades held vertically above them. They were watching him, these Frisians brought over by Radmer.

"Come on, then," Alfred said to Odda. "Let's see what she can do."

He led the way over a plank from the riverbank and stepped into the longship, the oarsmen leaning aside so that the two of them could clamber across to the sternpost.

To the helmsman he said, "Are we ready?"

"Yes, Lord King."

Alfred nodded and rested a steadying hand on the gunwale as orders flew, the plank brought on board, the longship pushed from the bank, and oars found the water.

All around, smaller craft full of happy, smiling townsfolk were being pushed into the river to follow the longships seaward. Amongst them, he saw Elswith given a helping hand into a small trading boat, with many others crowding on.

It was clear that no one wanted to miss the sea trial.

The three longships sailed slowly with the wind out of the River Frome and into Poole Bay. Each rounded the two small, grass-covered islands, then sailed slowly across almost to Hamworthy on the far shore.

The square sail of each longship was filled by the breeze, so that the oarsmen could sit back, chatting to each other or calling out to the other crews. More wagers were placed, more shouting of odds or insults.

Just short of Hamworthy the sails were brought down and oars set into the oar holes. With instruction from helmsmen, each were turned and manoeuvred roughly alongside each other.

Now they faced back towards the start point where the townsfolk of Wareham were waiting in their small boats.

Alfred stood with Odda by the helmsman of the Danish longship. He could feel the breeze on his face and see the water rippling, the warm sun glinting off the water.

Silence descended on the three longships, oars poised to

cut into the water.

Alfred reached out a hand to a young warrior holding a hunting horn. "Get ready."

With Noth's English oarsmen barely accustomed to the new longship, they were to be given a small advantage at the start.

Alfred glanced at Radmer in the Frisian ship and received a nod.

Then he looked across to Noth.

Noth smiled, then raised his arms. "Go. Go!"

And they were first away, aiming to claim the wagers at the end.

Alfred waited for several beats of the leading vessel's oars, then shouted, "Now."

The horn sounded and the Frisian and Danish longships pulled forward amid the cries from the two helmsmen.

Alfred held on to the sternpost and took in the sea air as it blew into his face.

This, Alfred thought, was quite different to the attack on the Danish longships. There was still the pounding of blood in the veins because of the desire to win, but today there was no fear. This was a good day.

His hair and beard felt the wind blown against it. He raised closed eyes to the sun, feeling the warmth, and slowly his other senses claimed more of their hold on the world, the beat of the oars cutting the sea, the cries of the gulls overhead, the feel of smoothed oak at the sternpost and the taste of salt on his lips.

He opened his eyes and gazed along the longship. The vessel, he thought, was around twenty-five paces long and at its widest about five paces. At the prow, the gunwales rose together reaching a peak topped by the intricate carving of the dragon-head. To his right, the great side-rudder was raised above the water-level, not to be used while the oarsmen were providing power and direction, only when the longship was under sail.

Alfred counted sixteen oarsmen on either side, each

sitting on a chest in the well of the longship. Most were bare from the waist up this warm summer's morning and their shoulder muscles moved in harmony. The spruce-wood oars projected through oar ports in the third plank down from the gunwale, and each oar along the dipping length of the longship was of a different length, so as to cut the water at the same moment. This was a wonderful craft, full of years of learning the ways of the sea. On the flat of Poole Bay, of course, this ocean-going longship would not show its true strengths, its ability to flex and bend with waves and swells, taking in the sea's power and using it. But even here, Alfred could only marvel at the skill of its makers.

"We're overhauling them."

Odda's words brought Alfred back to the present, and he looked across to the left. They were just ahead of the Frisian longship and level with the English longship.

Noth and Radmer were both screaming and shouting their orders to their oarsmen. Their voices carried across the water, just audible through the beat of the oars. But Alfred was more than content for the lead Frisian oarsman to mark time in the Danish longship, and to keep a regular pace.

Perhaps Noth's and Radmer's shouting were having some effect, as the English longship began to pull ahead and Radmer's was alongside again, gaining on them and looking to pass Noth's longship on the right.

Not too far ahead, Alfred could see the two small islands.

Turning to the helmsman, Alfred shouted above the noise of the oars and oarsmen, "Noth will probably take a wide sweep around that island, thinking that he'll push Radmer wider still. Let's see if we can take an inside curve."

"We'll be very close to the sandbanks."

"Worth the risk, I think?"

"If you wish, Lord King."

Word was passed down the oarsmen, and as Noth pulled wide, the Frisian lead oarsman on Alfred's longship shouted and the pace suddenly upped, with Alfred at last feeling what it must be like for a viking longship to be moving at full speed. They were almost through the gap before Noth notice the manoeuvre and redoubled his shouting at his own oarsmen for more speed. But Alfred's tactic had been a risk and suddenly the longship bumped and ground, as a sandbank reared to almost sea level, and the vessel very nearly came to a halt, only its own momentum carrying it over.

Alfred held on to the gunwale with both hands to steady himself.

In the meantime, Noth's and Radmer's longships had both careered on, neck and neck now, with both men laughing at Alfred's failed manoeuvre behind them, before turning to roar at their own men.

With the sea-trial lost, Alfred called across to the lead oarsman, "Let's catch them up at least."

It took several strokes before they were back in rhythm and coming up to speed, but they were spectators to the final moments of the race, as the two longships headed for the final turn at the western end of the island.

Noth held the inside run and it was clear that the shorter distance to cover would be to their advantage. Except that Noth was maybe too busy deriding the Frisian longship from the gunwale to concentrate on their own course. Suddenly it was the English longship, just before the final point of the sea-trial, which hit a hidden sandbank, and slued crossways to a halt, its bows catching the rear oars of the Frisian longship.

Radmer shouted at his own oarsmen to raise oars until they had slipped past the ailing English longship and then they were through, all the oarsmen standing and shouting as they passed Elswith's small boat, where every man, woman and child were cheering and laughing.

Even Alfred's longship skimmed over the final stretch of water as the English longship was still trying to free itself from the sandbank. Elswith would have no need to judge who had won.

When Alfred's longship eased to a stop by the Frisian vessel, all the oarsmen were standing and pointing, many with uncontrolled laughter.

Alfred looked back and saw that it was not the longship's situation they were laughing at, nor the oarsmen who had come so close to winning. They were laughing at the man who had been standing on top of the gunwale mocking the other longships at just the moment when his own struck a sandbank, and who was now being hauled back aboard, spluttering from the sea-water in his mouth.

"Noth!"

CHAPTER 6

From the doorway Alfred looked around the hall, crowded with friends and with children breakfasting on meats, bread and ale on the long wooden table. It was a happy scene, golden light sweeping through open windows and doors from the early morning sun and falling on smiling, animated faces after the sea trial the day before.

There was an unexpected face amongst those eating.

"Osric."

Osric rose from his place and walked to Alfred's side, the sun bright on one side of his face.

"I understand that was quite a demonstration yesterday."

Before Alfred could answer, he felt a warm body beside him.

"Osric," Elswith said, smiling at her husband's cousin, "tell me why you're here alone. Have you left your wife at home by herself?"

"Oh, we're not so often together, Elswith. Most of my time is spent on one or other border – somewhere along the Thames or in Kent. It's no life for a woman and my wife prefers to be at our home in Wiltshire."

"You should get home more often, Osric. Shouldn't he, Alfred?"

"I'll talk to Osric about it, Elswith."

Elswith's look at Alfred was steady. He turned back to his cousin.

"Osric, if the Danes don't come this autumn and are hunkered down for the winter, I'll get Noth or Wulfred to take over from you for a while. If they can be spared from their wives. I believe they have become very close, Ealhburh and Hild, living together in Somerset."

"There's no need, Alfred. And the Danes can't be trusted not to come at any time of year."

"No. That's what we'll do. Every few months."

"Well. Alright," he said, turning back to Elswith. "I suppose it will give me time to get the manor sorted out. But I can't be away from the border for too long. The Danes-"

"The Danes will come," Elswith replied. "I know."

It was two days later, with the evening meal about to be served.

Alfred was sitting with Osric when Elswith came towards them.

She said, "Your travels seemingly took you through Winchester on the way here. The abbey?"

"Yes, Lady Elswith, I stayed the night. Why?"

"Your stay has been the cause of another visitor to us here."

She turned and beckoned to a youngster standing in the doorway. With the light behind him, it was a moment before Alfred recognised the open, friendly face under its unruly, dark brown hair. Oswald.

Alfred looked at the young man, a boy that his second oldest brother had acknowledged as his own, although his brother had not been married to the boys' mother.

"Oswald! Good to see you. But why aren't you at the abbey at Winchester?"

"Well, I... You see, I heard that Lord Osric had come to

the abbey. And I decided I couldn't stay. If the Danes are going to come, I want to learn to fight."

"Come and sit with us."

Osric moved along the bench to make space for the newcomer.

As he sat, Alfred asked, "How old are you, Oswald?"

"Seventeen."

"You've only had training for the church? Any weapons-training?"

"No, Uncle Alfred. I mean, Lord King."

Alfred scratched at his beard uncertainly. "But you don't want to stay in the church?"

"No. Not now."

"Alfred," Elswith said, standing by, one hand on Alfred's shoulder. "He can stay with us, can't he? Perhaps Wulfred will help him with his weapons-training?"

Alfred nodded. "Yes. Yes, of course. Welcome, Oswald. It's time that we had the younger generations here. Did you see my other nephews at all?"

"Helm and Wold? Not often. They and their mother are with the Ealdorman of Hampshire."

Alfred nodded thoughtfully.

The great hall had been emptied of all but the Council. The table had been cleared. His friends were already sitting at either side. Alfred, standing at the end of the table, listened for a moment as they chattered, laughing and joking still at the outcome of the sea trial, with Noth the butt of the jokes. Oswald was listening, smiling, his eyes bright.

It was some minutes before they were all aware that Alfred was standing quietly, waiting for them. Wulfred was the last to understand. He bit off a comment to Noth, both grinning.

Finally there was silence, all eyes on Alfred.

"I'd like to formally welcome my nephew Oswald to the Council of Wessex." Alfred's voice was quiet and sober. "I think he knows that he's amongst friends here."

There were nods and murmurs of agreement from all at the table, and the youngster's face blushed.

"Oswald, you missed the sea-trial but I'll arrange for Radmer to take you out on one of the longships."

The youngster was round-eyed. "Thank you."

"I'd also like Wulfred to sort out a weapons-training regime for you. Wulfred?"

"Of course."

"Then later in the year, Noth will be relieving Osric for a while on the borders, and the two of you can go with him."

There were nods of heads from the two youngest members of the Council, one of them with eyes full of optimism.

Alfred turned to the older members of the Council. "Now, I hope you all enjoyed the sea-trial."

"Very impressive," Odda said. "When do you expect further longships from Frisia?"

"Within weeks," Alfred replied. "And over the next two months more of our own longships will be ready. It's not many, but it's a start."

"No, not many," Osric said sombrely, "to take on a whole fleet of Danes appearing on the south coast."

"We really need more shipwrights."

"Plenty in Southampton. Wulfhere's Southampton."

"So there are."

Odda said, "And what about the building of ramparts around towns that we spoke of?"

"That's not been an easy task." Alfred scratched at his beard. "The Ealdormen of Hampshire, Somerset and even Berkshire ignore my instructions. The eastern shires do what they can, but that's little enough. So it's only in your own shires where we have reasonable ramparts. And even here, well, I don't mean to be critical, but you've run into opposition in many places."

Odda nodded. "Townsfolk don't like being told to work on walls, or to pay for others to do so."

"So the towns of Wessex are still not well-protected," Alfred said. "And we only have the start of a fleet. Osric is right there. We're not in a good position to deal with an invasion."

Garrulf said, "Even if the Ealdormen around this table had strings of fortified towns, the lack of them in Somerset and Hampshire would still leave the heartland of Wessex wide open to attack."

"That's true. So can we bring the Ealdormen of Hampshire and Somerset back to the Council? Can we persuade them to work with us?"

"If they did return," Odda said, "would we trust them?"

Garrulf steepled his fingers. "It pains me to say this of fellow Ealdormen of Wessex, but I see no reason for us to trust either. There's no reason to think they've changed their view that Alfred should not be King. That Helm and Wold should be heirs to the Kingdom of their father, with themselves in real control."

Odda went on. "I'd go further. I can see no prospect of Eadwulf and Wulfhere joining us, unless they themselves come under attack and need our help. In the meantime, Helm and Wold are under the control of their mother and Wulfhere. I think Helm at least should be here, out of their influence."

Eyes turned to Alfred.

"You're right. It's time my nephews were here. Let me think about that. In the meantime, Noth, I have a gift of land for you."

"More land?"

"I want you to be a power in Somerset. Forthred here," Alfred glanced at his Secretary, "will draw up the charters."

Noth paused, his gaze steady on Alfred.

"Ealdorman Eadwulf is really not going to like that."

Elswith was sitting on a chair by the bed, with Gifu asleep and nestled against the bump of her stomach, the little one's eyes closed in peaceful acquiescence to warm milk and tiredness.

The room was lit by a candle on the table, the light not penetrating to all corners of the room, but enough to show Ethelflaed and Edward also asleep in their own small beds.

"I heard about the Council meeting." Her voice was quiet, as she looked down at the baby she cradled.

"Oh? Who from?" Alfred said.

She looked up, and pinpoints of candlelight reflected from deep brown eyes. "Wulfred. He says Oswald has a new hero."

He ran a hand through his hair, smiling sheepishly. "I don't know."

"I do. But don't you think you might be pushing him too far too fast?"

"There's a new generation coming through, my love – Oswald, Helm and Wold. We need to bring them on."

She sighed. "I know, but Oswald seems so young for his age, and you haven't seen Helm and Wold for four years. Not since their father's funeral."

"Helm will be fifteen and Wold thirteen." Unconsciously his voice had become louder. "It's high time they were here – Helm at least. But Winifred-"

"Shush, Alfred. Keep your voice down a little." She indicated the sleeping children, including little Gifu in her white linen. "Winifred will not have it, Alfred. She will still believe with all her soul that Helm should be King and not you. And while they're in Hampshire with the Ealdorman, there's not much you can do about that."

Alfred sighed. "You may be right. I liked Helm very much, although if truth be told, I never really took to Wold."

"They may have changed completely, my love. They've had four years of their mother's bitterness and of Wulfhere's loathing for you. Who knows what they'll be like?"

"You're right. I've no idea if they believe they've been cheated out of the kingship."

"Also, the question of who is your heir has never been

settled. It can't be Oswald, because he's illegitimate. So would it be Edward," and she indicated the sleeping three-year-old, "or Helm?"

"If I died now, Elswith, it'd have to be Helm. A three-year-old cannot be King of Wessex. Even a fifteen-year-old would be very difficult. Especially one who may be under the thumb of the Ealdorman of Hampshire."

Alfred could make out a half-smile in the darkened room. "Well, we'd better make sure you don't die now."

"I hadn't intended to, but I've had four older brothers die at around the age I am now. And there's the pains in my stomach. Still nobody can tell me the cause."

"Are you alright at the moment?" she said, the smile gone.

"Yes. It's better when I'm active, of course. But, well, as you know, it can just come on at any time. I think... Elswith, I think we'd better get young Helm out from under the skirts of his mother and away from Wulfhere's influence."

"So," Elswith said, looking up at her husband through the soft candlelight with a smile, "you've arranged to send our soft-handed Oswald to the Kentish border. What do you plan for Helm?"

Alfred leaned down and gently took the sleeping Gifu from her mother. He carried her carefully to the small cot at the end of their bed and placed her down. She snuffled, but did not wake. As he looked down at her, he felt Elswith beside him, and her hand found his.

"Well?" she said, very quietly, her eyes still on the baby.

"Helm, you mean?" Alfred turned to Elswith. "First we need to get him here."

"And I guess you've worked out how to do that?"

"I just might."

She brought the back of his hand up to her mouth, kissed it and said, "So are you going to tell me?"

"Probably," he said, and then winced as her foot kicked him deftly on the ankle.

***

He had had a bad night and a bad day.

It was early evening when Alfred woke properly, no pains, just a deep tiredness in his muscles. He had felt too weak to argue with Elswith about getting up until now and had slept, off and on, for hours, waking occasionally to find either Elswith or Oswald sitting by him.

Now they were both there.

Oswald was saying, "How are you, Uncle Alfred?"

Alfred gently moved his legs and stomach. "I... think I'm alright."

He felt Elswith put a cool hand on his forehead. "There's no fever at least."

"No, and the pain has gone."

Even so, he sat up slowly and gingerly, his mind waiting for another moment of agony. But it didn't come. He eased his legs over the side of the bed and waited. Still nothing. So he stood, one hand resting on the bed just in case.

He raised his eyes and found that Elswith and Oswald were watching him carefully.

"It's fine. I'm alright. Look." And he raised his arms slowly, joining his hands behind his head, and pulling his chest up to stretch his stomach. Good. He really was on the mend. For today, at any rate.

"Oswald, have you been here all the time?"

Elswith answered. "He's been such a good companion for me. Thank you, Oswald."

Oswald was blushing. "It's nothing. I just wanted to help."

"Thank you from me too," Alfred said to him.

He turned and found Elswith looking him up and down, then she called through the open door. "Wulfred."

He appeared in the doorway in a matter of moments.

"Alfred," Wulfred said, serious of face, "are you well again?"

"Yes. Much better. And I want to go down to the river."

"Are you able to walk there?"

"Wait." It was Elswith, laying a hand on her husband's arm. You may want to walk to the river, but I don't think the people of Wareham should see you exactly as you are."

"Not good?" he said, looking at their faces.

Wulfred grinned. "Perhaps it's best if Lady Elswith helps you clean up."

Alfred looked thoughtfully at Wulfred. His eyes then fell on his young nephew. Oswald stopped fiddling with his sword-hilt. He blushed as Alfred's eyes held his.

"Oswald, your cousin Helm. How well do you know him?"

"We meet from time to time. Helm and his brother live with their mother at the Ealdorman's hall in Winchester. I was at the abbey, but we did meet."

"Then it wouldn't be unnatural for you to visit him there. He is, what, two years younger than you?"

"Yes," Oswald said slowly, unsure where the questions were leading.

"Wulfred, I'd like you to take Oswald part way to Winchester. On your way to Southampton."

Wulfred nodded, while Oswald had a confused look on his face.

"I have a job for each of you," Alfred said.

CHAPTER 7

The weather was turning. A cool early autumn breeze from the east was blowing across the ramparts and fluttering tunics.

Three young men stood before him.

Behind them, alongside two more part-constructed longships in the boatyard, Alfred could see a new set of shipwrights moving their packs into the huts.

The Ealdorman of Hampshire would not be pleased to have lost them.

He returned his gaze to the three before him, the evening sun lighting faces flushed from a long ride.

He smiled at the contrasts between them. Wulfred was twenty years old now, blond hair kept quite long, face shaved smooth. With a ready smile, he was not the shy boy Alfred had first known. No, this was the young man who had stood by Alfred in battle after battle and who had been with him on raids against the Danes. He had so much experience compared to the two on his right and it showed as he leaned casually against the cradle holding the skeleton of another longship under construction.

Alfred nodded to him and then gestured to the shipwrights. "Well done," he said.

Then there was Oswald seventeen years old, but looking younger. He had a look of pride on his round, young face, beneath its flurry of wild, brown hair. He held his chin high, as he acknowledged Alfred's nod of thanks for a task he had completed.

And then the third young man. Helm, two years younger again than Oswald, but gangly and slightly taller. He had fair hair trimmed close to his head and hazel eyes compared with Wulfred's blue. His cloak was rich, a dark blue, but mud-spattered from a long journey. He stood with feet apart, looking uncertainly at his uncle.

"Helm," Alfred said to him. "It's good to see you. It's been too long."

"Oswald found me at Winchester and we were able to talk in private. Thank you for your message, Uncle."

"I meant it. And I hope the message was clear. If you're ready, you're welcome in the court of the King of Wessex. Wulfred here was fighting battles alongside me at your age. Here you'll be treated like a man, not a boy. A Lord of Wessex."

"Oswald told me that you've taken him into your household and that he's training as a warrior."

"That's quite right. Although my guess is that you'll have had more training in the arts of war than Oswald at the abbey?"

"Well, yes. I've had training with the sword, the shield and the spear. I'd like to use the bow as well, but the Ealdorman said that wasn't appropriate for me."

"Here you can learn to use a bow, if you wish, and you'll come with me when we hunt."

"I can?"

"Of course. Did you not hunt with the Ealdorman of Hampshire?"

"No. My mother wouldn't let us."

"Winifred wouldn't let you hunt?"

"The Ealdorman said that she kept us too much under her skirts, Wold and me. He teased her, but mother was adamant."

"She let you learn to use a sword though?"

"Only when the Ealdorman insisted that a..."

He tailed off, his eyes now on his feet.

Alfred looked at the lad thoughtfully. "Helm, you're among friends here. Why don't you finish what you were going to say?"

Helm raised his eyes to Alfred's, and the eyes held his as he said slowly, "The Ealdorman said that a King of Wessex must know how to wield a sword."

Alfred nodded. "And what did you say to that?"

Still holding Alfred's eyes, Helm said, "That Uncle Alfred is King of Wessex."

"Wulfhere wouldn't have liked that. Nor your mother. How old were you then?"

"Twelve."

"So tell me what happened."

"He thrashed me. For being an insolent boy."

Alfred frowned. "Has he often thrashed you?"

"He did, before I grew."

Alfred smiled. "Yes, you'll be taller than him now. That would put him off. He was always little more than a bully. You know that Wulfred is his nephew and was brought up there? I think he suffered the same treatment."

Helm glanced to his left and saw that Wulfred was nodding soberly.

"Wulfred told me on the ride back here," Helm said.

"And does Wold get thrashed? He's only thirteen now."

"No. Mother is much too fond of Wold for the Ealdorman to thrash him." He smiled, and it was a good smile. "I think mother would thrash the Ealdorman if he lifted a birch to Wold."

"But she wouldn't do that for you?"

The smile faded. "No."

Alfred pulled at his beard, unsure what to say to that.

"Do they know that you've come here?"

"I told mother I was riding to the abbey with Oswald."

"But you headed straight towards Wareham?"

"We met up with Wulfred and came on together from there with your shipwrights."

Alfred nodded. "I think I should send a message to your mother to say that you've decided that your future lies at court and that I've welcomed you here."

Helm chewed at his lip and said nothing.

"And then I anticipate a visit from your mother."

The lad frowned. "Yes, and the Ealdorman of Hampshire."

"Almost certainly. But you're a man now, Helm. You've a place here at court with me. They cannot force you to return against your wishes. Not while you're under the protection of the King of Wessex. Now, come up to the great hall. Elswith will be there and she'll want to see you."

Alfred held out his arm and gestured for Helm to walk with him.

Helm took a couple of steps forward. "Thank you, Uncle." He paused, close to Alfred, and – almost the same height as Alfred – he looked directly at him. "Uncle, my mother hates you, do you know that? And so does the Ealdorman. That's one thing they have in common. And Wold does as well – he hates you."

Alfred blinked, then nodded. He put an arm across the shoulders of his nephew, and drew him towards the town gate.

"I know. That's a lot of hate."

"My mother says you've stolen the Kingdom from me, and that... well, that she wouldn't be surprised if you killed my father to do that..." His voice tailed away.

They were walking slowly, Alfred's arm still across the lad's shoulders.

"And Wold believes that?"

"He was younger when it all happened. He didn't know you like I did."

"You don't believe any of that then?"

Helm stopped in his tracks and turned to face Alfred.

"No."

"I'm glad. Helm, I loved your father. I tried to save him, and it's been on my conscience for the last four years that I couldn't. But that's all my conscience talks to me of. I didn't kill your father and I didn't steal the Kingdom. Your father and your grandfather both willed that I should be King after your father."

"I know."

Alfred put his arm across the boy's shoulders again and turned him to carry on walking towards the gate. "Come on then, come and see Elswith. Oh, and Helm," he paused, and Helm looked across, "it's good to see you again."

Helm smiled, and they were silent now as they walked along together, stride for stride.

Elswith was sitting on a stool in the door frame of the great hall, her spinning abandoned on the ground as she held a sleeping Gifu at her shoulder. The low evening sunlight fell on her face. Alfred felt what a beautiful picture it made.

She looked up at the sound of their footsteps across the yard but with the sun in her eyes, it was a moment before she realised who was there.

"Helm!"

And then she was standing with Gifu supported by one hand, reaching out the other to Helm.

The boy grinned and walked towards her into an embrace.

"Helm, I'm so glad to see you here."

She pulled back to look at Helm better.

Alfred was about to step forward to take Gifu, when Oswald was there, saying, "Can I hold her for you, Lady Elswith?"

"Of course, Oswald. Thank you," and her smile was briefly on Oswald as he lifted the baby from her, before she turned back to Helm. "Come inside. Come in and tell me everything. How's your mother? And Wold? And..."

She stopped in mid-sentence and mid-step, just short of the door-frame. She turned back to him, more serious now, taking both his hands in hers.

"Helm," she said. "I'm so glad you've come. I just wish your mother... Well, I wish your mother had come as well. And Wold, of course."

"Lady Elswith, Uncle Alfred thinks you might see them very soon. And the Ealdorman of Hampshire."

"Oh. But I meant that Winifred... Oh, you know what I mean. But that's not to be." She led Helm by the hand to the table, and the sun found its way in behind them and cast long pillars of light across the floor and across them as they sat.

"Helm," Elswith said, still holding his hand, sitting next to the lad, the sun on their backs.

Oswald and Alfred sat down opposite, with Gifu now being carried away by Bennath into the private rooms behind, the young Cornish woman's voice soothing the little girl.

Elswith turned her attention back to Helm. "Did you come without Winifred's approval? Is that why she'll be following on with the Ealdorman of Hampshire?"

"I couldn't tell her," he said. "They wouldn't have let me come."

"I suppose not. She'll be angry though."

"Yes."

With a slight frown, she said, "Helm, you have a home here, you know. I don't mean just Wareham. I mean Chippenham, or Wilton, or wherever in the Kingdom of Wessex Alfred and I find ourselves. As with Oswald here, we'll be your home."

Alfred noticed Helm's lips tighten together and that his eyes were moist. Elswith put a hand up to his cheek. The boy took a breath and sat up straighter, raising a hand to wipe across his eyes, blinking several times.

"Thank... thank you, Lady Elswith. It... I, well... I haven't felt that I had a home since father was killed and mother took us across to Winchester to live with the Ealdorman of Hampshire." There was bitterness in his voice. "We should've been together, all of us. That's what I told them, but they said that Uncle Alfred had stolen the Kingdom from me. From me?" He looked incredulous. And angry. "What would I have done as King of Wessex when I was eleven? What would I do now?" He looked across the table. "Uncle Alfred. If I can stay, I'd like to learn to learn how to fight the Danes. Whatever I can do... Anything..."

He looked back at Elswith, who had withdrawn her hand from Helm's angry young face and was looking at him, mouth open slightly. Then Helm's gaze switched back to Alfred.

Alfred nodded to him. "From now on, Helm, your place is here with Elswith and me. Though we'll do more than offer you a home. You are the son of your father and you inherit the land he gave you in his will. Those manors and lands are not for your mother, who was given her own lands. And they are especially not for the Ealdorman of Hampshire. Even though I understand that the coin from them seems to be swelling the coffers of the Ealdorman at the moment. That is your land now and I'll see to it that your ownership, and the coin or food-rent, is verified at the next Council. What's more, I'll add to the land you have."

Helm was staring across the table at his uncle, whose voice had risen in strength.

"You'll always be welcome with us, but we'll also help you to step into your lands and manors. You will – in due course – have your own following of men. And, Helm," he paused, "then you can fight alongside me against the Danes who killed your father."

The feast was nearly ready when Alfred found Elswith in the hall directing the servants.

"No, Helm will be between the King and me," she was

saying, casting a searching look at the top table. "With Oswald on Alfred's left, then the Bishop of Sherborne and Noth. Wulfred will be on my right."

There was a happy screech and Ethelflaed ran through the great doors, her long yellow dress held up to her knees so that she didn't trip.

Immediately behind came a red-faced Bennath, her hair loosened from its veil as she chased the little girl in.

"Ethelflaed," Elswith called. "Stop. Enough."

The little girl did stop, taking in Alfred and her mother.

"You should be with Bennath and your brother and sister. What are you doing? Go back outside, and be good. Bennath, are you alright?"

Bennath had also come to a halt, breathless. "Yes, my Lady, I'm sorry, I tried to stop her."

Alfred stepped towards his eldest child and crouched by her. "Ethelflaed, if you're good, you can stay up to watch some of the entertainers before the feast. But you have to go with Bennath and promise to be good."

It was a small, contrite voice that said, "I will, father." A pause, and then the little girl ran back out the great door, Alfred smiling behind her. From outside she heard the girlish shout, "Bennath, there's a feast!"

"You spoil her, Alfred," Elswith said. "She should be learning how to be the daughter of a King of Wessex not chasing around with the boys. One day we'll need to find a husband for her and I can't imagine a future husband wanting the skills she has been learning. Did you know she was found climbing the trees down by the river? Throwing stones at the boys."

"Was she?"

"Yes. And stop smiling."

"Sorry, Elswith."

"I really don't know what'll become of her."

***

In the centre of the hall a wild boar on a spit was being turned slowly by a young boy, the spitting fat dripping into the fire below, while on the tables spread around the hall were platters with pork, duck, swan and hare meat. There were plates of salty cheese, bowls of hazelnuts and walnuts, hunks of white bread.

At each table were the warriors and household of a King of Wessex, ale to hand. The noise level was high, shouting and calling, the children sent off with Bennath to bed – if they could sleep with this noise.

Alfred was feeling as happy as he had been in some time, with Helm on one side and Oswald on the other. The young men who might lead Wessex one day. Might. He frowned. Might. God knew there were many things that might stand in the way of that.

There was a sudden quietening of the hall and he realised that Bishop Athelheah was standing in the middle of the hall. The warriors around also seemed to sense that something was happening and that quiet would be needed.

The Bishop beckoned Alfred to join him.

As Alfred rounded the table end, he saw Helm and Oswald approaching from the other end of the table.

Now there was silence in the hall.

"Lord Ethelhelm, Lord Oswald," the Bishop was saying. "Now is the time."

Helm moved to stand in front of Alfred and sank to one knee. Oswald followed, a pace behind.

Helm reached a hand towards Alfred, who now understood, and took Helm's hand in both of his.

"Before the Lord God," Helm spoke, hesitantly at first but with growing confidence, "I will be faithful and true to Alfred, King of Wessex. I will love all that he loves and shun all that he shuns, according to God's law and to the laws of Wessex. I will never, willingly or intentionally, by word or deed, work against Alfred of Wessex while I am in his service and at his command."

There were cheers and shouts around the hall as Helm stood and stepped to one side while Oswald knelt.

Silence descended again as Oswald repeated the oath.

And then the hall erupted with noise - shouting, calling, singing, a joyful mix of warriors and ale.

Alfred found himself grinning, though still a dark cloud seemed to lurk just out of reach.

CHAPTER 8

It was three days later, mid-afternoon, when Alfred saw Ethelwulf letting himself into the great hall, pulling the oak door closed behind him on a grey and windy day.

There was a great commotion from the far end of the hall, where Oswald and Helm were throwing a leather ball between them, with younger children shrieking and running between them.

Elswith was sitting by him, little Gifu was being bounced on her knees, arms upstretched as she watched the older children excitedly.

On the long table by them, candles flickered in the many draughts from the unshuttered windows and the candlelight seemed lost.

Ethelwulf walked across to them and squatted on his haunches by Alfred.

"Alfred," Ethelwulf said. "They'll be here in an hour. The Lady Winifred and the Ealdorman of Hampshire. A scout has just come in to report."

Alfred's face lost its smile and he nodded. "So be it."

He stood thoughtfully, Ethelwulf joining him, and together they went outside into the relative quiet.

"How many warriors with them?"

"Forty. All mounted."

"Mail and helmets?"

"Yes. Nowhere near enough to use force against us. More for show, I'd say. And travelling openly."

"Very well. Ethelwulf, I want around fifty warriors lined up either side of the north gate – that's where they'll come?"

"Yes."

"You greet them there. Tell them to tether their horses outside and that they may bring, what, ten warriors into the town. In the great hall we'll have Elswith and myself, you and Wulfred, and twenty warriors, with more within easy call."

"You think there might be trouble?"

"Almost certainly not. But Hampshire's temper isn't to be trusted. And are his sons with him?"

"I don't know. There was no report of that, but they might be amongst the warriors. Wold is there, though."

"Wold?"

"Yes, riding next to his mother."

Alfred nodded. "Right, let's get our youngsters out of the way."

"What about Helm and Oswald?"

"Ah, well, I suppose this is the moment when we find out if they're still boys or are now men."

Alfred looked around the hall carefully. The visitors had arrived at the gate, he had been told, and all was ready. The long table had been moved to one wall and the fire was unlit, so there was room for him and Elswith to greet them in the centre of the hall. Immediately behind would be Wulfred – mail-coat, sword in scabbard, but no helmet. And behind him Helm and Oswald.

Around the walls were the twenty warriors, mailed like Wulfred, but helmeted and each with a spear as well as a sword and long-knife.

Alfred looked at Elswith. She had been to change as

soon as she heard of Winifred's arrival, and here she was in a long dark blue dress, its half-sleeves revealing the long white sleeves of her linen underdress. Her dark brown hair was tied behind her, and at her neck she wore a necklace of blue stones to match her dress. Four years ago, she had refused the title of Queen. Now, standing there, still known only as Lady Elswith, she looked a Queen in all but name, her head held high, confident in her place and her position. He saw her glance behind, taking in Wulfred standing tall in his mail-coat, left hand resting on sword-hilt, and then she smiled at Helm and Oswald.

Helm was the taller, despite being younger by almost two years, and his fair hair contrasted with the shock of dark hair belonging to his cousin. New clothes had been found for them — woven tunics, belted at the waist, but with no scabbards and swords. Not yet. Both looked very nervous.

There was the sound of footsteps and talk at the door. Alfred turned to see the Ealdorman of Hampshire striding through the doorway. He stopped, looking at the scene around him, the warriors lining the walls, with Alfred and Elswith some ten paces into the hall. He did not greet them, but stood to one side, his eyes not leaving Alfred.

Behind him stepped Winifred, and here there was such a change. When Alfred's brother had been King of Wessex and they had two growing sons, Alfred remembered her as jolly and charming and funny. He remembered brown lively hair tossed back in laughter, sparkling eyes and the soft spot she had for her husband's younger brother.

The woman who walked into Wareham's hall now was quite different. She did not glance at the Ealdorman, but walked straight ahead towards Alfred and Elswith. He took in the unsmiling face, more lines than he remembered. Her hair was mostly hidden in a linen veil, but it was a wisp of grey-brown hair that escaped, not the bold dark brown of four years before. A travelling cloak hid most of her clothes, but it was clear that there was no brightness here, no sign of joy.

Two paces in front of them, she stopped, with the Ealdorman and his sons just behind. Wulfstan and Wulfhard both wore mail-coats and had swords in scabbards at their belts.

It was Wulfhard who was resting a protective hand on the shoulder of Wold, now a lad of thirteen, dark haired, with a serious, intense face.

Ethelwulf had followed them in and moved around from behind them, then stood watching from close to the warriors along the wall.

In the doorway stood Hampshire's warriors, though it seemed that Ethelwulf had insisted they leave weapons outside the hall.

Winifred ignored them all. "Where is my son?" she said.

"Winifred," Alfred said, keeping his tone even. "You are welcome." He glanced behind him and Wulfred stepped to one side, so that Winifred had a clear view through to Helm and Oswald. "Lord Helm is with us and is well. As you can see."

"I've come to take him home."

"Helm has asked to stay with Elswith and myself and we've agreed."

"You have no right to. The boy is mine." She paused and her voice grew bitter in the absolute silence around the hall. "Haven't you taken enough from me Alfred?"

"Winifred, he's not a boy. He's a young man and he has made his decision."

"Rubbish. Oswald has obviously filled his head full of tales. I will not have this, Alfred."

Alfred was silent a moment, then said, "Winifred, you have no choice. Helm is fifteen. As from today he comes into his own lands and into his rights and duties as a Lord of Wessex. He'll have a place on the Council and in due course no doubt he'll become a captain of the Kingdom of Wessex with his own warriors."

"He should be King." Her voice was hard, the words clipped.

"No." Alfred's voice had also taken on a controlled vehemence. "By my father's will and my brother's intent, I was my brother's heir. As you well know, Winifred. But look," and with a softer voice he turned and looked behind, "we'll ask your son. Helm, would you please step forward."

Every pair of eyes in the room looked at the young man. He was tall and thin, despite his young age. His dark blue tunic looked rich and well-suited for a Lord of Wessex. His fair hair had been newly cropped, and new leather boots found. But for all the preparation and fore-knowledge of this moment, the youngster walked uncertainly towards Alfred.

Helm looked at his mother briefly, eyes blinking nervously, then stopped by Alfred, turning to face him.

"Helm," Alfred said, returning Helm's look. "Your mother maintains that you should be King of Wessex. The Ealdorman of Hampshire almost certainly agrees. Do you wish to claim the Kingship of your father?"

Helm glanced at his mother, then turned his eyes back to Alfred and his answer dropped into the silence around the hall. "No," he said, and although his voice was quiet, there was not one man or woman in the hall who did not hear.

"Very well. Do you think that I should be King of Wessex?"

"Yes." This was louder, more confident. "I swore an oath and I meant it. Every word."

Alfred nodded. "And then there is a choice for you. Your mother says that you should return with her and the Ealdorman of Hampshire. Do you wish to?"

And now he had found his voice, "No. I wish to remain here."

"Well, I think that's clear. Now, Oswald."

He beckoned his other nephew over.

Oswald flushed, his round face almost scarlet, then walked towards Alfred. "There's a scabbard on the table over there. Would you please bring it over?"

There was some shuffling of feet in the room and exchanges of glances, nobody quite sure of the purpose of Alfred.

Oswald returned with a leather scabbard, finely made, and passed it to Alfred.

"Thank you, Oswald. Helm, if you're to be a captain of the King of Wessex, as you've asked, you'll need a sword. This is your father's, brought from the battlefield where he received the wound that was to kill him. It's yours."

He held out the scabbard and Helm reached out two hands towards it.

"Helm." The voice was broken, but still high. Wold had stepped towards his older brother. "He's tricking you, Helm."

Helm's hands wavered in mid-air, held out towards the sword.

A much deeper voice added to Helm's hesitation. "Wold is right, boy."

It was the Ealdorman of Hampshire, chin out, feet planted wide, an aggressive stance. "That sword is yours by right not by gift of your uncle. You are the son of a King and should be his heir. Just as my sons will be my heirs."

"Helm," his mother said. "You have a sword at home. Come away now."

Helm's eyes remained on the scabbard Alfred held before him. He raised his eyes to Alfred's, who did not flinch or react in any way, but just stood there.

There was almost a minute of tense silence as all there waited for Helm to move, his eyes back on the scabbard.

Helm blinked and looked away, the hands dropping slightly, then turned back to his mother. She held out her hand to him, but he did not move. He raised his eyes to the Ealdorman of Hampshire's and the older man try to smile at him, though it was more grimace than anything. Then Helm looked down at his brother.

"Come home, Helm," Wold said.

"I'm sorry," Helm replied. "Mother, I'm sorry." And he

turned back to Alfred and lifted the scabbard into his hands. Then he smoothly drew the sword from the scabbard, feeling the balance of the blade in his hand, before looking up at Alfred again.

"Lord King," he said formally to Alfred, "I'd like to serve as a captain for Wessex," and Alfred smiled and nodded.

There was an explosion of noise from the Ealdorman of Hampshire. "This is ridiculous."

Around the hall and in the doorway, warriors moved to the balls of their feet.

The Ealdorman went on, his voice still too loud for that hall in this company. "He has been duped."

Behind him, some half dozen of the Ealdorman's men laid hands where sword hilts should have been, though finding none there.

"No!" and it was Helm's voice that stilled the movement. "No. I haven't been duped. I've lived for four years in the home of the Ealdorman of Hampshire, where he treated me like an insolent boy. Now I choose the life of a warrior for my uncle who is King of Wessex."

His mother still had her hand reached towards him. "Helm?" she said, and this time there was pleading in her quiet voice.

But it was Elswith who moved first, in quick paces coming over to her former friend and laying a hand on the outstretched arm. "I'll look after him, Winifred," she said.

The movement and words of the Lady Elswith seemed to calm the tall mail-clad men around them.

Winifred looked blankly at Elswith, then drew her arm away as if burned. She stared at her older son, then turned to walk toward the door, the Ealdorman's sons and his warriors making way for her. Wold was first to follow, catching up with her by the door.

Alfred found himself facing Helm again, the boy still with his father's sword in his right hand and scabbard in his left.

"Is this really my father's?" Helm asked.

"Yes."

"Then... thank you." He paused. "Uncle."

The Ealdorman, watching, said, "This is not the end."

"No, Wulfhere. It's not," Alfred said. "My men will be making sure that in future Helm receives the coin from the lands that he is due, rather than it flowing your way. I suggest that you do not interfere."

The Ealdorman's mouth opened, but no words came out. Then he turned and stormed towards the door, his sons and his warriors scattering out of his way.

CHAPTER 9

Yule was just a month away.

The woodlands around Chippenham had lost their leaves as the nights grew colder, while the harvest had been stored away for the winter.

It was evening, the meal over, their younger children asleep in their cots, though Bennath and Ethelflaed were playing a quiet game in the corner of their room.

Candles on a table cast a gentle light, with a waxy aroma suffusing the room.

From the great hall, just the other side of the wooden partition, there was the murmur of voices and an occasional laugh or a call to close the door to the wind.

Alfred and Elswith were talking quietly, sitting up on the bed, straw-filled pillows behind them, a blanket across their laps.

"How was the journey?"

"Cold. Wet," Alfred replied.

"And Kent?"

"Windy."

He glanced at Elswith and she smiled.

"So is the Archbishop any happier with you?"

"Not really."

"But the Danes have held off on attacking there?"

"For now. Hey, you." He raised an arm and Elswith sank beneath it, her head tucked into his shoulder, a hand on his chest. "It's good to be back."

"I'm glad you're home."

"Home? Here in Chippenham is more home to you now, isn't it?"

"After the Danes took over Wilton, yes. It won't ever feel right there. Not for the family. Will he come back? Guthrum?"

"Yes. Yes, he will."

"When?" Elswith asked.

"I hope not till the spring."

"I know he said five years. But will he really wait? He must know about the confrontation with Wulfhere and Winifred. It's just what the Danes have exploited before."

"Yes, like in Northumbria."

"Is Guthrum still in East Anglia?"

"So far as we know."

"And Halfdan?"

"Said to be in Ireland."

"So we are reasonably safe for now."

"I hope so. Though I do keep plenty of warriors close to the border with Mercia."

"I know you have Cuthred based here. He's been with you from the start, hasn't he?"

"He has. His father was killed in that skirmish in Kent. He wasn't very old and my warriors looked after him. It seems a long time ago now. He's been with me ever since. I trust him."

"One of your captains now?"

"Yes."

"And Osric is in Berkshire?"

"He has most of my warriors there. It's the most likely point the Danes would attack."

"Like when they took over Reading."

"Yes."

"And Noth?"

"I suggested he spend Yule at his manor in Somerset with Ealhburh."

Elswith tapped him on the chest. "I think I suggested that."

Alfred smiled. "Perhaps you did."

"I also suggested Osric spend time with Mildthryth."

"Ah, Osric isn't quite so easy to pin down. Besides, I need at least one of them on the border."

Alfred and Elswith were breakfasting at the table at one end of the hall, when Wulfred ushered a man in.

He looked exhausted. His cloak, trousers and leggings were filthy, his boots caked in mud.

Wulfred said, "Alfred, you need to hear this. He's from the Ealdorman of Surrey."

Around the outside of the hall, men stopped talking and examined the messenger.

Alfred pushed his platter away.

"What's happened?"

"It's the Danes, Lord King," the messenger said. "A horde of them arrived in London, camped overnight, then headed into Wessex."

"Into Wessex? How many? And in which direction?"

"Hundreds. All mounted. When I left, they were riding south west. Through Surrey and towards Hampshire."

"Not Berkshire then. Not Reading. Do we know who it is?"

"The word is, Guthrum."

"Of course it is. Do you know any more?"

"No, Lord King. I set off as soon as I could to warn you."

Alfred turned to Wulfred. "Any news from Osric?"

"Nothing."

The messenger spoke up again. "The Ealdorman of Surrey was sending messengers all over Wessex as well as sending me to Chippenham. So if Lord Osric is in Berkshire, he will know by now."

Alfred nodded and turned back to Wulfred. "Noth, Oswald and Helm are still in Somerset?"

"Yes, Alfred."

"And Ethelwulf in Pewsey?"

"I believe so."

Cuthred and Forthred had followed Wulfred and the messenger in and stood to one side. Cuthred was tall and had filled out in the last few years. Next to him, Forthred was a head shorter, thin and studious-looking.

Alfred considered.

"Cuthred, we need scouts to go out from here. Across the whole border area. And send messengers from me to my manors and to the Ealdormen to raise their warriors, plus to Noth, Ethelwulf and Osric. Forthred, I need you and your clerks to write messages for Cuthred's men to take. Wulfred, you and I need to head south with whatever warriors we can and gather more along the way."

Wulfred said hesitantly, "Alfred, I..."

"What is it, Wulfred?"

"What if this is only a feint? If there is more than one army? And besides, we don't know where Guthrum is going."

"Yes, true."

Cuthred said, "Lord King, sending out all those messengers and keeping a good number of warriors to defend Chippenham will mean there won't be too many men for us to take south."

"For me to take south. Cuthred, you'll be in charge here. You'll need to raise more men once we have gone so as to guard Chippenham and watch the border here. Wulfred and I will go to Pewsey and hope to find Ethelwulf and maybe Osric, then head towards Winchester if there's no sign of where Guthrum has gone. Winchester or even Southampton would make tempting targets for him, although they're very deep into Wessex. At least the

Ealdorman of Hampshire will join us for any threat to Hampshire."

Elswith put a hand on his arm. "What about us? The children and me?"

"You're too close to the border here, in case there should be another army to the north coming our way."

"Then where should we go?" She turned to Wulfred. "To Somerset where your Hild is with Noth and Ealhburh?"

Alfred considered. Somerset to the west, Dorset far to the south, the breadth of Wiltshire and then Hampshire to the east and south.

"Dorset. Sherborne. Go to Bishop Athelheah. Forthred, as well as a message to the Ealdorman of Hampshire, write another from me to Winifred. Tell her that Elswith and the children are going to Sherborne and suggest from me that she takes Wold there. It will be safer than Winchester."

"Yes, Lord King."

"Will she come?" Elswith asked.

"I don't know. I hope so."

"I suppose it depends on what wins out in her mind. Her fear of the Danes or her hatred of you."

"Is it that bad?"

"It could be."

Alfred and Wulfred had taken a day to get the men organised, pack up provisions, prepare weapons and send out scouts and messengers. Then a day's ride through a cold November saw them arrive at Pewsey in Wiltshire.

Alfred's own warriors were very well armed. Each had his own horse, a pack with provisions and a helmet attached to the back of the saddle, a mail-coat and weapons: sword and long-knife in scabbards fixed in a belt or a baldric, shield and spear on straps behind their backs.

There was anger amongst them; the Danes were back in Wessex.

As Alfred and Wulfred rode slowly into the marketplace,

Pewsey seemed a hive of activity. Men were arriving from all over Wiltshire, most not as well equipped as Alfred's. All had a spear and a long-knife and while some had a helmet, fewer had a sword and very few had a mail-coat. Horses were being gathered, but again, there were not so many.

Alfred was relieved to see one particular face. Ethelwulf appeared to be attempting to organise the men into groups that could ride onwards and groups who would be marching.

"Ethelwulf!" Alfred shouted across the marketplace.

Ethelwulf was involved in a deep discussion with a warrior holding the bridles of two horses, but he looked up, saw Alfred and smiled.

"Alfred!" he called across. "Lord King, I mean. Glad you're here. Come across to the hall and we can talk properly."

Alfred dismounted, taking care that the shield and spear on his back didn't knock his horse. A hand reached out to hold the horse's bridle.

"Thank you," he said and he made his way across to the large thatched building.

As they met at the door to the hall, Alfred shouted over the noise from the warriors crowding around the marketplace. "I'm glad to see you. What news of the Danes?"

"Let's go on in," Ethelwulf said, pushing the heavy oak door open.

"Wait."

Alfred lifted the straps holding his shield and spear over his head and found Wulfred doing the same.

With both spears and shields left leaning against the door frame, Ethelwulf lead the two of them into the semi-darkness of the hall.

When Alfred's eyes became accustomed to the dimness, he made out that the walls were lined with hangings, some plain, others with scenes of hunting or from the bible.

"You've made this homely, Ealdorman of Wiltshire."

"Ha," Ethelwulf replied. "Not so much me, more Leofe."

"Is she here?"

"Yes, at the moment." He looked around and called, "Leofe. It's Alfred."

The young woman who came from behind the curtained area at the end of the hall had the look of her grandfather, the previous Ealdorman of Wiltshire. It was an honest, assessing face.

"Lord King," she said.

"Please, 'Alfred' when we are just us."

"Alfred then."

There was something different about her.

Ethelwulf laughed. "Yes, Alfred, we expect our second towards the end of the summer."

"That's wonderful. Congratulations."

"Thank you. Early days."

Leofe said, "Is Elswith with you? I was worried with you being so close to the border."

"No. Elswith and my three are on their way to Sherborne in Dorset."

"Sherborne?" Ethelwulf interrupted. "That may not have been the best choice. I'm leaving Leofe here. So far as we know, she'll be as safe here as anywhere. There's another messenger come in, so we know now where the Danes have gone."

"You do? Where?"

"Wareham. On the Dorset coast. So anywhere in Dorset might not be the safest place."

Alfred felt Leofe's hand on his arm.

"Oh, hellfire," he said.

The messenger from Wareham had been brought in. He stood in front of Alfred, nervously wiping his hands on his tunic.

"So there was no-one to marshal a defence?"

"No, Lord King. Ealdorman Garrulf was at Sherborne and the town reeve was, um, occupied."

"The Danes just walked through the gates?"

"Well, yes, Lord King. Then they locked the gates behind them."

"And the people of Wareham?"

"I don't know. When the reeve was roused, I was told to ride to Wilton. There was fighting behind me in the town, but he said not to wait. To just get there as fast as my horse could take me. At Wilton, they said to come on to Pewsey."

Alfred ran a hand over his face, breathed deep and asked, "So the Danes all arrived by horse, travelling through the night? No longships?"

The messenger shook his head. "Not before I left, but of course the river at Wareham runs into Poole Bay, so..."

"So they could have been on their way. Do you know any more about the Danes? How many? Who's leading them? We heard from the Ealdorman of Surrey that it might be Guthrum?"

"I'm sorry, Lord King. I'm just one of the messengers sent out for help."

Alfred pondered, "Guthrum was in Cambridge. It's a very long way from Cambridge to Wareham, right across half of Wessex. If it is him, why would he do that?"

Ethelwulf said, "Alfred, I've had news via traders that a fleet of longships has been gathering in East Anglia. Not just that, but Halfdan's longships from Northumbria would join them. I had been going to send a messenger to you at Chippenham, but you're here now."

"A fleet. How many?"

"We don't know. A good number though. It may have nothing to do with this, of course."

"It may, but it's a coincidence if so. In fact, I can't believe Guthrum would ride away from his 'Kingdom of East Anglia' and leave Halfdan behind him with a fleet unless..."

"Unless they have an agreement. Perhaps an agreement to meet up at Wareham. One army by horse. Another by longship."

"So there could soon be two armies of Danes on the Dorset coast." Alfred turned back to the messenger. "Tomorrow, at first light, can you ride onwards?"

"Yes, where to?"

"Sherborne in Dorset. Lady Elswith is on her way there with my three children. She needs to be away from there. It's too close to Wareham and God help them if Guthrum or Halfdan catches them."

Alfred watched as a group of mounted men led a force of marching warriors into Pewsey's already busy market place, the morning sun silhouetting them. Their leader rode his way through warriors already preparing for a move south and worked his way across.

"Alfred," he said.

"Osric, I'm glad you're here."

"We set off as soon as we realised the Danes had bypassed us. Do you know any more?"

"Yes, they're at Wareham."

Osric dismounted and clasped arms with Alfred.

"Wareham? I had imagined Winchester. We heard you were here though so came to join forces."

"What else have you heard?"

"Only that the Danes were moving at great speed. Not stopping to loot or fight."

"So the towns between London and Wareham?"

"More or less intact. They either rode through them if it looked like there was no opposition, or around them. Anything to be fast."

"What do you read into that?"

"That they're not a raiding party, but they hadn't enough warriors to do battle and were meeting up with another force. Not that I've heard another army is on the move, but I've left half our warriors in Berkshire just in case and told the Ealdorman to raise his warriors."

"Who's leading the Danes? Is it Guthrum?"

"Oh yes, Guthrum, 'King' of East Anglia. When do we leave, Alfred?"

"Now, if you're ready to go. Ethelwulf and Wulfred are finishing sorting those with horses to set off in advance, with those on foot to follow."

"We've come through the night but we'll water our horses and let the men have something to eat and then we'll be ready."

"Good. And you know about Halfdan's fleet?"

"Halfdan?" Osric replied. "He's in Ireland. Or was, last I heard."

"He might or might not be, but we're told he has longships in Northumbria ready to sail south to join another fleet in East Anglia as soon as he gets there."

Osric frowned. "That's it then. We can expect Halfdan and his fleet at Wareham some time soon."

CHAPTER 10

It had been a cold ride, with a wind from the east finding its way through cloaks. But they were well on their way south now, stopping at Wimborne to feed and water the horses and men.

Alfred had not been to the abbey here since his brother's funeral. Even now, the memories were painful, though he tried to put them to one side.

It had seemed likely that the Danes would torch the abbey and the town on their way past to Wareham, but nothing had been destroyed.

"They rode past at speed, Lord King," the Abbot said. "Your brother's grave is untouched."

Alfred nodded. "Good. I should... I should see it."

"Of course. This way, Lord King."

Alfred turned to Ethelwulf, Osric and Wulfred. "Would you get the men ready to move on? I won't be long." To the Abbot, he said, "I'll follow you."

The Abbot led the way into the high-roofed church. Each wall was decorated with a biblical scene, dim in the gentle light from the high windows.

The church was quiet and cool, but a relief from the wind.

A scent of burning candles lingered in the air, with around the walls a number of them casting a faint glow.

Towards the east end, not far from the altar, the Abbot stopped and gestured to the floor.

"He is here," he said.

In the floor was set a larger flagstone than the others around and on it burned a single candle.

"Thank you. Would you please leave me for a moment?"

The Abbot backed away and Alfred stood there alone.

He unbuckled the baldric holding his scabbard and sword over his tunic and laid them to one side. Then, facing the candle, he went to his knees and stretched out face down on the cold stone, arms wide, eyes closed.

"God forgive me," he said aloud. "I couldn't save him. I tried."

He thought of his brother, of all his brothers. All dead. And his father and mother. None left. Now it was just him.

Even with his eyes shut, the candle seemed to pierce into him. He opened his eyes slowly.

It wasn't just him. Elswith. The children. Noth, Ethelwulf, Osric, Wulfred.

He prayed quietly. For them. For himself. For Wessex.

At last he found himself repeating the prayer said at almost every church at every service, "Deliver us, Oh Lord. Deliver Elswith and the children. Deliver them from the wrath of the northmen."

He paused, thinking that the messenger must have got through, that Elswith would be heading away from Sherborne to somewhere safer.

He heard gentle footsteps. Ethelwulf's voice said, "Alfred."

He pulled himself to his knees on the hard, cold stone. "Yes, Ethelwulf, I'm coming."

Osric was reading a message. "Wulfhere is gathering Hampshire's warriors and will meet us at Wareham."

"Good," Alfred said.

"Not all of them though. He knows about the Danish fleet and says it could make landfall anywhere along his coast even if it is on its way to Wareham."

"Ah."

They were talking quietly in the refectory of Wimborne Abbey - Alfred, Osric, Ethelwulf and Wulfred. Around them, warriors were being served food by the monks and taking it outside. There were far too many to eat inside.

"There's more. This is from the Ealdorman of Surrey. Halfdan's fleet is still delayed, he says. Halfdan is still fighting in Ireland."

"What?"

"That's what he's written."

"Show me."

Osric passed the parchment to Alfred, who scanned it and said, "So Halfdan is still in Ireland and hasn't yet joined up with his longships in Northumbria. And there's rumours that he won't. That's what the Ealdorman of Surrey understands from traders out of London. He says there's been jostling for control but the fleet may well still sail and that Guthrum's fellow 'King' Anwend seems to have taken the lead."

"Anwend?" Wulfred asked. "Who was with Guthrum in the battle at Wilton?"

"Yes, while Oscetel is at Wareham with Guthrum. All of them 'Kings' apparently."

Ethelwulf said, "There's been no report of the fleet around Kent or Sussex, has there?"

"Not that we've heard," Osric replied. "But with a fair wind the fleet would move much quicker than any messenger would find us."

Alfred said, "Thank the Lord there has been a delay. We'd better get Radmer and his longships out looking for them. We could do with some advance warning. Osric, can you get word to him and tell him to meet us somewhere near Wareham?"

"I will."

"And have we heard from Noth or the Ealdorman of Somerset?"

"Nothing."

"I hope I haven't disturbed a hornet's nest by sending Noth, Helm and Oswald there. We don't need any trouble in Somerset with the Danes holed up in Dorset and a fleet of longships on the way."

They were riding through woodland, still some way from Wareham, when shouts ahead alerted them to something going on.

"I'll go," Osric said.

"Alright."

The column came to a halt, Osric bypassing it.

Alfred called out to the warriors around, "Stay alert."

His men were scanning the woods around, but there was no sign of the enemy.

Osric reappeared. With a frown, he said to Alfred, "It's families fleeing north from a village up ahead. The Danes in Wareham have sent out raiding parties to scour the land. These have been burned out of their homes. As they fled, they saw their animals and the few possessions they had being taken off south."

Alfred said, "Garrulf won't have enough warriors raised to stop them yet."

"No, we'd better get to him as soon as we can."

"Where are the families going?"

"I doubt they know. They're just getting as far away from the Danes as they can. Most of them have probably never been much outside their own village."

The first of the families trudged past the mounted warriors. Babies and small children were being carried by the women on their hips, faces huddled into shoulders. Older children were walking, several tearful, others looking around at the warriors on their horses, wide-eyed and scared. One or two had a bag with some small possessions in. There were two older men, one limping and leaning on the other.

Alfred called to them, "Will you make for Wimborne? To the Abbey. Tell them I told you to go there and that you would receive help."

The two men stopped, one mumbling, the other saying, head bowed, "Yes, Lord."

"Where are the rest of your men?" Alfred asked them.

"They tried to fight, Lord. To stop the burning."

"Oh, God."

The two men and the rest of the sorry group trudged on past.

They could smell the burning before they could see anything.

Osric and Ethelwulf had ridden to the front, with Alfred and Wulfred still side by side in the centre of the column.

Around and in front of them the horses were jittery, making the warriors wary, each man looking into the woods either side in case of ambush.

Ahead of them, the trees were thinning, light filtering through, with what seemed to be smoke rising beyond.

"I think we've reached the village," Alfred said to Wulfred.

Wulfred said nothing, but was peering forward.

Alfred fell silent, guessing what they were about to find. He wasn't wrong.

As they came out of the trees, he found that many of the warriors had dismounted and were bent over bodies lying where they had been felled amongst the smoldering remains of a small village.

Ethelwulf rode over to him.

"We've found their men. Not a single one alive."

Alfred fought to contain his sense of anger. Just now, he needed a clear head.

"Leave a small party behind to bury them," he said. "We need to press on."

He lifted his eyes to the road beyond the village where it led into more woodland and saw, dismayed, more smoke rising.

Ethelwulf, next to him, followed his gaze. "Every village between here and Wareham will be the same," he said.

"Come on," Alfred said, and he shouted to the warriors, the anger free now, "Ride on!"

Village after village was the same. Farm after farm.

The Danes had been in a hurry to get to Wareham and had not taken time to torch and pillage the land and people on the way. Once inside Wareham though, the raids into the surrounding country were clearly much different.

Small groups of sorry families moved north along the road or emerged from hiding as Alfred and the warriors rode south. The sense of urgency grew.

Some villages were just empty husks, all of the villagers having sensibly run on the sight of smoke from the next village south. Other villages were a mix of death and sobbing families.

By the fourth village, Alfred stopped telling his warriors to stay and help bury bodies. There would be too few warriors arriving in Wareham if all of the bodies along the way were to be buried.

Wareham's north gate stood on the far side of a boardwalk. In summer the River Piddle would have been little more than a stream through marshland. Now, with winter drawing in, the whole area was a quagmire, with the boardwalk the only access to the northern side of the town. Before long it might well flood over.

The gate itself was tall and made of heavy wooden planks. It was shut fast.

On either side of it, just above river level, ramparts ran west and east. The ramparts were supported at the front by stakes buried into the ground. On top of the ramparts ran a palisade of more stakes, all fresh, new wood, at shoulder height.

Garrulf had been following Alfred's instructions to strengthen the fortifications of his towns. "He's been busy," Alfred said to himself. "Unfortunately." The Danes had the perfect defence.

A defender behind the palisade could easily duck into safety if spears were thrown, or could stand and throw his own spear or a stone at any attackers who dared to try their luck over river and rampart. Not that approaching the rampart from the north would be easy, with the land part flooded and with just a boardwalk the width of a cart as access.

Osric and Wulfred stood with Alfred, while Ethelwulf, with some scores of warriors, had been sent around to the west gate to join Garrulf. The land was drier there and Alfred didn't want to suddenly find himself hemmed in by an attack from the Danes at that point.

The south side of town had had no rampart when he had been here before, but it did have another river, the Frome. Wider and deeper than the River Piddle, the River Frome and the marshy land around it had always been thought to be enough of a barrier, but messengers from Garrulf had told him that the Danes had thrown up a small rampart there, back from the river and with a palisade on top.

The area between that rampart and the river, Garrulf had said, was wide enough to beach Danish longships arriving via Poole Bay. There were none so far. But the Danes had captured the three merchant ships that were berthed at the riverbank.

There was also an east gate that led beyond the boatyard into marshy fields surrounded by water where the two rivers ran into Poole Bay. From that direction he could hear the lowing of numerous cattle and the neighing of horses.

Alfred watched as peaceful smoke rose from fires warming houses within the ramparts. An observer might think the whole town was at peace. It was not. Behind the wooden palisades, Danes watched from the ramparts.

He heard a rider approaching and, turning, he saw Garrulf.

"I've left Ethelwulf in charge at the west gate," Garrulf said.

"What more can you tell me about what happened?"

"I wasn't here, of course. The Danes appeared from nowhere, moving fast. The gates were wide open and there was no warning at all. They were inside before the guards had even thought about shutting them. There were very few warriors in town at all. Those few who fought were heavily outnumbered and were soon corpses piled outside the west gate."

"Are the bodies still there?"

"No, the Danes let our women go forwards and bring them away."

"What's happened to the townsfolk apart from that?"

"Well, we don't really know. There's been nobody released. My guess is that they're being used by the Danes. The bakers will be baking for them. The woodworkers will be mending shields or making spears for them. The women..." He shook his head. "The Danes will do whatever they want with the women and the other townsfolk. At least until we can get them out of there."

"And food? There are a lot of them."

"After the initial taking of the town, they sent out raiding parties and brought in cows, goats and sheep from the surrounding farms."

"We know. We've seen all too many villages and farms raised to the ground and everything stolen. And bodies. Too many bodies."

"The Danes were mostly after food - livestock especially. You can hear the cattle packed on to the land to the east of the town. Between the rivers."

"Preparing for a siege?"

"It seems so. They've brought a lot in. Also, the nunnery will have had quite a stock of grain and the like."

"Any sign of the fleet of longships either here or in Poole Bay?"

"Not so far. Radmer has our longships out patrolling. They've seen nothing so far."

"So the Danes are just sitting there waiting for them?"

"Apart from the raids for food and livestock, yes."

"And have you been in contact with the Danes? Are there any demands?"

"Yes, Alfred. One so far. They want to see you."

Alfred stopped on the road, Osric and Garrulf next to him, just over a spear's throw from the western gate. Danes were watching them from the ramparts, and in particular watching Wulfred as he approached the gate, fair hair dull as low clouds loomed over them.

There came some sounds of heavy wooden spars moving. The gate eased open. A man stepped through, mail-coat and helmet making him anonymous in the shadows.

Wulfred and the Dane spoke together, out of earshot, but only briefly, for Wulfred was soon walking back towards his friends, the Dane holding his ground behind him.

"Alfred, they want to talk. I've told them you're here and they say they'll come out to you soon, if you'll wait here."

"Who was the Dane, Wulfred?"

"Well, I think it was Guthrum himself, although he didn't say so, and his helmet and the shadow made it difficult to tell."

"I wouldn't be surprised. Go back and say to King Guthrum that we'll wait for him here, the four of us. But that he should bring no more than three men with him."

Wulfred's conversation with the Dane was again brief and within moments three men were accompanying Wulfred back along the road. All wore mail, swords belted at their waists, and helmets, but as they approached Alfred and his friends, one removed his helmet. The face was familiar, five years - very nearly - having added some weight, but no beard and no scars.

Guthrum. Pagan 'King' of East Anglia.

The two men accompanying Guthrum stood either side of him, hands on sword hilts. Alfred knew who they were. The first was Oscetel, one of the Danish 'Kings' who had been with Guthrum five years before. And Huda, the Saxon working with the Danes to interpret for them.

Huda was looking pleased with himself. He was wearing a tunic, dark red and with an embroidered edging, and his boots looked new. All probably looted from Wareham.

Oscetel, bearded with long and dirty dark hair, was clearly wary, glancing now and then at the warriors a hundred paces back from Alfred.

Guthrum himself showed no signs of wariness and his face had a grim smile.

"King Alfred," he said. "We meet again on the soil of Wessex."

"Indeed we do, King Guthrum, not quite the five years of our agreement."

"Ah, but I don't believe your payments have come to me as they should and so our agreement is of course terminated."

Alfred struggled to control his temper. "Guthrum, you've bled this country dry. And no doubt you've come back for more. But you'll have nothing."

The Dane, with unconcerned face, replaced his iron helmet on his head. As his hands came down, a heavy silver arm ring slipped to his wrist. He ignored it, but Alfred's eyes were drawn to it. It was open-ended with Odin's ravens sculpted at each end, Huginn and Muninn, ravens who would fly the world each night and report back what they had seen.

Fortunately, Alfred thought, Guthrum had no such ravens and surely would know nothing of the whereabouts of the fleet.

He said, "The shires are being raised. Within days you'll be trapped here. You've made a mistake this time."

"We shall see, King Alfred. You're not prepared, then, to negotiate."

"No."

"Then let's wait those days you spoke of and we'll talk again."

To Alfred's surprise, he turned and, with a brief word in his own tongue to his companions, began to walk back down to the gate.

"Guthrum," Alfred called, and the Dane turned. "Will you release the women and children?"

Guthrum pursed his lips. "No. Not yet. Not until you're prepared to deal sensibly with me." He continued his return towards the gate. The shadows swallowed him, before the thud came of the gate closing.

"He's very confident."

Osric spoke for them all. "If there is a fleet of longships coming, he can afford to be."

CHAPTER 11

Alfred was disturbed from his sleep by Wulfred shaking him. Sitting up he felt chilled and temporarily disoriented. He took in the tent walls with only a little moonlight filtering through and the sounds of warriors preparing.

Shouts.

The grunting of warriors putting on their heavy mail, their baldrics and belts, their scabbards and swords.

"What's the noise? What's happening?"

"The Danes have made a sortie out of the north gate. A group have broken through and headed north on the Roman road through Wareham Forest towards Bere."

Alfred felt sleep fall away. "Gather the men."

"Just ours?"

"How many Danes?"

"I was told about a hundred, but it's dark, they were mounted and moving fast, so who knows?"

"A hundred. A full raiding party. Hellfire, they should never have got through."

"So do we follow them?"

"We have to."

"By the time we're ready to go, they could be miles ahead and daylight hours are short."

"We can't just wait for them to return. Where are Osric and Ethelwulf? And Garrulf?"

"Each preparing his own warriors."

"Get messages to each of them. Garrulf and Ethelwulf to stay here. Garrulf and his Dorset men at west and south gates on alert. Ethelwulf with the men of Wiltshire at the north gate. We'll take Osric and all our warriors after the Danes."

"Yes, Alfred."

"And Wulfred, I want scouts that know the area from Garrulf. We'll be following the Danes through the dark for a few hours yet."

In that dark the men and horses seemed to take an age to get organised. There was shouting, neighing, the stamping of hooves, oaths and orders.

Osric had finally arrived. His horse slewing to a halt in front of Alfred.

"Alfred."

"Where were you?"

"With Garrulf. I'm here now and your warriors are ready."

"Good. Let's go."

Alfred pulled himself up onto his horse. "You lead."

"Alright," Osric said and he called out to the warriors. "We head north. They're on the Roman road. Keep tight. Scouts ahead in case of ambush. Away now."

Osric kneed his horse and it moved ahead of Alfred.

Alfred followed, with Wulfred alongside, aware of a column starting to form around and behind them.

"Alfred," Wulfred had stopped and was looking back, the horses behind whinnying and jostling for space. "Fire. Look."

Alfred reined his horse to a halt too. From inside Wareham, flames were rising from the east side of the town.

There were shouts and more oaths from the warriors in

the column. Some were looking back, clearly afraid that the town would be destroyed with all those in it. Others were just trying to find space, their legs crushed between horses.

"What do we do, Alfred?" Wulfred was shouting.

It was Osric who answered. "It could be a ruse. A distraction to stop us following the raiders, or at least to slow us up. And it's working. Every moment we sit here, they are further away."

Alfred nodded. "Doing God knows what. Osric, move the men on. Ethelwulf and Garrulf are in charge back there."

The pace seemed too slow to Alfred.

The road, what was left of it after so many years, ran straight but was rutted and broken. The men of Rome had built this too long ago. Even so, it was the straightest way and generally above any swamp and marsh.

Through woodland it was still quite dark and the column slowed each time they passed under the trees of Wareham Forest. When out in the open, the riding was easier going with the sky starting to lighten. Even then a horse could lose its footing and go lame or fall. Twice they found a horse with its throat cut on the road. No doubt left behind as the Danes moved on.

Then they saw flames ahead.

"Slow," called Osric.

There were no shouts of warning from the scouts ahead, so the column continued. Just off the road a farmstead was burning, the thatch almost gone now, the walls collapsed.

Alfred looked on but rode past. There was nothing he could do.

About two hours in and shouts were heard from the scouts ahead. One seemed to be making his way back towards them.

"Lord King. Lord Osric."

"What is it?" Osric was saying.

They were under trees here and the darkness had closed around them so that Alfred could barely see the scout's face.

"The Danes have gone off the route. East. Another track joins just ahead and they have turned that way."

"East?" Alfred broke in. "What's east of here?"

"Some villages. Morden the closest, on the north road. Further on of course there's Wimborne."

"Wimborne?"

Osric said, "If it's Wimborne, we've no warriors in any numbers there."

Alfred turned back to the scout. "You say Morden is on the north road. Do you mean the north road out of Wareham?"

"Yes, Lord King."

"So the Danes could get to Morden and ride straight back to Wareham, leaving us still in their wake?"

"I suppose they could."

"Which would make this a ruse. A feint. While the real raid goes out somewhere else."

"But what if they are going to Wimborne?" Osric said. "They could destroy the Abbey, take whatever they can find, then head further on again, expecting to be collected by the fleet."

Alfred paused.

"It could be either. Do we follow them thinking they're heading to Wimborne in the hope we can catch up with them before they get there and we can save the town and Abbey? Or do we go straight back down this road here to try to get ahead of them before they reach the gates of Wareham again, taking Ethelwulf's men out on the way? Ethelwulf won't expect them from the north. Not yet at least."

"What's the biggest danger?"

"I don't know. Wimborne, I suppose. Even if I think this is a feint. But if it's not, then Wimborne will be destroyed. We'll follow them east, but send a messenger back down this road to Ethelwulf as fast as he can get there."

Wulfred, his horse a little way off from Osric and Alfred, made his way over.

"Alfred," he said. "There's another scout here. He's heard something. On the road ahead."

"What?"

"Horses, he thinks."

"Here? Riding through the night?"

Osric moved first.

"Men, quiet." he said in a low voice.

The warriors gradually fell silent, aware that something was happening.

"Dismount, everyone," Osric said. "Some of you take the horses further back down the road. The rest, shield wall. Get beyond the junction then spread across the road and to either side, unless it becomes too boggy. And do it quietly."

Alfred slid off his horse, a hand in the dark taking the bridle from him.

He moved to Osric's side, the two of them staring into the night. "Danes?" he said.

"This is what they do. Arrive by night. Nottingham, Repton, Reading."

"I know."

Alfred felt Osric's hand on his arm, leading him quietly to the junction where a smaller trail led off to the right. In front, in the darkness under the trees, the Roman road was almost invisible.

Their men were forming up, shields overlapping, helmets in place, swords and knives loosened in scabbards, spears in hand. All without talk. Ahead though, Alfred could begin to hear riders approaching. It sounded as though there were many of them, and their loud voices suggested they had no idea they were riding into a trap.

"Wait till we can see them."

Osric was speaking in a low voice to the rows of warriors in front of him, each with a shield overlapping his neighbours. Each with spear to hand.

"They still don't know we're here. When I say 'now' beat spears on shields, shout, make as much noise as you can to spook their horses. Then walk steadily forward."

There were one or two murmurs of 'Yes, Lord,' but otherwise the men were silent in the darkness under the trees. These were Osric's men, King's men, trained before by Noth and Alfred, but now under the discipline of Osric.

Alfred could feel the tension. Almost smell it. If these were Danes riding towards them, they would be seasoned warriors. If they weren't, well, why would they be on the road at night if they weren't Danes?

There were a great many horses coming towards them. Any talking amongst the newcomers drowned out by the sound of hooves on the track. They were going at no great speed, seemingly, but then they appeared, a vision of horses and men almost ghostly in the dark.

"Now!" Osric shouted, and the air was filled with the crashing of spear on shield and the shouting of 'Wessex, Wessex'.

The horses at the front of the column reared and broke sideways, men falling.

Alfred felt rather than saw their own shield wall begin a slow march forwards.

Still the noise, the beat of spears, the shouts.

Ahead was confusion and pandemonium, horses lurching into each other, men panicking.

The warriors in the shield wall now placed their spears above and between the front row of shields, ready to push into Danes, and the noise level dropped.

And then there was a voice. So loud it cut through the shouting of the shield wall.

"What do you mean, 'Wessex'?"

Alfred paused. He knew that voice. "Stop," he shouted. "Stop."

The shield wall fell silent and held their place.

From the darkness, the voice called, "Alfred?"

Alfred smiled. "Noth, what in the name of God are you doing here?"

A figure loomed towards them on foot, his horse seemingly gone.

"Me? What about you? And if you've hurt my horse with all this, you can bloody buy me a new one."

Osric was off re-organising. Men were being reunited with their horses and the newcomers were being brought through and given a place in the column.

A messenger had been sent back to Wareham to warn of the Danish raiders possibly attacking Ethelwulf's men of Wiltshire from the rear - if he could be back there in time.

Alfred stood to one side, with Noth and young Helm and Oswald by him.

"Seriously, what are you doing travelling at night?"

"Speed, Alfred. That's what the messenger said. So we've ridden most of the day, had a few hours sleep at Bere then come on from there. What are you doing here, facing away from Wareham?"

Alfred explained about the raiders and Noth nodded. "So shall we join you going east?"

"How many men do you have?"

"About fifty. Some of my own following plus a few from new nearby manors when your message found us."

"What about Ealdorman Eadwulf? Is he sending any of Somerset's warriors?"

"I don't know. To be honest, I doubt it. He's not altogether pleased with me or with you. I imagine he will think that defending Somerset's northern border is more important."

"Well, perhaps it is. We thought you were another army of Danes on the way through Mercia to join Guthrum in Wareham."

"No sign of another army from that direction. Though there are stories from the traders of a fleet and army around the coast of Wales. Led by Halfdan's brother Ubba."

"You know Halfdan's still in Ireland?"

"Thank the Lord for that."

"Guthrum is more than enough. Helm, Oswald, how have you got on with this oaf here?"

"Hoy," Noth said.

In the gloom, Alfred could see Oswald smiling. "He's been teaching us. Weapons. The shield wall. And how the Council works, with the Ealdormen of Somerset and Hampshire and so on."

"Alright. Not entirely wasted getting you to spend time with him. Now, find your horses. It looks like Osric is ready and we've lost more time here. Time we might not have if we are to catch up with the Danes."

The track east had not been as wide as the Roman road to Bere, and it had twisted around hillocks rather than running straight over them. Gradually the sky had lightened though, with the sun soon to break the horizon, and they seemed to have made good speed.

One of Garrulf's scouts came back from the front of the column.

"We're almost at the north road, Lord King."

"Take it slowly then, in case there's a trap of any sort."

"Yes, King Alfred."

The scout rode forward again.

"Alfred," Noth said, "have you thought about how the Danes would have known about this track?"

"Yes. They clearly have local guides, just as we do."

"And that's not a good thought."

Some minutes later they found themselves on another straight road, this one heading north in one direction towards Wimborne, south back to Wareham in the other.

Osric was there. "They turned south, Alfred."

"Ah. Not Wimborne then. Well, I'm very pleased for the people of Wimborne, but this was clearly a feint and it's worked. They've tricked us. Come on, let's get back to Wareham and see what damage has been done."

By the time they reached the north gate, it was clear that the messenger had not arrived in time.

There were warriors being treated for wounds, bandages drenched in blood, while Ethelwulf was helping carry a limp body across to one side of the road.

Alfred and his friends halted, watching on.

"Hellfire," Alfred said. "We're too late."

Ethelwulf, with the body laid carefully on the ground, looked around.

"What happened, Ethelwulf?" Alfred said, swinging down from his horse.

"Those raiders fell on us from behind and as soon as the Danes on the ramparts saw it, they sallied out as well." He wiped bloodied hands down his tunic. "It was all over in minutes. Many of our men were cut down from behind. No time to form a shield wall or even defend themselves properly. Then the raiders were through us and the gate swung shut. The Danes in Wareham have been singing away ever since."

Alfred shook his head. "But why? Why would they risk it? Has something else happened?"

"You could say that. I've heard from Garrulf. There was what seemed to be another group of raiders out of the west gate. Garrulf called his reserve in to hold them, but that was also a feint. Some hundreds of Danes used the merchant ships as a makeshift raft across the river on the south side of town. Garrulf's men couldn't hold them. They were loose in Purbeck for a while. No doubt raiding wherever they wanted. Garrulf sent a detachment after them, but didn't dare send all his warriors. Then the Danes reappeared, driving cattle across the river and into the town. Again with warriors coming out to hold off Garrulf's men."

"So they've more food to keep them going till the fleet

arrives."

"So it seems."

"And once they have a fleet, they can raid anywhere along the south coast."

CHAPTER 12

"How's your stomach, Alfred?"

"I'm trying to ignore it, Noth."

They were alone in Alfred's tent, Alfred lying on his couch bed, Noth sitting on a stool. It was cold and gloomy, with only a dim light filtering through the tent fabric.

Noth said, "Three days since that raid and nothing stirring from inside Wareham."

"They're waiting," Alfred said, stifling a wince as a pain jolted his stomach.

After a pause Noth said, "Can we afford to let them sit there?"

"We've still not enough men for an assault. And even with more men, it could turn into a disaster if we're not careful."

"Like Reading."

"I wouldn't make the same mistakes as were made at Reading. Even so, an assault would be dangerous."

"So what do we do?"

Another painful jolt. Alfred breathed in and out slowly, mastering himself. "I don't know."

"How much does that hurt?"

"Enough, Noth. Enough."

"You know Wulfhere is due shortly? And Odda."

"I know. I'll be alright. I'll have to be."

The Ealdorman of Hampshire was quieter and more thoughtful than usual. His finger-nails were scraping across an unshaven chin as he looked across at the town of Wareham.

A low sun was casting a golden glow on the ramparts.

Odda of Devon, too, was restrained. These two opposites, one usually loud in his bitterness and suspicion, the other more often loud in his enthusiasm and conviviality, stood side by side, concern on their faces. Alfred stood a pace behind them, one hand across his stomach, the pain now more of a dull ache.

"How many are there, Alfred?" Wulfhere asked.

Alfred felt that the ache was under control and said, "Over a thousand, I would say. Perhaps fifteen hundred. It's a guess though. And those that saw them might have exaggerated."

"We've more than that anyway," Odda said, "or soon will have once my men and Wulfhere's have all arrived."

Alfred said, "Plus Eadwulf's Somerset warriors, when he arrives."

Odda said, his back to the others as he inspected the deceivingly quiet town, "Don't expect the Ealdorman of Somerset in a hurry, Alfred. He's not well. He might send men, but he won't be leading them."

There was a noise from behind and Garrulf was there, his face red, his eyes on fire. Alfred moved to restrain him, but there was no time and in any case, he wasn't sure he was in a state to.

"Wulfhere." Garrulf sounded furious. "Why the hell was there no warning? How did Guthrum get across Hampshire to Wareham without you knowing? Or did you know but not think it worth telling us?"

The Ealdorman of Hampshire seemed to grow in height

as the attack came and to revert to type. "Don't think you can blame me for this mess, Garrulf," he said, his growl with the venom of old. "They came through my shire at night, but what happened when they crossed the border into Wessex in the first place? Where were the famous warriors of Alfred's, supposedly defending the Thames?"

Garrulf opened his mouth to attack again, but the Ealdorman of Hampshire overrode him. "And where were you, Ealdorman of Dorset, when the Danes walked into Wareham without a fight? No, you can look elsewhere for someone to blame."

"Ealdormen," Alfred interrupted, his hand on Garrulf's arm to prevent an answer. He felt a jolt from his stomach but contained it, aware that Wulfhere was watching him closely. "We're all tired and there's nothing to be gained by fighting amongst ourselves. I propose that we retire to our own men and get some sleep."

Odda spoke for him. "Till the Council tomorrow then, Wulfhere. Garrulf."

He placed a hand on the arm of each and gently manoeuvred them in opposite directions.

The two Ealdormen gave brief nods to Alfred and turned away.

"Thank you," Alfred said quietly to Odda.

Odda looked at Alfred. "Tomorrow," he said.

"Are you sure you're up to this, Alfred?"

Noth was holding the bridle of Alfred's horse, the first, cold light of day rising to the east behind them and beginning to hit the ramparts of Wareham to the south.

"I'm sure. I need to see what's what from higher up. Before the Council meeting."

"Alright. Don't you go collapsing on me though. You've already done for one of my horses."

Alfred smiled. Just a dull ache today. "Where are Osric, Ethelwulf and Wulfred?"

"Waiting for you. Like me."

The five of them rode west, Osric leading the way, with the land rising into heathland of scrubby bushes and grasses. After no great distance, Alfred turned his horse and was able to see across and down to Wareham town.

With the new day's sun now filtering into the town, Alfred could see two of the gates set into the town's ramparts. The west gate was closest, made of oak planks, not high, but high enough, he thought, with those ramparts on either side manned by Danes. There were a good number of them, their helmeted heads silhouetted against the lightening sky behind.

The north gate, closest to where he had camped and where he had met Guthrum, was equally strongly guarded. On that side too, the flooded river Piddle was a barrier.

Alfred looked beyond to the south side of town. He could make out the river there, wider and deeper, with the three merchant ships tied up at the bank close to the nunnery. No sign of Danish longships though. Thank the Lord for that. The new rampart built by the Danes just back from the river was out of sight, but it was another barrier against an attack.

Alfred glanced around him. His friends were also staring down at the town.

He said, "We'd struggle to get in there to drive them out, even if we had men enough."

He lifted his eyes. Beyond the town, in the fields between where the two rivers met, were so many animals, it seemed like one body swaying in the sun. Horses on the south side, cattle on the north.

"They're not about to starve, Alfred," Osric said.

"They'll need feed for the horses before long. They'll surely soon run out of the stores in the town and at the nunnery. You're right though. They think they just need to wait till their fleet arrives."

Noth said, "Then there could be many times the number of warriors they have now."

"And mobile enough," Osric replied, "with that fleet to get armies of warriors anywhere along the coast. Hampshire, Dorset, Devon. The whole south coast would be vulnerable. And via Southampton Water they could be at Winchester before we know it. From Portland they could be at Dorchester. From the river Exe they can be at Exeter. And everywhere in between."

"Remind me what's south of Wareham," Alfred said.

Osric replied, "The road from Wareham leads through more marsh and over heath towards the gap in that line of hills. The village in the gap is Corfe and there's a gated manor on the hill in the gap. With the marshes, the heath and then that row of hills, Purbeck is almost like an island. That's the way the locals think of it, anyway. Then off to the east of Corfe there's Studland. A good, wide flat beach. Further south there's the village of Swanage on the coast."

"Also with a beach? Could the Danes land longships there?"

"Yes, if for whatever reason they didn't come into Poole Bay or land at Studland. It's not a wide beach for a large fleet though, and they'd have to watch the cliffs on either side. There's danger in getting too close when the tide and wind are wrong."

"Are there cliffs on both sides of Swanage?"

"Yes, there's a rocky point on the north side between Swanage and Studland with great white standing rocks in the water. Beyond Swanage to the south there are high cliffs around most of the coast stretching a long way west. The dancing ledges are particularly lethal."

"Dancing ledges?"

"Flat shelves of rock that stick out into the sea for a good long way. When the tide covers it, you'd have no idea what was there."

"So, really, if the captains of the Danish longships had some local knowledge, they would head into Poole Bay and not risk the cliffs around Swanage? Unless it's calm weather, or they have someone to guide them in."

"That's right."

"Can you get lookouts placed on the cliffs to send us warning of sightings?"

"Already done," Osric said. "With beacons to light and pass the word down the chain. They will come, Alfred. We just don't know when."

Alfred pondered and said, "I think Guthrum hasn't made a mistake at all. If his plan worked, he would have Wareham as a secure base in the centre of Wessex for his horses and warriors, linked by river to Poole Bay and space there for this new massive fleet of longships. If that were to happen, he knows he could end Wessex from here."

Back where they had camped, his warriors had a fire going and he moved towards it, hands out to take whatever heat he could find.

Smoke was rising from warm homes within Wareham.

He missed Elswith. Yule with Elswith and the children.

"Am I getting too old for this, Noth?"

"Too old? No, you've just gone soft."

Alfred smiled and took a small loaf of bread that one of the warriors offered him.

"Let's get the Ealdormen and the rest of the Council here as soon as we can."

"I'll send word out."

Alfred took a bite of the loaf, chewing thoughtfully.

"I hope Wulfhere was as uncomfortable as me last night."

"I doubt it. He was going off to find a manor to stay in. In Wool or Bere probably. It's only idiots who would be the ones to stay close to Wareham to make sure the Danes don't break out again."

"Thanks for that, Noth."

***

"Bishop Athelheah," Alfred said.

They were standing on the heathland west of the town, with a blustery east wind blowing low cloud above them.

His friends stood on his right, Osric and Noth, Ethelwulf and Wulfred, with the Ealdormen of Dorset, Devon and Hampshire opposite. On his left were his secretary Forthred and Athelheah, the Bishop of Sherborne.

Behind each of them were warriors and clerics, each listening as best he could.

Not so far off, the west gate of Wareham stood solidly closed.

"Thank you, Lord King." The Bishop raised his hands wide and looked around, his voice commanding now. "The bible says, 'Be strong; fear not! Behold, your God will come with vengeance. He will come and save you.' Put your trust in the Lord. Be strong against these pagans and we will overcome."

Alfred bowed his head.

"Amen," came from those around.

Looking up, Alfred said, "This must be a hasty Council. We must make some decisions quickly. First, is there any news of the Ealdorman of Somerset arriving?"

Wulfhere spoke up. "He's not well, Alfred. But a force of his warriors is on its way with his cousin, Eadred. He is to be under my command, Eadwulf says."

Alfred frowned. "So be it."

"He won't send them all. He needs to be wary of another fleet coming out of Wales. Rumour has it that Ubba is there."

"That's something we can do without. I sent a message to Elswith and the children to go northwards. Now I'm not sure. Where are Winifred and Wold?"

"Still in Winchester. For now."

"Nowhere is safe," he said. "Osric, is there any more

news of the Danish fleet off East Anglia?"

"None since yesterday. When last we heard, it was still beached in East Anglia. Radmer has our own longships strategically placed along the south coast, which should hopefully give us some warning. Not much, of course. The Danes can move fast when they start."

"But we still think that Guthrum arrived here when he did because he was expecting the fleet to meet him here?"

"It's the only conclusion I can come to."

"So your advice would be to deal with Guthrum before he is reinforced?"

"That's all very well," Osric said, "but I've looked at every possible means to get warriors inside, and we could face the same odds that led to defeat outside Reading. We have no option but to negotiate and, if we can, pay them off."

Wulfhere shifted on his feet, that defeat - and his blaming of Alfred - clearly still rankling, though he said nothing.

Ethelwulf said, "I'm sorry, Osric, but I disagree. I admit that I wasn't at Reading. But I was at Nottingham even before that, when no attack was made at all. The King and Ealdormen of Mercia simply capitulated, paying off the Danes. Because we didn't fight, the Danes came back and came back. And what state is Mercia in now? No, we must fight. Must."

Alfred frowned. These were two men whose views he respected. Both were right, and how could they resolve that? "Garrulf," he said. "What do you think?"

"It is a question of the balance of dangers."

He fell silent and the Ealdorman of Hampshire was too impatient to wait. "Meaning what, Garrulf?"

The Ealdorman of Dorset's voice was again quiet and contained. "Attacking the ramparts of Wareham could work, of course. But honestly, I think it's unlikely. I had those ramparts built up, new palisades on top. And giving Guthrum silver to go? Why would he take it, when he's expecting a fleet of longships any day? Which he hopes will win him a Kingdom."

"Very helpful, Garrulf," Wulfhere said. "So what would you have us do?"

"Wait. Wait and see if the fleet does materialise. With Halfdan still across in Ireland and without his leadership, perhaps the fleet will disperse. In the meantime, we blockade the town, not allowing any more raids. They may have meat from those cattle for the warriors, but they will soon run out of feed for their horses."

"So that's your advice, is it? Do nothing. What do you think of that, Odda?"

The Ealdorman of Devon, usually pugnacious, was sitting quiet. "I don't know," he said. "I do think that we shouldn't do anything too hastily."

"But that," Ethelwulf said, "just allows them to build the ramparts higher and better if they feel the need to. To dig a ditch in front of the west gate perhaps. And it leaves the people of Dorset on the inside of those ramparts. Alfred, we must do something now. We must attack."

The eyes of all those there turned to Alfred and he turned over in his mind three conflicting pieces of advice. To pay the Danes off, if they would take it. To attack. Or to do nothing and to hope that the Danes, or at least their horses, started to go hungry, cutting off their means of escape if the fleet did not appear. He fiddled with a ring on his finger, twisting it absent-mindedly, and paced.

"We wait," he said, facing the Ealdormen. "We wait." He ran a hand over his face. "Ealdormen, we wait."

Eadred, the young cousin of Ealdorman Eadwulf and his nominated 'heir' to Somerset, was standing facing Alfred.

"Lord King," the young man said.

"Thank you at least for acknowledging me as King. Your cousin still struggles with that, I think. Even after these years and in these circumstances."

"I'm sure Ealdorman Eadwulf would acknowledge you in the same way, Lord King."

"He hasn't so far, Eadred. Did he tell you to acknowledge me?"

"I... well, I can't speak for him."

"No. No, you can't. But you are here with his warriors?"

"Yes, Lord King, though not all of them. Eadwulf believes he needs to keep most of his warriors to hand in case of invasion from the north."

"I see. And your warriors are to be put at my disposal?" Alfred asked, already knowing the answer.

The young man coloured. "Eadwulf said they were to be under the authority of Ealdorman Wulfhere of Hampshire."

"So really nothing has changed with Eadwulf. Tell me about yourself. What experience do you have of battle, Eadred?"

"I have trained with the Ealdorman's warriors."

"You've been involved in no real battles or skirmishes so far?"

"Not yet."

"But Eadred has nominated you as heir?"

"He has no children. So, yes, I am his heir. He says..."

"Yes?"

"He says it's much like you were your brother's heir when you had no experience of battle."

"I see."

"I will..."

"Say it."

"I will make a good Ealdorman for you, Lord King."

"How old are you?"

"Seventeen. About the same age as when you became heir to the Kingdom."

"Alright, let's leave it at that for now. Take your men around to the camp near the north gate. You will find Wulfhere there."

"Yes, Lord King."

"But you understand, Eadred. A King appoints

Ealdormen."

The young man blinked.

"Yes, Lord King."

CHAPTER 13

"Alfred, wake up."

It was Wulfred's voice in the darkness. Through the tent fabric.

Alfred pulled the blanket away from himself.

"What is it? What's happening?"

The tent flap was wrenched away and Alfred felt rather than saw Wulfred appear in the door of the tent.

"Something's happening on the south side of town. With the merchant ships. They're trying to be silent, but we've watchers close in."

For twenty days and nights there had been no change. A miserable Christmas day had come and gone. The days had become colder. The nights more so. Men were fretting, frustrated, unhappy.

The Danes had waited.

Alfred had waited.

Only Wulfhere had run out of patience the previous afternoon, stumping away from Alfred and muttering about being needed further east. Which was possibly true, Alfred had to admit. If and when the Danish fleet finally arrived, they could do a lot of damage along the coast before they reached Poole Bay. So Wulfhere's warriors had set off for

Hampshire and Wulfhere had sent the small number of Somerset warriors, along with Eadwulf's cousin, back to Somerton.

Of Wulfhere's sons, the younger Wulfhard had gone with his father. The older son, Wulfstan, was said to have been left at Wimborne with a large group of warriors, ready to counter any move out of Wareham eastwards towards Hampshire.

Meanwhile, more warriors had arrived from elsewhere in Devon, Dorset and Wiltshire and were camping where they could find dry ground. The main problem would be feeding them and any horses they had brought.

In the darkness, Alfred felt around for his boots and pulled them on, tying the toggles by feel.

"Let me out, Wulfred."

He rose and followed Wulfred outside where he found it was no lighter than inside the tent. Low cloud, no moon and cold. No sign of sunrise. An ideal moment for the Danes to raid out of Wareham.

Alfred had moved his tent to the west side of town, so as to be able to deal with raids more easily than where he had been on the north side. Even so, it would take a while to take warriors around to the south side beyond the river and marshy flooded ground.

"Is Garrulf there?"

"Yes, he's quietly gathering his men so as to ambush the Danes once they cross the river. He sent a messenger to tell us what's happening. I've sent word on round to Ethelwulf and Osric at the north gate in case it's another feint."

"Noth's here?"

"Yes, with Odda, Oswald and Helm. They're getting our men in place in case of an attack out of the west gate."

"We're spread too thin if it's a large-scale raid."

"Garrulf thinks it's not a large raid. It's too quiet for that. There's some stealth in the movements."

A figure appeared and Noth's voice said, "How are you, Alfred?"

"I'm fine."

"Your-"

"Fine."

A pause. "Good. Alfred, I was thinking to take warriors round to support Garrulf."

Two figures appeared next to Noth.

"No, you stay here with Oswald and Helm. Make sure they're safe. I'll go. But only with a handful of men. This is the obvious place for any major raid on horseback, so we can't thin out our warriors here. You've raised them?"

"Happening now. As quietly as we can."

"Are the horses within easy reach in case we have to follow mounted Danes?"

"Yes, I've kept them near to hand."

"Well done. Alright, Wulfred, let's get round to Garrulf."

Garrulf's man had his hand on Alfred's arm and was guiding him down a slight slope towards the river.

"This way, Lord King. Do you see the coracle?"

The tiny boat was tied to a low post and he could just make out more coracles slightly upstream.

"Yes, I see it. How many do you have here?"

"Four, Lord King."

"Good. Take me in the first and Wulfred in the second, then ferry the other warriors over."

"You'll need me to show you the way on the far side. It's marshland and the paths would be impossible for you to find. It's a black night."

Alfred stepped down and his boot found water.

At his oath, the man said, "Have you done this before?"

"Used a coracle? In the Somerset marshes when I was hunting with Lord Ethelnoth, yes, but not in the dark."

"Let me go first then."

The man let go of Alfred's arm, turned and stepped backwards quickly into the coracle.

"Now you."

Alfred tried to repeat the process, with limited success, and flopped on to the small wooden seat next to his guide, the boat rocking alarmingly.

"It's alright, you're in. Just sit still."

They waited a moment and the rocking subsided. Two back and forth strokes from the man's paddle in front of the coracle and they were away from the riverbank.

Just then, a commotion came to them from some distance downstream. Shouting, something heavy hitting water. All too far away to see what was going on.

More shouting, another great splash. Then another.

Alfred said, "Wait. What do you think that was?"

The man paused in his paddle strokes, listened, then said, "They had the merchant ships pulled up on the riverbank. I'd say that was three merchant longships being pushed back down the bank into the river."

The sound of wood clattering on wood.

A drum started, two drums, three. Each beating out a time.

"That's to keep oarsmen in time in the dark."

The sound of the drums very gradually began to diminish.

"And that's the sound of three ships full of warriors going a-viking. Probably fortunate, Lord King, that they're rowing away from us, rather than towards us."

The sky was finally beginning to lighten when Alfred found Garrulf standing on top of a ridge south of the town.

Oak and ash woods obscured the view back to the town, despite the bare branches of winter, but eastwards beyond wide marshes lay Poole Bay. Even so, there was nothing now to be seen in the dimness of the early morning with low cloud above them threatening rain.

"They'll be well out across Poole Bay by now, Alfred," Garrulf said.

"Not a raid to get feed for the horses from Purbeck

then."

"No, but it could easily still be a raid. If I was them I'd be heading for Hamworthy, Poole or some such, across the far side of the Bay."

"We've none of our longships to hand?"

"Radmer has one along at Arne near the river mouth to keep watch and another on the sandbanks by the entrance to the Bay. The rest are scattered east of us along the coast."

"So not enough to deal with three merchant longships full of Danes."

"No."

"God help Hamworthy and Poole then. What about when they come back?"

"My guess is they'll offload whatever they have downstream, where the horses and cattle are. Maybe leave the longships there for now."

"Can we get at them when they're there? The longships?"

"Not very well. There's marshland on both sides of the river, but the locals have long had paths and hidden boardwalks on the far side so that they can offload before the town so as to avoid the reeve. Even if we brought our longships back and crammed them with warriors, we'd be trying to land against a well-armed group of hundreds of Danes. And then we'd have fewer longships to give us a warning when the Danish fleet arrives."

"Hellfire."

"It's going to be almost impossible to stop them raiding using those longships around Poole Bay."

"Alright," Alfred said. "In the meantime we should get word out to all the villages and farms around the Bay to withdraw inland."

"And burn."

"Burn?"

"Burn. Destroy. Anything that can't be moved inland."

"This is your shire. Will you do that?"

Alfred looked at the grim expression on Garrulf's face.

"Anything that needs doing."

***

It was late in the afternoon, the winter sun low in the sky behind them, when the Danish longships returned.

Garrulf had brought Alfred and Wulfred back to the ridge.

The three of them stood together watching the three heavily loaded longships being rowed upstream on the River Frome. The rowers were singing, chanting in time to their oar strokes, clearly pleased with themselves.

Garrulf had his warriors with him, but unless the Danes came close to the solid ground that Garrulf had occupied on the south side of the river, the Danes could clearly simply offload what they had brought slightly downstream.

Behind Alfred, the warriors were restive, some beginning to shout at the Danes.

The Danes ignored them and pulled the longships across to the north bank well beyond where spear or arrow from the men of Wessex might reach them.

As the Danes began to unload what seemed to be mostly feedstuffs for horses, one man stood out. Alfred recognised him. Tall, unkempt, an air of authority.

"Oscetel."

Wulfred said, "Again."

"Yes. 'King' Oscetel." Quietly, he said, "What have you just been doing, Oscetel?"

Oscetel looked towards them. He seemed almost to give a slight bow, then turned and disappeared into the reed beds towards Wareham.

"Radmer, what can we do?"

Alfred had borrowed a horse from Garrulf to ride down the Arne peninsula to meet up with Radmer close to where the rivers ran into Poole Bay. It was the day after the Danish raid and word had come back that Hamworthy had indeed been raided. Men, women and children had been killed if they had not fled, while Oscetel's Danes had filled the three merchant longships with hay and grain, meat and valuables.

From the mud bank at Arne where Radmer's longship was pulled up, there was smoke in the air on the far side of the Bay.

Burning.

Garrulf would now be there, doing what he said he would do. Burning.

"To stop them raiding, you mean, Lord King? Give me more longships and I will stop them getting out of the river. Bottle them up."

"How many would you need?"

"Three. Four would be better."

"We don't have those without taking them away from your watching of the coast."

"Better, I think, that we have those longships here. And we do what we can to give you warning of the Danish fleet. Perhaps the fleet won't come?"

"I still believe they'll come. And when they do, keep your few longships well out of the way. We'll need them."

"If our longships are in Poole Bay watching the river here, a fleet of Danish longships entering Poole Bay would simply destroy them. It would be a death trap."

Alfred paused. "Whatever I do, people will die."

"What's your decision, Lord King?"

"Three longships here, based at Arne. Another where you have one now on the sandbanks. At the first sign of the Danish fleet, the sandbanks longship gets here with all speed. Then you sink our longships."

"Sink them?"

"Sink them so they can't be used by the Danes. And run."

CHAPTER 14

"There's a Dane come through the gate, Alfred."

"What do you mean, Noth?"

"Just standing there."

"Do you think they want to talk?"

Two long, slow months on from Oscetel's raid and there had been no movement from inside Wareham.

The days were longer. In the woods around Purbeck, where men were sent out to hunt, the snowdrops were giving way to primroses. Butterflies with orange and black wings were fluttering in search of warmth and nectar. And birds unaccustomed to a Wessex winter were returning from across the sea.

The camps around the outside of Wareham had developed almost a feeling of permanence. No Dane or Saxon had emerged from the gates. The merchant ships had stayed pulled up on the riverbank. Only on the eastern side was there often movement, with the numbers of cattle and sheep being whittled down as the Danish garrison and - hopefully their Saxon hosts - were fed.

Wulfhere was away at Winchester. Garrulf came and went. Ethelwulf and Osric were north on the border.

Still the fleet had not come.

"Shall I see what he wants?" Noth asked.

"We'll both go. We have plenty of warriors on alert?"

"Wulfred is seeing to it."

"Good. Come on then."

As they approached the western gate, Alfred recognised the man. Not a Dane, but Huda, the Saxon interpreter. Alfred suppressed a feeling of anger.

"You speak to him, Noth. I don't trust myself."

Noth gave a sort of smile. "You trust me to deal with him then?"

"Just don't kill him."

"I'll try not to."

Alfred stopped fifty paces back from Huda. Wulfred moved alongside, numerous warriors behind and around. On the ramparts, the Danes were several deep.

All watched Noth walk towards Huda.

"Lord Ethelnoth." Huda's voice seemed full of disdain.

Huda, as when they had seen him before, was richly dressed, this time in a blue tunic with woven edging. A large silver brooch was pinned to it. At his side was a sword, its hilt richly decorated with jewels.

"It's Alfred I want," he said. "Send him over, would you?"

Noth said, and his voice carried back to the watchers, "King Alfred will decide for himself whether he wants to lower himself to speak to the likes of you. Give me the message from your 'king' and he can make that choice. I assume you have a message?"

"Oh, yes. Tell him that Guthrum needs feed for the horses and food for the people in Wareham. But that he doesn't necessarily need all the people."

"Meaning what?"

Huda raised his voice slightly, clearly intending for all those listening to hear.

"That unless you supply us with food and feed, we will

need to find a way to reduce the numbers of people eating. And I don't mean letting anyone go. So this is the message from King Guthrum and King Oscetel: you have until tomorrow morning or you will begin to see bodies come over the ramparts."

Huda turned and stalked back towards the gate. Noth seemed to watch him go, then walked back to Alfred.

"I'm not sure we have a choice, Alfred."

"You don't think Guthrum's bluffing?"

Noth thought about it. "I doubt it. He's clearly kept all the townsfolk of Wareham there for a purpose. And this is it. To use as hostages."

"How ruthless is he?" Alfred asked, more to himself than to Noth.

"Do we want to test that?"

"But if we feed them, we can never starve them out."

"Did you think we could?"

"No, I suppose not. We are running out of options though. So be it. We'd better let Garrulf know. These are his people. In the meantime, would you arrange feed for their horses and food for them. At least it gives us time to think."

By first light the following day, carts were drawn up at the western gate.

Alfred and Noth looked on, morose warriors behind them.

The Danish warriors on the ramparts, however, were clearly in a very good mood, laughing and pointing.

It was Huda that pulled the gate open. He was followed through by a large group of Danes. They approached the first cart, which was rapidly abandoned by the Saxons who had been pulling it.

Huda made a low bow to Alfred, a grin on his face, and watched the Danes as, one by one, they pulled the carts rumbling through the gate.

The Danes on the ramparts cheered each cart and when the final one was through, Huda called across to Alfred. "Until tomorrow, King Alfred."

Noth, speaking quietly, said, "Now that we've started, we can't stop."

Alfred said, "Perhaps you should have just killed him."

"The longer this goes on without the Danish fleet arriving, the more strength we will have to negotiate."

There were loud voices from all around Wimborne Abbey's refectory.

"But if the fleet suddenly appears in Poole Bay, it's over. Alfred will have nothing to negotiate with. We have to negotiate now. Get them out of there."

"I still say we need to attack Wareham. To take it back."

"No-"

"Stop." Alfred came to his feet at the end of the table.

Around him, the voices came to a halt.

He was about to go on when the Ealdorman of Hampshire interrupted, "Alfred, we-"

"Enough, Ealdorman. We have been over this too many times. Everyone has an entrenched view. It's time for a decision."

Alfred's friends, the Ealdormen, the Bishop, Elswith, they all waited. Silent now. Long months into the takeover of Wareham by the Danes.

"We negotiate."

Elswith was watching Alfred from the bed in the guest room at the Abbey. Candles burned on a small table next to Elswith, giving a soft light in the darkening room.

Alfred stood by the door.

"Am I right?"

"There's no right and no wrong in this. Just a decision."

He nodded. "Are the children alright with Bennath?"

"Yes, of course. Wilton is a long way from Wareham. And they love Bennath."

"Thank you for coming."

She smiled. "Moral support?"

"Something like that."

He sat down on the end of the bed, saying nothing, but taking off his boots and unwrapping his leggings. He stopped, sitting there.

"What?" she said. "What is it?"

He swung round to face her.

"I need not just to get Guthrum out, but to keep him out. And to stop the fleet."

"Yes. So-"

"I can give him silver. Maybe enough to get him out, if he's starting to believe his fleet isn't coming. But even if it is enough, I need something to stop him coming back." His voice softened. "For our children and their children. I need a way that I can trust him. And he would need to trust me. He needs to know they can ride out of here and we will simply escort him to the border, not attack him. I have an idea, but... many won't like it."

"Tell me."

He took a breath. "When we take oaths to one another, we each do so on a bible. Or on a holy relic. Together. Face to face. It holds us. Binds us."

"They're not Christians. Why would that bind Guthrum?"

"No. They're pagans. So... what if Guthrum and I take an oath on a pagan symbol?"

She was quiet a moment.

"You and he would swear an oath on a pagan symbol?"

"I told you people wouldn't like it."

"The Bishops, you mean? Athelheah will surely understand."

"I'm not so sure. But it goes much beyond that."

"What would you swear on?"

"You remember what I told you he was wearing when

we first arrived? The arm ring?"

"With Odin's ravens on it?"

"Yes."

"You, the Christian King of Wessex, would swear a sacred oath with a pagan on Odin's ring?"

Alfred looked into her eyes but said nothing.

The candles flickered in a draught, threatening to blow out, but then steadied.

Elswith looked down. "Do whatever you need to do."

He still sat there, unmoving.

"There's more," he said.

"Tell me."

"I'm going to need hostages from him. So that we know he means what he says."

"Good."

"And he will want hostages from us."

"Oh."

She waited, but Alfred sat silently.

"Who?" she asked.

"I don't know."

"But significant people. They would have to be. Alfred, if you get this wrong, you... we could lose everything."

"Yes, that I do know."

The Bishop stood with his back to Alfred.

"You want my support for swearing a sacred oath on a pagan arm ring?"

"We need to bind Guthrum in the same way it would bind you and me if we swore an oath on a Christian relic."

Bishop Athelheah turned to face him.

"Lord King, I have supported you in many ways until now."

"I know."

"Even when you were taking land and silver from monasteries and abbeys to pay off the Danes last time."

"Yes. Thank you."

"When the Archbishop condemned you for it."

"Yes, you did."

"And threatened to excommunicate you."

"Yes."

"But this..."

"Athelheah. Please."

The Bishop looked down, took a breath and, when he looked back at Alfred, said, "The best I can do is not condemn you for it."

"I would also have both of us swear on a Christian relic. On something that even Guthrum would recognise."

Athelheah looked thoughtfully at Alfred. "I could bring a relic from the holy St Aldhelm, founder Bishop of Sherborne. Even Guthrum might recognise the power and authority of God in that relic."

"Good. Yes. Thank you, Athelheah."

"Bishop, you cannot let this stand."

"Ealdorman Wulfhere, I will not condemn the King for seeking a way to end the invasion."

"You say he should swear an oath to Odin?"

"No! Absolutely not. The King will be swearing an oath, yes, but not to Odin. In his heart it will be to our Lord and he will swear that oath on a relic of the holy St Aldhelm. It is Guthrum that we will expect to swear an oath to Odin and on the relic."

"Wulfhere," Alfred interrupted from his end of the table, "I am open to better ideas."

"Like the hostages?"

"If we and they have hostages, an oath sworn on Odin's arm ring and on the relic of St Aldhelm and we agree a payment of silver, how can he not take his warriors out of Wareham and out of Wessex? The hostages will be returned at our border and the oath to Odin might just make him pause before returning."

Osric said, "There's still the fleet, Alfred."

"Which still has not arrived. I'm beginning to think it's not coming. And Guthrum must be thinking that by now. He can have had no word. All this time. He must believe that it's not now coming at all."

The Ealdorman of Hampshire said, "Who are you proposing to let them have as hostages, Alfred?"

"We will see who they demand."

"Yes, but there is also who you will let them have."

Alfred frowned. "Well, we will see."

"And who do you want from them?"

"I know one. Oscetel."

Alfred and the men of the Council stood well back from the western gate. Across the top of the ramparts, rows of warriors watched them, spears to hand.

Wulfred walked forward and, as he did so, the gate swung partly open.

A man stepped through. Oscetel.

The discussion between Wulfred and Oscetel was brief. Wulfred walked back to Alfred, while Oscetel slipped back through the gate, which quickly closed behind him.

"Well, Wulfred?" Alfred said, and he was aware of all those close hanging on every word.

"Oscetel says that Guthrum will meet you. As you said, I proposed six from each side."

"And..."

"He wants to meet just you. No one else. And no weapons."

As Wulfred finished, the gate swung part open again. Two men stepped through, each carrying a short stool. They carried the stools half way between the watching men of Wessex and the gate, placed them a pace apart and returned to the gate. Again, the gate closed behind them.

Alfred faced his Council. Wulfhere in particular was looking unhappy.

"It seems I am not being offered a choice," Alfred said.

"For now at least. I'll see what the man has to say and then we can talk again as a Council."

Wulfhere frowned, but Alfred turned his back and walked slowly towards the stools.

Osric's voice stopped him. "Alfred, your sword and knife."

"Ah, yes."

Osric stepped forward and took both from him. "Good luck. And good bluffing," he said quietly.

The gate swung part open and this time Guthrum stepped through. The Danish King appeared also to have no weapons. Alfred noted though the arm ring with Odin's ravens.

Alfred reached the stools first and waited as Guthrum made his way there, clearly assessing Alfred.

Once the Dane was a short distance away, he came to a halt and said, "King Alfred."

"King Guthrum."

Guthrum gestured at the stools. "Not really fit for Kings, but shall we?"

They both sat, hardly a sword's length apart. Alfred glanced around. The Danes lining the ramparts. His own men ranged either side of the westward road.

Guthrum started. "You asked for this meeting, Alfred. What is it you want to say to me?"

"You have been waiting on a fleet of longships, Guthrum. Would you like to know why it has not come?"

The Dane pursed his lips. "I think you are going to tell me."

"Halfdan is still in Ireland."

"Ah."

"Without him, the fleet has not sailed and now never will. It has disbursed in argument and rancour, each captain or king searching for easier pickings. That changes the balance of power here from what you had anticipated. If I am not mistaken, you rode with your men across Wessex to the best harbour in southern Wessex to meet up with the largest fleet of longships every assembled. Instead, you find yourselves blocked in, with no means of escape, with decreasing amounts of food for your men and feed for your horses."

Guthrum bowed his head. When he looked up, he said, "If that is all true - if, I say - what do you propose?"

"We want you out of Wessex, Guthrum, not just for now, but forever. We will allow you to walk back to where you have come from. We will accompany you using your horses and we will hold hostages for your good behaviour until the border. And, Guthrum, I want an oath from you not to return."

Guthrum smiled. "An oath? Do you have a relic there for me to swear on?"

"You will swear on your arm ring. Swear to Odin himself that you will never return to Wessex, not you or your men."

Guthrum looked down at his arm ring and, when his eyes met Alfred's again, they were not smiling.

"Alright, King Alfred, now let me tell you what I propose. You may or may not be telling the truth about Halfdan and the fleet. I cannot tell. Perhaps I will ask you to swear on a relic that what you have said is true." He raised an eyebrow.

Alfred did not react.

"So be it. But you do not hold all the power here to be able to demand that we give up what we hold."

He raised his hand and clicked his fingers in the air.

There was the sound of struggling on the ramparts near the gate and then of talk and dismay from the men of Wessex.

Alfred looked up at the ramparts and saw a man being held on the outside of the palings, just above the gate, hands tied in front of him, a rope around his neck and a long knife close to his throat.

"King Alfred. This is the reeve of Wareham."

Guthrum raised his hand again and once more clicked his fingers.

Alfred watched as two women had the same treatment, one on either side of the reeve.

"One is the woman the reeve was with when we stormed the gate. The other is his wife. I don't know which is which."

The three were now trying very hard to keep their footing, each gagged and tied.

"Guthrum, stop this."

The Dane raised his hand again and even before he had clicked his fingers, a body came over the palings, screeching through his gag. A boy, not yet a man.

Guthrum glanced up. "Ah, the reeve's son. Would you like to see his daughters, Alfred? He has three. Quite young."

"Alright, Guthrum, you make your point. Stop this."

Guthrum turned on his stool to face the ramparts and shook his head.

"So let us negotiate properly, Alfred. You want us out of here. Yes, we are prepared to go as of course we cannot know why the fleet has not arrived. We will both swear an oath to Odin on this arm ring, I that we will ride away and not return, you that you will not hinder us. You will swear the same thing before your God. And you will pay us to go, just as you did before. Hostages, yes. From both sides. I think that is how you do it in Wessex."

It had come back to this. Perhaps it was always going to.

"Within bounds," Alfred said, "I think we can agree that."

Guthrum stood. "Tomorrow, Alfred. Here again. And we will hammer out what is to happen. The oaths, the amount of silver, the names of the hostages each of us will demand. I will propose four."

"You already know who."

"I already know."

As Alfred watched him, the Dane stood, turned and marched back to the gate, while the four on the palings were pulled back inside the ramparts with no gentleness, tumbling back over.

BOOK TWO: VENGEANCE

A young girl's voice was screaming for her mother.

CHAPTER 15

"Alfred, how do we know which hostages to ask for from Guthrum?" Noth asked quietly as they sat in Alfred's tent.

"Demand, not ask for," Alfred replied. "Oscetel, we know."

"But other hostages?"

"If Anwend was here, then he would be one."

"He's with the fleet. So far as we know."

"I think we demand three other captains and see who they demand of us."

The following day, stools had been placed outside the gate again. The same implacable faces on the ramparts. The same men of Wessex facing the Danes. Alfred and Guthrum facing each other, the two having just sat.

"Ealdorman Ethelwulf."

Alfred paused. "No."

"Lord Osric."

"No."

"Lord Ethelhelm."

"No."

"And Lord Ethelnoth."

"No."

"Then this is not a negotiation."

The Dane stood from his stool, turned his back and stalked off.

At the gate, he shouted back, "Two days time, Alfred. We start again."

When daylight finally came the following morning to a day of low cloud and heavy rain, the reeve's body hung limply from the ramparts.

By mid-morning a messenger had arrived, wet and exhausted, from Kent.

"The Danes, Lord King. The longships out of East Anglia. They are coming."

"Ealdorman Ethelwulf."

"No."

"Lord Osric."

"No."

"Lord Ethelhelm."

"No."

"Lord Ethelnoth."

"No."

"Alright, wait, Alfred. Ealdorman Garrulf and Ealdorman Wulfhere."

"No. No Ealdormen."

"The Bishop of Sherborne."

"No."

"Then one of Ealdorman Wulfhere's sons and Ealdorman Garrulf's daughter. Also one of your Abbots - Wimborne or Sherborne." There was a moment's silence before he went on. "And Lord Oswald."

Alfred waited, letting the names sink in.

"I... I will need to consider. To consult."

"And who do you demand from our side?"

"Oscetel. And three of your captains."

"Three captains, yes. Oscetel, no."

"Then we start again tomorrow, Guthrum, and let me be clear, there must not be another body hanging from the ramparts."

"Or?"

"Don't do it, Guthrum."

They were all present, Alfred's friends, the Ealdormen, Bishop Athelheah, Helm, Elswith. Plus Wulfhere's sons Wulfstan and Wulfhard, Garrulf's daughter Gunhild, the Abbots of Sherborne and Wimborne, Oswald.

Alfred had brought them away from Wareham's ramparts and they stood on a small hillock, Alfred in the centre.

The wind was strong but the rain had stopped for now. Dark clouds blew overhead.

"Osric, tell everyone what the messenger has said."

Osric moved to join him. Looking around the Council, he said, "There is a vast Danish fleet on the move. It was seen at Thanet off Kent, which led the Ealdorman to send us his messenger. In the time the messenger has taken to get here, it could easily be nearly here."

"But no word of it from anywhere else closer?" Wulfhere asked.

"None. The wind has been against them, though they could be creeping along the coast."

Alfred said, "We need to conclude the negotiations and get Guthrum's army out of Wareham before the two can join up. Is there anyone who disagrees with that?"

Silence.

"Of course, Guthrum does not know this. Must not know it. Radmer, can you redouble your efforts to stop any longships coming into Poole Bay before Guthrum is gone?"

"Yes, Lord King. Can I say something about the fleet?"

"Please."

"The wind has been blowing strongly from the south west, west and north west," Radmer said. "It looks set to continue, blustery and wet. The Danish fleet may struggle to make headway along our coast, whether sailing or rowing. They would have to shelter at various places."

"But we have no word of them on the coast since Thanet."

"No. So perhaps they are not coming along our coast. Perhaps they have crossed the sea and will come along the Frankish coastline. Then straight north, so far as they can, to Poole Bay. We would have no warning at all."

Alfred frowned. "Yes. Yes, you could be right. Is there anything we can do about that?"

"Honestly, no, Lord King."

"Guthrum must not hear any of this. Ealdorman Garrulf, can we be certain that no one can get into Wareham over the ramparts or through the gates? We cannot know if Guthrum has spies here, but must assume he does."

Garrulf nodded. "We'll redouble the guards both close to Wareham and on the roads in."

"Next then, I propose offering Guthrum half of the silver that he accepted when he left Wessex last time. Offering more might suggest we are desperate for him to go. Does anyone here object to that?"

Again, silence.

"The oaths. You all know that I have agreed to swear an oath on Guthrum's Odin arm ring. I know some of you are unhappy with that and I'm not going to say I am happy with it either. However, if it holds Guthrum to his word, I am prepared to do it."

Silence.

"Lastly, the hostages."

"Not my sons." Wulfhere's voice was not loud, but it reverberated around the company.

"Wulfhere-"

A woman's voice interrupted. "I will do it. I will be a

hostage."

Alfred turned to find the source of the voice. It was a young woman, very young, hardly more than a girl, standing in front of Ealdorman Garrulf, his hand on her shoulder.

He recognised her. Gunhild. Garrulf's older daughter.

Garrulf stepped forward. Quietly, he said, "Gunhild and I have discussed this. She is prepared to be a hostage in order that we rid ourselves of the Danes."

The Abbot of Wimborne also stepped forward. "And I also accept what fate offers."

From next to Wulfhere, his son Wulfstan moved into the centre of the ring.

His father said, "Wulfstan, no."

"If the Lady Gunhild and the Abbot are prepared to offer themselves as hostages, then how can I refuse?"

Then all eyes turned to Oswald, standing by Elswith.

His face coloured. Elswith took his arm and she turned her eyes on Alfred.

But it was another voice that said, "I will be a hostage."

"Helm," Elswith looked with horror at him. "No. Alfred!"

"No, Helm. I have already said 'no' to Guthrum.

Oswald detached himself from Elswith's arm and came to stand by Alfred. "Yes," he said. "Yes, I will do it."

"Alfred, you can't let Oswald do this," Elswith said.

She had taken Alfred to one side and was speaking quietly and earnestly to him.

He reached both hands forward and took hers.

"I do believe he will be safe, Elswith. I do."

"Then why did you not say 'yes' to the others? To Helm?"

He dropped his hands and turned away from her.

"Say it, Alfred."

He turned again to face her.

"Because it is not entirely safe. And Wessex can afford

to lose an illegitimate son of a King, but not a legitimate one. No matter how attached we are - you are - to Oswald."

He realised that she was silently crying, tears rolling down her cheeks, and he took her in his arms. She sobbed into his shoulder.

After a minute he said, "We have to be brave, Elswith. Like Gunhild. Without her bravery earlier..."

"I know. I know the fleet are coming and we have to make sacrifices. But Oswald-"

"What else can I do, Elswith? Honestly, what else?"

She stood back from him and looked into his eyes.

"Nothing."

"You can march your men to the border, Guthrum. There we will pay you half of the value of silver that was agreed after the battle of Wilton. And you can have the hostages you named - Wulfstan, the son of the Ealdorman of Hampshire, Gunhild, the daughter of the Ealdorman of Dorset, the Abbot of Wimborne and Lord Oswald, my nephew."

"Good."

"There are conditions."

"Tell me."

"As a hostage, we must have Oscetel. And three of your main captains. You will swear an oath on Odin's arm ring that the hostages you hold of ours will be handed back to us unharmed once we have you out of Wessex. And you will swear to Odin that you will leave Wessex and not return."

"I need your oath in return. You will swear not to harm Oscetel and my captains. You will swear to allow us to march freely through and out of Wessex. You will swear to raise and give us the silver. All sworn twice, once on Odin's ring, once on a holy relic of your own. Then if you break your oath, there will be no hiding from any of the Gods."

"We have an agreement."

"We have an agreement, Alfred. Bring the hostages here

this afternoon and a relic you propose to swear on. We will walk out of here tomorrow morning. Northwards."

The two stools were not present. Instead, a table had been placed in front of the western gate to Wareham.

By it stood Guthrum, Oscetel and three men.

Guthrum looked unconcerned, while Oscetel was clearly angry. The other three nervous. Fearful, perhaps.

Alfred led Wulfstan, Gunhild, the Abbot and Oswald towards them. None were armed, though the Abbot carried a small silver casket.

As they approached, Guthrum said, "King Alfred." He gave a slight bow, then looked at each of Alfred's companions. "Yes, these are them."

"King Guthrum. I know Oscetel, but these are...?"

"Captains of my longships. I don't think you need their names."

Alfred frowned, but no, perhaps he didn't.

"Abbot," Alfred said, "the relic."

The Abbot, in his robes, stepped towards the table and carefully placed the casket on it, saying, "A relic of the holy St Aldhelm." The box was finely worked in silver and had precious stones inlaid.

"St Aldhelm?" Guthrum asked.

The Abbot said, "The peace and mercy of our Lord God flowed through St Aldhelm."

Guthrum shook his head. "Abbot, you should know that my god, Odin, is a war-god, seeker of wisdom, a King's god. He has these two ravens," he said, pulling the arm ring from his wrist and placing it by the casket, "that fly the world, watching and listening, then whisper in his ear everything he needs to know."

"A powerful god, then, Guthrum," Alfred said, "who will know if you are not true to your oath."

Guthrum smiled and placed his hand on the arm ring. "I swear to Odin that I will not harm these hostages, that we will walk out of Wessex and return them safely to Alfred of Wessex, so long as our hostages are not harmed, that we are not hindered and that we are paid the promised silver. Does that satisfy you, Alfred?"

"So far as it can."

Alfred placed his hand on the casket and, looking into Guthrum's blue eyes, said, "I swear to the Lord God that, if Guthrum holds to his oath, we will not harm these hostages, that we will allow him and his men to walk out of Wessex unhindered and that we will pay the promised silver."

"And now on the arm ring," Guthrum said.

Alfred hesitated, glancing at the Abbot, then put his hand on the cold silver of the arm ring. Once more looking at Guthrum, he repeated the words. In his mind, he said, 'Forgive me, Lord'.

To Guthrum, Alfred said, "And now you swear on the relic of St Aldhelm. Our God is a God of peace and mercy, the Abbot says, but our Bishop says he is a vengeful God."

"Very well, Alfred." He placed a hand on the silver casket and, with perhaps a smirk on his face, said, "I swear on this bone, or whatever it is, that I will not harm the hostages and that we will walk out of Wessex. Enough?"

"Enough."

"Then we are finished. Oscetel, take our captains and go with King Alfred."

Alfred took a breath. "Wulfstan, Gunhild, Abbot, Oswald, thank you. We will see you very soon."

Guthrum picked up his arm ring and replaced it on his wrist. He made a mock bow to his four hostages and waved them towards the gate.

"So tonight we can all rest easier, Alfred," he said, and he raised his voice so that all around could hear. "Perhaps your warriors can have some mead, some ale, knowing the oaths each of us have sworn. Mine certainly will."

He raised his arm to the Danes on the ramparts, miming drinking from a flagon, and received cheers in return. From some of the warriors behind Alfred, there also seemed to be a ragged cheer. Perhaps a sign of relief that this was nearly over.

Guthrum spoke more quietly direct to Alfred. "Until tomorrow morning then."

Alfred watched the five of them until they reached the gate, which was opened wide from within. Through it stepped all bar Oswald, who looked back, meeting eyes with Alfred, before he too disappeared from view.

"I'm not happy about this, Alfred," Wulfhere said. He, Odda, Garrulf and Alfred were standing apart from the others. "Wulfstan is my eldest son."

"He made the choice himself in the end."

"Only under pressure from..."

Wulfhere's voice trailed away, but Garrulf finished the sentence. "My daughter."

"Alfred, I was going to say."

"No," Garrulf said, "I believe it was my daughter's courage that gave us the agreement."

Odda said, "I think that's true. We owe her a great deal. Now, Alfred, with this agreement, I will set off back towards Devon. We don't know, of course, whether the Cornish were meant to be part of Guthrum's plans or whether Ubba is over in Wales with a fleet. I will make my way back to Exeter. Do you have enough warriors to escort Guthrum and the Danes northwards?"

"Would you leave a portion of yours here with Garrulf?"

"Of course."

"Thank you. I'll send messengers to let you know what happens. Wulfhere, are you staying?"

The Ealdorman frowned. "No, Wulfstan can follow on when he is released, but I should go back to Hampshire with my men. Who knows where the East Anglian fleet is now? They may not be coming to Wareham at all. It could be Southampton. Or Portland. Or Exeter. Or nowhere. A messenger will find me at Southampton."

"Alright, well, we seem to be in agreement, Ealdorman Wulfhere, which has not always been the case. I hope we can keep it like that."

Wulfhere looked briefly into Alfred's eyes, nodded, then turned and left.

The other two Ealdormen seemed to exchange a look, then they too nodded to Alfred and set off for their own men.

Alfred found Elswith by his side. Quietly he said, "I know you're not happy with this."

"No. It shouldn't have been Oswald."

"What other choice did I have? If I had declined Oswald, the Ealdormen would have refused and that would have been the end of any agreement."

"I know, but he's so..."

"Young? Not any more. He's not a boy now, Elswith. He's old enough to make up his own mind."

"Please God he and we have made the right choice."

"Amen."

"Alfred, I need to get back to the children. I'll ride as far as Wimborne and go on from there."

"Yes, good. Wulfred can come with you with an escort."

"Thank you. Please, Alfred, take care. I don't trust the Danes at all."

The noise of celebration from within Wareham kept Alfred awake till late. Singing, drinking, shouting. His own warriors were also clearly in celebratory mood. Then the wind got up and his tent door started to flap. It never seemed to quieten.

Utterly tired, Alfred finally fell into a restless sleep, half-waking now and then with uncomfortable dreams. Once he felt for where Elswith would be, before remembering that Wulfred had escorted her to Wimborne Abbey.

So when he heard shouting and the sounds of horses' hooves, many of them, he was at first confused, uncertain in the darkness of where he was and what was happening.

Then his name was called.

"Alfred! Alfred!"

Noth.

The tent door was ripped back and the wind whipped in.

"Alfred, the Danes!"

He sat up. "What? The Danes?"

He heard more thundering horses, screams, shouts.

"The Danes are breaking out."

"They can't be."

Alfred stood, then bent to pick up his sword and long-knife in their scabbards, before heading outside into complete confusion in the black night.

Men were running everywhere - his own warriors - with streams of Danes on their horses driving past them.

There were so many of them, galloping horses, the smell of animals and men, and there was no stopping them.

Alfred stood frozen.

Then there were more screams from behind, horses' screams, men's screams, shouting.

The horses. Their own horses.

He ran, half tripping over tree roots and stones, towards where their horses had been corralled.

He knew as soon as he got there.

The noise, the stench. It was carnage.

Wessex's warriors and horses were dead or dying, rolling in agony or lying still, while a last few Danes rode away into the darkness.

CHAPTER 16

Perhaps Alfred's eyes were now more accustomed to the darkness or perhaps it was the first glimmering of a dawn beyond the low cloud being driven across the sky on a strong wind.

Either way, he could make out more of the carnage where the horses had been held. 'Keep the horses close', he had said to Noth, so that they could deal with any raids out of the western gate.

How wrong he had been. All the noise, the drinking, it had been a sham. A cover. He had been so wrong. On all of it.

Guthrum had sworn his oath to Odin knowing that he was going to break it that same night. That the Danes would ride out and...

The hostages. What about the hostages? Oswald, the Abbot, Gunhild, Wulfstan.

He stumbled back towards the town's gate. All around were stunned warriors, standing, uncertain. Though now he could begin to hear voices of authority.

Osric's voice. "Form up by the gate! You, get your weapons. Then get to the gate."

Then Noth. "Osric, I'll round up the horses. We need to

get after them."

"Good. Where's Alfred?"

"I'm here. The horses have nearly all been slaughtered. Those we had close by. Is that gate open, Osric? Have the Danes all gone?"

"Must have. The gate's swinging open and there's no Danes on the ramparts either."

"What about the hostages?"

"I don't know. I'm getting warriors together to get inside and search now."

"And the Danes we hold?"

"I've sent one of our warriors for them."

"Send messengers round to Ethelwulf and Garrulf. They have horses there. Get them round here. Which way did the Danes go?"

"Hard to know. Westwards from here, but the closest way to the border is north."

"Oh, God. Elswith. She's gone north."

Noth put a hand on Alfred's arm and said, "We can't follow without horses, Alfred. We need Ethelwulf's and Garrulf's if our own here have been killed. Even then, we wouldn't have enough to take on the Danes. All we could do is follow."

Alfred said, "Let's get inside the town. Perhaps Wulfstan and the other hostages will know which way they are going."

"Unless the Danes took the hostages with them," Noth said.

"You're assuming," Osric said, "that they are still alive."

There was silence between them, thinking the almost unthinkable.

"But we hold Oscetel and his captains," Noth said.

"Do we? The Danes knew where the horses were. Perhaps they also knew where Oscetel was. Or didn't care."

As they pulled the gate wide open, some of the inhabitants of Wareham were beginning to emerge. Pale anxious faces.

"Have they gone?" a woman called to Alfred and his

friends from her doorway.

"Yes, they seem to."

The woman fell to her knees. "Thank the Lord," she said and she began to sob. A youngster appeared and clung to her.

Osric said, "Let's try the great hall."

He led the way through the town, more townsfolk now appearing either side. There was relief, but still fear.

At the hall itself, in the market square in the middle of the town, no faces appeared. There was silence from the half-open door.

"I don't like this," Osric said. "I suggest you wait here, Alfred."

He pulled at the door and disappeared inside.

It was a matter of moments before he was back.

"I'm sorry, Alfred."

"Tell me."

"They're dead. All four. Plus the reeve's family."

"Oh, hellfire."

"Their throats..."

Alfred thought of young Oswald. How could they? And Gunhild. The Abbot. Wulfstan.

"The reeve's children?"

"All of them."

"No."

Alfred walked slowly past Osric towards the great hall. He stood in the doorway, the smell taking him back to battles he had lost or won, the smell of blood.

He stepped inside.

It was dark, the faintest light coming from small windows. Even so, he was able to make out the bodies, hands tied behind them.

He felt such anger and desolation. As if he was responsible, and perhaps he was. It had been his agreement with Guthrum. His hand on Odin's arm ring. His hand on the relic of St Aldhelm. And this was the result.

Noth was standing facing him, though his face seemed

hazy.

"Alfred, you didn't do this."

"Noth..."

"You didn't kill them. The Danes killed them."

Alfred tried to turn away, but Noth had hold of both his arms.

"Alfred. Now, more than ever, you're needed. Don't look inside yourself for blame. Look outside. Look at the Danes. And remember what the Bishop said. Ours is a vengeful God." A pause. "Alfred."

"Alright. Yes, alright."

With one hand on Alfred's arm, Noth was leading him outside.

From off to one side a voice broke his thoughts.

"Lord Osric, we have the Danes here. The hostages."

"Bring them," Osric replied.

"Yes, Lord. Guthrum's men had searched for them before they rode off, but we had them hidden and kept them quiet."

Alfred tore himself away from his own thoughts and found himself looking at Oscetel and the three other Danes surrounded by a group of warriors. Each had his hands tied behind his back and ankles hobbled by looser rope. Oscetel was at the front. Where before he was confident, head held high, now his face was heavily bruised and he shambled, limping.

They all had similar injuries. They had, as the warrior had said, been kept quiet and Alfred had no sympathy whatsoever.

"Oscetel, did you know?" Alfred said, his anger boiling inside him.

The man just looked at him.

"Did you know what was going to happen? And do you know where Guthrum is going?"

A fist from the Saxon warrior hit Oscetel in the side of his face and the Dane stumbled.

Alfred felt Noth's hand on his arm again.

"Wait," he said. He forced himself to breathe. To calm down. "His English is not good. He had a Saxon interpreter when we saw him before."

He turned to the other three hostages. "Which of you speaks English?"

Silence from all of them.

To Osric, he said, "Get someone who speaks their language. Radmer if possible."

He looked at the hostages and said slowly, "Osric, show them what their comrades have done inside the hall. We need information. Quickly. So... do what you need to do."

Osric signalled to some of his warriors and they led the hostages into the hall, there was the sound of scuffling and a long wail that was suddenly cut off.

Alfred turned as he heard a horse from the direction of the northern gate.

"Alfred!" Ethelwulf's voice.

The horseman came to a halt by Alfred, and Alfred caught the bridle.

"Ethelwulf, the hostages. They're dead. All of them."

"Oh, dear Lord."

"And if they're heading north, your sister will be in their path. Where are your warriors and how many have horses?"

Ethelwulf was still staring at Alfred. "The hostages."

"Ethelwulf. We need to catch up with the Danes before they come across Elswith."

"Yes. Yes, Elswith." He shook himself. "My warriors are preparing to ride, those with horses, but there's nowhere near enough with horses for us to take on the Danes. Where's Garrulf?"

"Not here yet. Do you have spare horses? For Osric, Noth, me and at least some of the warriors here?"

"Not spare ones. But you take what you need. We'll need warriors here anyway. In case the fleet arrives."

"Oh, God, the fleet." Alfred took a deep breath. "One thing at a time. Osric has the Danish hostages in the hall there and is trying to find out what they know."

Garrulf and Radmer came hurrying in from the southern side of town, clearly having heard the last words of Alfred and Ethelwulf.

Garrulf asked, "What about Gunhild and the others? Oswald? The Abbot? Wulfhere's son?"

Alfred put a hand on Garrulf's arm.

"I'm so, so sorry, Garrulf. They've been killed. By the Danes as they left."

Garrulf went rigid. He said, "Alfred, my daughter?"

"Garrulf, I am so sorry."

"Gunhild..."

He made for the door to the hall.

"Garrulf, no," Alfred said, but it was too late.

Alfred and Noth watched the door for a moment, but there was silence now.

Ethelwulf said, "How could they... Why?"

"I suppose the Danes thought their hostages might have picked up on some or all of their plans. Like which way they are heading now. Radmer, we need you. Osric has the Danish hostages in the hall there, but we need someone who speaks their language."

"I'll go in."

"Good. Ethelwulf, your warriors. Bring as many as you can around to the western gate. We'll bring everyone together there."

"Yes, Alfred. And we think they are heading north, out of Wessex?"

Osric appeared, replacing his knife in its scabbard. "They're going west, Alfred."

"West?"

"To Exeter."

"Why Exeter?"

"They still have hopes for the fleet, but also believe the Cornish might ally with them."

"Oscetel told you this?"

"No, one of the captains. I... well, we have two hostages left."

Alfred nodded. "And Oscetel?"

"Still with us. For now."

"Is he talking?"

"Nothing."

"Alright, make it plain to him through Radmer that if he helps us in some way, he may live. If he doesn't, he won't."

"You'd keep him alive? After what the Danes did to our hostages?"

Alfred looked at his friend.

"No. We won't. But for now, he might be more useful alive."

Noth turned to Alfred. "I know you want to get straight after the Danes, but we can't forget that there's a huge fleet of longships on its way here."

"You're right, Noth." He paused. "If there are that many mounted warriors on their way to Exeter, we won't be able to stop them anyway. Even if we could catch them with the horses we have here, we're too few to take them on."

Noth said, "We could try to get a messenger to Exeter to warn Odda and Exeter's reeve. Garrulf..."

The Ealdorman had emerged from the great hall, a stunned look on his face. Realising Noth was speaking to him, he shook his head and said, "What?"

"Garrulf, I'm sorry, but how long would it take ride to Exeter from here?"

The Ealdorman glanced back at the doorway behind him, then turned back again. Taking a deep breath, he said, "For the Danes? There are a lot of them and the horses will be carrying weapons and supplies, not just men. Maybe four days if they push their horses."

Alfred said, "I suspect the Danes may catch up with Odda. He won't have been in the sort of hurry the Danes will be. But yes, let's get messengers away to Odda, to Exeter and to any other towns in the path of the Danes. They have to be warned, if we can. And Exeter could maybe hold out if the gates are closed on the Danes. The town still has its walls."

Alfred had seen Exeter's walls before. Many generations before, the Romans had built great thick walls encompassing a promontory close to the River Ex. The town had grown since then, making it a busy port for merchant longships from the Kingdom of the Franks, Frisia and further afield.

So there really were 'walls' at Exeter, not earthen ramparts and fences, and Alfred knew that Odda had been filling in gaps and increasing them in height where the wall had broken down. Defended in numbers, they would be almost impossible to scale. But only if the gates had been closed on the Danes.

If not, Guthrum had chosen well again.

"The other towns, and even Odda, won't be able to take them on," Osric said. "Our forces are all too scattered."

"No," Alfred said, "I mean that the messengers should tell the people on the way to flee."

An image of Oswald's youthful face came to him. That last look as he walked through the gate into Wareham. To his death. Alfred did not want Oswald's fate to be replicated along the route to Exeter.

He went on. "So send out warnings as fast as we can. To Exeter, Dorchester, Honiton, everywhere along the route. Tell the people to flee. But at Exeter, if they can, close the gates. In the meantime, we need to work out how we would deal with a fleet of longships. "

Osric went on. "Wherever they land, we will be too scattered. If they had come along the coast we might have had warning of where their target was. But they haven't. We think it is probably Wareham, as they will have no idea that Guthrum has gone. But it might not be."

"Alright," Alfred said. "Osric, gather all the mounted warriors we have. From them, pick the fastest and send them off as messengers to try to get ahead of the Danes. Then follow them when the main body is ready."

"Yes, Alfred."

"Garrulf," Alfred said. The man was quiet, his look far

away. "Garrulf."

"Yes, Alfred. How could they...?"

"Garrulf, you need to be here to try to prevent the same thing happening to others if the Danish fleet arrives."

"Yes, yes, I need to be here."

"But we need horses to get after the Danes. Will you help with that?"

"Alfred. After what I have just seen, anything."

"Osric, send messengers back to me and to Garrulf. Dorchester would be on their direct route. The Lord knows what they will have done there."

"You're not coming with me?"

"Not yet. First, there's the fleet to think about."

A stronger gust of wind caught them. It was carrying rain. Large drops spattering them as they stood there.

"Lord King." It was Radmer. "I was on my way to tell you when this happened. We have word from the Franks. The fleet are now there, but not raiding. I believe they are just resting up before they sail to Wareham."

"They won't know yet that Guthrum has escaped. They will still be planning to relieve a siege."

"Yes, Lord King. I think they will watch for a drop in the wind, then come."

CHAPTER 17

Day had come but the light hardly with it. The clouds were low and the wind was gusting even more and carrying rain.

Osric and Ethelwulf had left with as many warriors as they could find horses for, following a trail clearly westward. Fast-riding messengers had gone off to try to warn those in the path of the Danes.

Garrulf and his warriors were beginning the grisly process of moving the dead hostages, including his own daughter, to the church by the northern gate.

Others in the town had also suffered. There had been deaths, destruction and in particular there was the fate of many of the nuns at the hands of the Danes. Athelheah would have to be told of that, as well as of the death of the abbot.

Another messenger was on his way to Wulfhere from Alfred. The eldest son of the Ealdorman of Hampshire had been murdered in cold blood and the Ealdorman's anger would likely know no bounds.

Then, Alfred could barely to think of it, Oswald was dead. A young man, scarcely more than a boy. His nephew. His brother's son. A messenger had gone north to find

Elswith and to tell her. She would be devastated. And, Alfred thought, it was his fault.

Even so, the fleet was coming.

He shook himself. "Radmer, I need to get more of a sense of the lie of the land for when the fleet arrives. I want to see anywhere else it might land rather than come into Poole Bay."

"They could beach their longships at Swanage or Studland. Both have a sandy beach. Then they would come on to Wareham from the south."

"So I understand. And then they would expect to catch our besieging forces in the rear and by surprise. Noth, would you find us horses? Radmer, can you take us there."

He looked to the sky, the rain spattering his face, the wind blowing his hair and beard.

Noth was also contemplating the weather. "Will the Danes come today, Radmer?"

"No. They will wait. And this weather could be set in for some time."

Alfred frowned. "I'll spare a day, but then I think I have to follow Osric and Ethelwulf."

Noth said, "Are you sure?"

"No. No, I'm not sure of anything. Almost every decision I have made has turned out to be wrong. And look at the result. But we know we have Guthrum and his Danes heading through Dorset and Devon towards Exeter. I could wait here for the fleet and it might not come."

Radmer said, "It is coming, Alfred. I just don't know when."

Alfred, Noth and Radmer rode south on a track through open heathland.

Garrulf had provided a guide and provisions for the day's ride, while a warrior had brought their cloaks against the rain.

The ground was sandy in places, with damp wet peat

elsewhere being recharged by gusty showers, which also soaked into the cloaks pulled over their heads.

Alfred pushed them on. He begrudged the time not chasing Guthrum westwards, but he needed to understand what might happen behind him.

A long, low ridge faced them, broken by a gap only part filled by a lower hill with a ring of palings around the top, inside which were a number of thatched houses.

The guide said, "That's the manor for the village of Corfe, Lord King. We head east from here."

He led them on another track over and around hills and woods. After some way, dunes rose up and the guide said, "We should walk from here."

They hobbled the horses and strode through the dunes, their feet sinking into soft, golden sand.

When they came out at the top of the beach, the sand stretched away northwards, the wind whipping it up despite the squally rain. On the southern side of the bay an arm of the ridge made a wooded promontory projecting out into the sea. Through the squalls, Alfred could see high, white teeth of rocks standing tall from the water, waves breaking and crashing on them.

"What are we looking at?"

"Handfast Point, Lord King. And around the point is another beach and the village of Swanage."

"Another beach where the Danes could land."

"Yes, Lord King."

"Take us out to Handfast Point, then over the ridge to Swanage."

Back through the dunes, they came to the horses and rode through woodland and out to the point. From here, they were looking across gaps to the tall stacks of white rock, waves rushing in and breaking with force, high, high into the air.

"Alright, enough," Alfred said.

The guide led them on again, up to the top of the ridge. The wind here was stronger, plucking at their tunics and cloaks, but the rain had gone and they could see further. The Isle of Wight was a smudge on the horizon while to the south they looked across another beach to a small village clustered at the far end of a bay.

The way down was steeper and they dismounted, leading their horses carefully on slippery grass and mud.

A path wended through dunes, the horses' hooves slipping sideways in the soft sand.

Alfred reined in his horse and looked back. The cliffs were a mix of white and green, high and imposing, but the bay had a gently shelving beach.

"They could land here," Alfred said to Radmer.

"It's not a wide beach and there are those sea rocks either side. I wouldn't choose it in bad weather."

"You'd choose Studland? That's more open to the wind."

"I would choose Poole Bay if the wind was right."

Alfred nodded.

They rode into the tiny village of Swanage, a cluster of thatched huts for fishermen and their families above a small stream.

Small boats were pulled up above high water level. The smell of seaweed and salt air was strong here and seagulls wheeled overhead. No one was in sight.

At the stream they dismounted and let the horses drink, while from their packs they took food and water for themselves. The rain grew heavy and through it Alfred could just see a further ridge to the south.

"What's beyond there?"

The guide replied, "The sea, Lord King. Steep cliffs for miles westwards with barely a beach."

The day was wearing on. "One last ride then and back to Wareham."

The horses took them up the ridge, where the guide said, "We should walk again from here."

At the very brink of high cliffs, wind and rain drove in, buffeting Alfred. He crouched at the edge and looked down on huge waves breaking at the foot of the rock, white spume flying high in the air and crashing down again.

"Take care, Lord King," the guide shouted into the wind to him.

Alfred stood and took a step back, looking along the line of cliffs.

"How far do these cliffs extend westwards?"

"A very long way. Almost to Weymouth and Portland with only a few small bays before there. Not enough for a fleet of longships."

Alfred could see that. The cliffs and rocks would be death to any longship that found its way there in an onshore wind.

Radmer, standing by him, shouted against the wind, "We can keep lookouts on the cliffs as well as the sandbanks. It could give us long enough to get warriors to Corfe or Studland and try to hold them there. If that's the way they come."

"Yes. Alright, let's get back and talk to Garrulf."

"Garrulf, how are you?" Alfred asked, swinging down from his horse.

He felt cold and wet. Chilled through.

"Angry," Garrulf replied.

"With me?"

"No. Never. These Danes. I hate them, Alfred. I want to destroy every last one of them. Especially Guthrum."

"I understand."

"Do you?"

"They killed young Oswald as well."

"Yes, of course. I'm sorry, I can't get Gunhild out of my head. And there's her sister, my younger daughter. I can't think how it will affect her. Alfred, I want to ride west and hunt the pagans down."

"I know, but we need you here, Garrulf. This is your shire. You need to raise as many warriors as you can as quickly as you can. That huge fleet could arrive here as soon as the weather drops a little according to Radmer."

Garrulf took a breath. "I know. I know that really."

"So you need warriors ready to defend Wareham's ramparts should they come by river. If they land at Swanage or Studland, you may have enough men to meet them in battle instead. Either way you will need lookouts all along the coast with beacons ready to light to warn you."

"Yes, yes, I can see that. But you, you won't be here?"

"I need to follow Guthrum."

Garrulf nodded and he seemed to come back to closer to his usual self, eyes on Alfred. "Messengers have come back from Osric," he said.

"Saying?"

"Guthrum has passed through Dorchester. Not too much damage, Osric says. My people fled as soon as word came of the Danes approaching."

"Thank the Lord."

"The Danes weren't wasting time stopping to destroy or kill. They clearly want to be in Exeter before messages can get there."

"Does Osric think he can get ahead of them to warn Odda and Exeter?"

"I don't know. Odda maybe. Exeter, it depends how fast the Danes are riding."

"We must just thank the Lord that Guthrum left before the fleet could get here. Guthrum's mounted warriors and the fleet together..."

"We need more miracles yet, Alfred."

"Garrulf, Noth, Radmer, come in the tent and talk to me. This wind and rain is just not stopping at all."

Alfred pulled aside the tent door flapping in the wind and stepped for the moment out of the wet. The others followed, Noth holding the tent door behind him so that they could hear each other.

"How nearly ready are we, Noth?"

"Almost there. We don't have anywhere near enough horses for all the warriors of ours, but Garrulf may well need our men here anyway. So we're quite a small party going west."

"Alright. And Garrulf, are your men away to keep watch along the cliffs and the dunes?"

"Yes, they left yesterday evening. They'll try to set up beacons, but how they will manage that in this weather, I don't know."

"Your longships, Radmer, can they be out in this?"

"No, not until the wind drops. It's too strong and the waves too high."

"So the same would apply to the Danish fleet. They will be stuck where they are?"

"Yes, for now, but the weather is coming from the south west. They will be released before we are. And the wind will be in their favour. We may have very little warning."

"Then we do need a miracle."

Garrulf said, "What about you, Alfred? How far do you expect to ride today?"

"Beyond Dorchester. We've lost at least a day's riding on the Danes, because they set off in the night and then had all day yesterday. You guessed at four days to Exeter, Garrulf, with that many riders plus weapons and supplies? We'll try to beat that."

"You're a smaller party travelling light. You should be able to."

Noth said, "And we don't know if they will have met any resistance along the way. From Odda, for example, or any of the towns. That could slow them."

"I don't think anything much between here and Exeter can slow them," Alfred replied. "Imagine that number of mounted warriors riding at you. The best anyone can do is just get out of the way. No, I suspect we might have another siege, so we need to gather the warriors of Devon and Somerset for that. Your warriors are needed here, Garrulf, plus more from Wiltshire and hopefully from Hampshire."

"If Wulfhere will let his come. Who knows what mood he'll be in with the news of Wulfstan's death?"

"Who knows, indeed?"

"And you need Somerset's warriors. Eadwulf's."

"Yes. Yes, I do. Come on, Noth, we need to go. Garrulf, Radmer, keep safe and good luck."

The afternoon was wearing on by the time they approached Dorchester. Some low earthen ramparts filled gaps where the old Roman town walls had fallen. In most places, there were more gaps than wall.

With the rain blown into them in gusts, their cloaks and trousers were soaked through. The track had been heavily broken down by the Danes and had mostly turned to mud, so horses and men were all filthy.

Even so, Alfred had not planned on them staying in Dorchester.

Warriors guarded the road into the town, but on seeing Alfred, Noth and their men, the warriors pulled the gates wide.

"Lord King," one shouted. "There are messengers waiting for you at your hall."

"Good," Alfred said to him. He dismounted, wanting news.

"And the Bishop is there as well. With the reeve."

"Bishop Athelheah?"

"Yes."

"What happened when the Danes came through?"

"We had no warning, Lord King. There were just a handful of us at the gate. And there were hundreds of the Danes. So we spread out through the town and told people to run. North, south, anywhere. Just to go."

"And they did?"

"Mostly. Then the Danes rode through. They raided houses for provisions and the like. But then they just rode on out again. On the Roman road over the downs."

He had ridden that way before. The Danes would be able to go even faster on the old Roman road. Even though much of it had turned to mud or undergrowth, it still led straight west above the woodland and villages for some miles before dropping down into the valley at Bridport. After that, there was less left of the old Roman roads and progress would be slower for the Danes until Honiton. Then the Fosse Way, the men of Rome's principal route into the west, would take them directly into Exeter. With the lead the Danes had on Osric and Ethelwulf, there didn't seem much chance of Guthrum being caught up with before Exeter.

Alfred led his horse onwards into the town, passing thatched houses and workshops where the townsfolk were assessing damage and losses to the Danes.

One house had been burned to the ground and a small family sat consoling each other on what had been their doorstep.

The lanes were now a mess of mud and Alfred's boots stuck and slipped as he followed the lane into the market place. The King's hall was on the far side, larger than the other buildings around, including Garrulf's and the reeve's.

The hall was oak-framed, with wood panelling around the outside and wooden tiles on the roof. Alfred had happy memories of the place, having spent more than one Easter and Christmas here when his brothers had been Kings. As youngsters he and Noth had played right here where the invaders had ridden through only the day before.

Today was very different. He felt cold, wet and dispirited.

A servant came and took his and Noth's reins. He dismounted, Noth alongside him, and he pulled the heavy door to the hall open.

Candles guttered as the wind took them and he heard an oath from the semi-darkness.

"Bishop, is that you?"

"You may find that was the reeve."

Alfred's eyes gradually became accustomed to the dimness which was only faintly relieved by candles on the table in the centre of the hall.

"Athelheah, good to see you. It seems we need your prayers more than ever."

"I have been praying to St Aldhelm."

"Thank you. If your prayers would be answered for the Lord's assistance for the people of Wareham and Purbeck and for the people of Exeter, then that would be good."

"They are indeed very firmly in my prayers."

"Reeve, what news is there?"

"The Danes have passed through, followed later by Lord Osric and Ealdorman Ethelwulf with their warriors. Messages came back to say that the Danes camped along at Eggardon Hill, close to the Roman road where the old earthworks are, then moved on at first light. Lord Ethelnoth was sending riders to try to get ahead to warn Ealdorman Odda and the reeve of Exeter. We don't know if that has been successful."

Alfred suddenly felt weary and a spasm of pain came from his stomach.

Noth took his arm and the Bishop said, "Alfred, are you alright?"

"Yes. Just a... Noth, we should carry on."

"No, Alfred. Look, we won't come anywhere near catching Guthrum before he gets to Exeter. We should stay the night here. Get warm. Sleep. Then we'd be better placed to deal with what we find at Exeter."

A little light-headed, Alfred put a hand down to the table to steady himself.

He took a moment, then said, "Yes, perhaps you're right."

"Reeve, would you call the King's servants please?"

"Yes, Lord Ethelnoth."

"Then I think you will have duties to attend to?"

"Ah. Of course."

"And Bishop, if you would wait here, I will see Alfred to his room."

Alfred felt Noth take his arm and allowed himself to be led to the curtained-off room at the far end of the hall.

It was very dark in there, the bed a dim but welcome sight as tiredness seemed suddenly to take him. He had another spasm of pain and almost fell on to the bed where he lay on his side, knees curled to his chest.

"Alfred-"

"I'm alright. Just... just leave me, Noth. Please."

Then he heard movement and felt hands taking off his wet boots and clothes, sitting him up, moving his arms, legs. Each time his pains came, the hands pulled back, but finally they had him in a dry linen tunic and he was able to lay on the bed and turn his back, a cover pulled over him.

He closed his eyes praying that sleep might overtake the pains.

Slowly, too slowly, they did.

Weak daylight was filtering into the room as Alfred came awake.

There was a voice from behind him. By the bed. Speaking softly. Noth.

"Alfred, are you awake?"

He waited for pains, spasms, but nothing came. He felt drained though.

Without moving in case he set things off again, he said, "Yes, I'm awake. What time is it? It looks like daylight outside."

"It is. Late morning. I've been in several times, but each time you were so deeply asleep that you didn't hear me at all."

"Late morning." He rolled carefully on to his back and looked at Noth. "You should have woken me. We need to-"

"No, we don't. We need you well."

"But-"

He made to move, to sit up, but found Noth's hand pushing him back and had no strength to resist.

"No," Noth said.

"Alright. Tell me, is there news?"

"No word yet on whether word got through to Odda or to Exeter of the danger they are in."

"And from Wareham?" Alfred asked.

"Nothing."

"What's the wind doing?"

"It's dropped a bit."

"Ah."

Noth said, "So the fleet may be on the move."

"Shall we go west or east then?"

"For the moment, I think we need to stay here. Partly until we hear more definite news. Partly so that you have chance to recover. You're in no condition to ride anywhere for now."

Alfred thought a moment. "I suppose you're right. What does Athelheah know? About me, I mean? And the reeve?"

"I've told the reeve you're tired but fine and waiting for more news before continuing. What he suspects, I don't know. Bishop Athelheah knows everything."

"Are he and the reeve here?"

"The Bishop's out and about with the townsfolk. I don't know where the reeve is. Probably raising men to send back to Wareham to Garrulf."

"Then perhaps someone can bring me food and dry clothes. I'll try to appear a bit more respectable before I see them."

"Respectable? Well, I suppose they didn't know you when you were younger."

By late afternoon, the wind had returned in force, moaning through the roof of the hall, rain slanting down across the market square.

The reeve had sent as many warriors as he could eastwards to Ealdorman Garrulf, while more warriors had marched or ridden through the town in the same direction.

Alfred sat at the long table, fingers drumming as he waited for news from east or from west, his strength gradually returning, but getting more irritable with the delay.

"Noth, one way or another we need to be away from here in the morning. I just can't sit here doing nothing."

"There must be news soon," Noth said. "If not tonight, then tomorrow morning."

"Alright, tomorrow morning then. If there's no news of the fleet arriving or on its way, we ride westwards."

"Fine. So long as you-"

"No. We're going."

"Give it another hour, Alfred."

"For what? I've already waited longer than I wanted."

The horses were ready, their warriors set. Alfred had seen to that.

The market square was awash with mud, the horses churning it up and the warriors up to their ankles in it. But the rain had finally gone and the wind was no more than a middle strength.

"For word to come from Wareham. What if the Danish fleet is on its way now the weather has eased and we are riding west rather than east? We need word from Wareham. One way or another."

Alfred sighed.

"Alright. Yes, I know. You're right, Noth. Stand down, all of you. One hour. Then back here."

It was less than an hour before Alfred, back in the hall, heard horsemen arriving to shouts and cheers from the townsfolk of Dorchester and the warriors Alfred had brought.

He pushed the door open on to a glorious commotion as a large group of newcomers were being mobbed. Arms were raised as if there had been a great victory and there was whooping and laughing.

Mystified, Alfred, Noth and Athelheah walked out into the market square. All around, grinning faces moved aside and he found himself face to face with Garrulf himself.

"Garrulf, what are you doing here? The fleet-"

"Is gone. Smashed. Smashed into the smallest pieces."

"What do you mean?"

"I mean smashed. Destroyed. Gone."

Alfred could hardly hear amongst all the calling and shouting around them.

"Come inside and tell me."

He led them back into the hall, where the noise from outside was diminished, then turned back to Garrulf.

"They came yesterday, Alfred," Garrulf said. "They were too impetuous. One break in the weather and they set off, a vast fleet it seems."

"And?"

"It looks like they were heading for Poole Bay, but the wind really got up, banking up the waves as well, rain pouring down. We think they gave up on Poole Bay and instead tried to get into the bay at Swanage, but it was a storm, Alfred, and it blew them the wrong way. You remember those cliffs we looked down on?"

"Of course."

"The entire fleet was caught on the wrong side of Purbeck. The longships were thrown on to the rocks and cliffs. The whole fleet were blasted on to them, warriors, weapons and all. We had watchers above and they saw it, the carnage."

"Every ship? Every single one?"

"The watchers can't swear to that. They could only see what they could see, perched on the cliff tops. But if more than a handful escaped, I would think it unlikely. Possibly none escaped. Even when the watchers climbed down the cliffs after the storm eased, they found only two alive amongst the broken planking and casks and bodies. And them more dead than alive."

"What happened to them?"

"My men took them back to Wareham. Do you know how many longships they say there were? One hundred and twenty. Imagine if they had landed all their warriors."

Alfred turned to Athelheah. "I can hardly believe it. It really is the miracle you prayed for."

"Yes, Alfred, and He has delivered. Will you pray with me?"

"Pray, yes."

The Bishop opened the door and walked out into the melee, Alfred and the others just behind him.

Alfred expected Athelheah to move towards the church, but he stopped in the midst of the warriors. Standing there in the mud and the rainwater, the Bishop raised both arms to the sky.

"Lord God," he called, and around him men quietened and began to stand and listen. Even the wind seemed to pause.

"Lord God, we thank you for delivering us from the great fleet of pagans."

Men shouted, but he went on, "You heard us, Lord. You heard me call on St Aldhelm to beseech you to save us and to wreak vengeance on the heathens who kill and destroy. St Aldhelm, on whose relics the heathen King of the Danes swore an oath and which oath he then broke. The Lord God said 'Vengeance is mine, and I will repay. In due time their foot will slip; their day of disaster is near and their doom rushes upon them.' For these pagans, these heathens," his voice rising, "their doom has fallen!"

"Amen!" rolled around the market squared.

"Lord God, I will build a church on those very cliffs in your honour and in honour of St Aldhelm that all may know your glory and your power."

"Amen!"

"And now let your glory and power assist our Lord King Alfred as he seeks to expel the pagans from our land of

Wessex."

The Bishop stood there, feet mired in mud, arms outstretched, slowly lowering his eyes to find Alfred's. Around them, 'Amens' turned to cheers and shouts, while Athelheah and Alfred stared at each other.

Alfred nodded. "Amen," he said.

CHAPTER 18

"My men are ready, Alfred."

"Thank you, Garrulf. A question for you. Where is Oscetel?"

"Tied to a stake in the middle of Wareham. The townsfolk have been told that they can throw whatever they want at him, so long as they don't kill him. He will smell pretty ripe by now." Alfred smiled grimly and Garrulf went on, "I'm forced to agree with you that he might be more useful alive than dead."

"Does he know about the destruction of the fleet?"

"Yes, but I'm not sure he believes us how complete the destruction was."

"Alright, will you send some of your men back to Wareham, take Oscetel to the cliffs and show him the destruction on the rocks below? Then bring him on to us at Exeter."

"Yes. Yes, that's a good plan."

"What about the survivors you spoke about? Two of them?"

"Tied to the same stake as Oscetel and the remaining captain from the original four hostages."

The Bishop, listening, said, "I will go with your men,

Ealdorman. This really has been a miracle. I will take brothers from the Abbey to begin building a daughter church on the cliff as thanksgiving to the Lord. It will be a reminder to any other heathens who approach our shores."

"Good. And, Athelheah, perhaps you can persuade Oscetel that Wessex is defended by a more powerful God then their own gods. A vengeful God, you said."

"Yes, Alfred, and a vengeful God I meant."

"And then, Garrulf, when you bring Oscetel to Exeter perhaps he will persuade Guthrum of that."

"I can assure you, Alfred, vengeance is not just for our Lord."

A larger party of warriors now, they rode out of Dorchester on the old Roman road, the way fairly flat at first with the going quite fast. Then the road began to climb and they were following the ridge high above the valleys below.

There were stands of trees and scrubby bushes on either side, blown by a strong wind. The sun had reappeared though, by now past its highest point in the sky. Where they could see the sea to their south, the light gleamed off the water.

As they finally reached the end of the ridge, Alfred made out the age-old ramparts of Eggardon Hill, where the Danes had camped. But before that, the road swung steeply downwards into the valley below and he held the reins tight to stop his horse getting ahead of herself.

"Woah, now. Careful," he said to her.

Garrulf had ridden alongside him.

"Alfred, my men are going to need to stop soon. They've ridden a long way. The horses won't carry them much further."

"Yes, of course. Where do you suggest?"

"The town of Bridport is not far ahead."

"Alright, we're better to get to Exeter in good shape rather than at speed."

A short few miles past woodland and farms, still on the Roman road, they arrived at the town. The road ran straight and true into and out of the town, with a market square off to the left. They dismounted there, with the nervous town reeve reporting to his Ealdorman that the Danes had come and gone.

"We need as many beds as you can give us," Garrulf told him. "Plus food for the men and feed for the horses."

"But the Danes took almost everything."

Frustrated, Garrulf said, "Then look further afield, man. But find us what you can. We are staying here overnight."

"Yes, Lord."

The reeve set off into the market square.

"Alfred," Garrulf said. "That's the reeve's house over there. Get yourself inside. The reeve will have food there at least, I'm sure. Then rest. We're going to need you in good shape, not just my warriors."

Riding into Honiton early the following evening they found the town was already packed with warriors searching for somewhere to spend the night, even before Alfred, Noth and Garrulf had arrived with theirs.

In the market place they found Eadred amongst a swirl of men, all of them seeming to ignore their young leader.

"Eadred," Alfred said, "is Ealdorman Eadwulf still unwell?"

"He is, Lord King."

"So are you in charge of the warriors from Somerset?" Alfred asked, gesturing to the large numbers milling around the town.

"I am."

"Then perhaps you can take all these men out beyond the town to camp for the night? There are far too many for any lodgings here and I can see that the townsfolk are not going to be happy."

"But I have already arranged for a bed for myself at the

reeve's house."

Eadred gestured to one of the larger properties near the church. It looked prosperous, oak planked, with the thatch quite new and still golden. Two men on the doorstep were fending away other warriors clearly also hoping for a bed.

From behind Alfred, Garrulf said, "Young Eadred, if your men are camping outside the town, their Lord should show an example and be with them. As will I."

"Oh, yes, of course."

"Arrange things then, Eadred," Alfred said, and the young man turned and set off, calling the captains of Somerset to him.

Noth's voice also came from behind Alfred, quietly. "Are you really camping with your men, Garrulf?"

"No, I just didn't want to share the reeve's house with any relative of Eadwulf."

"You know I'm also Eadwulf's cousin?"

"Far enough removed, I think, Noth. Far enough removed."

By the following morning messengers had arrived from Osric, Ethelwulf and Odda.

A forward party of the Danes had got into Exeter and effectively barricaded the gates so that a large number of the townsfolk were trapped. Then the main body of Guthrum's men had arrived and were now manning the walls.

"So we were too late to stop the Danes getting inside?" Alfred asked one of the messengers.

"Yes, Lord King. I was there. I am from Exeter. Some of the townsfolk, including myself, were able to escape out of the west and north gates before the heathen closed them. Why would they trap our people?"

Alfred knew the answer. He had seen the same at Wareham.

***

The walls, when Alfred saw them later that day, were even higher than he had remembered. Perhaps the height of four men standing on each other's shoulders.

Or at least that was the height of the wall by the south gate that Alfred was staring at from a suitable distance away.

Most of the wall was of large dressed stonework, a purple-blue shade. Each stone had been chipped and carved into an oblong shape and each row of stones carefully placed, level, heavy, unmovable. Alfred marvelled at what the Romans had achieved here. Only in some places were there patches of more higgledy-piggledy stonework.

"Your repairs?" Alfred asked Odda.

"Some of it. Some older, when it was the Cornish who we were more concerned about than the Danes. The newer repairs were meant to keep the Danes out, but they caught the town off guard, the gates open and undefended."

"I remember the walls as being very wide as well as high?"

"Very. Two, sometimes three good paces wide."

"And those gates?"

"You won't break those down too easily either. Replaced or repaired within the last few years. Heavy, thick timber."

"This is the South Gate?"

"Yes, there's five altogether, North, South, East, West and the Water Gate leading down to the river."

"They're all as strong as this one?"

"I'm afraid so."

"No obvious weaknesses we can take advantage of?"

"Sorry, no. The whole point of the walls and the gates was to hold out against attackers."

"No chance of storming the town then?"

"None, Alfred. None."

***

Odda was back. He had gone to oversee his warriors while Alfred and the men with him had food and some rest after their ride.

"How many men do you have now, Odda? Enough to keep the Danes inside there?"

"Hard to say. I've raised Devon and you have your warriors. We have some of Eadwulf's warriors from Somerset come down with his cousin Eadred. Then we have Garrulf and a part of the warriors of Dorset. Is that enough? It depends what they try."

The two of them were stood back from the south gate, taking in the walls and the camped groups of Saxon warriors behind them.

"You have men outside each of the gates?"

"Yes, mine are on the north and west sides. Yours, Garrulf's and Eadred's the south and east plus the water gate."

Osric appeared by them. "The men are settling for the night here and by the east gate. With plenty of sentries."

"The horses?"

"Well back from the gates."

"Good, we can't afford another break-out where the horses are killed."

"I've put your tent further back than at Wareham as well. We also can't afford to lose you."

"If you must."

"And there's a message just in. Wulfhere is on his way with his warriors."

Odda said, "Well, it swells the numbers we have. Though they will need feeding and Wulfhere might have his own agenda for being here."

"He'll blame me for Wulfstan's death," Alfred said.

"Without doubt."

"When is he due, Osric?"

"Tomorrow."

"Alright, let's do a circuit of the walls and see how things stand here, then have a Council meeting tomorrow when Wulfhere is here. We need to hear what he has to say."

"I want vengeance, Alfred. For my son."

Wulfhere had stalked towards Alfred, stopping too close to Alfred's face. His son Wulfhard was just behind him.

"I understand that, Wulfhere. And I do understand your feelings; we lost Oswald."

Wulfhere took a step closer, spittle flying from his mouth as he said, "No, you don't understand. Oswald was not your son. What if the pagans were to slit the throats of Ethelflaed or Edward or Ethelgifu? Then you would understand."

Alfred stepped back and bowed his head, trying not to see images that would be hard to shift.

"Yes, alright. Then I can only say how sorry and angry I am."

"We should never have given them hostages. I was against that."

"You-"

"Those negotiations were badly done. No son of mine is ever going to be at the mercy of the Danes again. Whatever a King of Wessex says."

"I'm sorry but-"

"From now, I decide what happens to my family and my people."

"Alright. But we must work together, Wulfhere. To get the Danes out of Exeter."

"I don't want them out. I want them dead."

The Ealdorman turned on his heel and walked off, his son trailing him.

***

The room was not big and was dim with little light finding its way inside. They were inside the farmhouse that Odda had found for the Council meeting. It smelled of pigs.

"Eadred, are you representing Ealdorman Eadwulf at this Council?" Alfred asked.

"Yes, Lord King."

"Then please sit."

The young man took his place on a bench at the table.

Odda, Garrulf and Eadred were at one side of the table, Osric, Noth and Ethelwulf at the other. Wulfhere sat at the far end on a stool, shifting in some discomfort.

Around the walls more were crowded in. Helm, Forthred, various lords and churchmen from around Exeter.

Alfred was standing, leaning on the back of the one chair at the head of the table. "Odda," he said, "what do we know?"

The Ealdorman of Devon was unusually subdued. "We estimate there are over one thousand Danes inside Exeter. Enough to man the walls anyway, if we try to scale them. And the gates are very secure."

"This is a mess," Wulfhere broke in. "How could this be allowed to happen? After Wareham as well, where they just walked in. They did the same at Exeter!"

"Wulfhere," Alfred said calmly, "how it happened and how we can stop it happening again must wait. Odda, go on."

The Ealdorman of Hampshire was about to continue, but Odda went on quickly.

"Some of the townsfolk escaped. Not all, by any means. The Danes will have some stock of food there, especially if they take it from the remaining townsfolk. They can probably survive on that for a while. But feeding their horses will be more difficult. For every Dane there was a horse and all the horses are inside the town, without the fields that they had at Wareham."

"So they are likely to use the townsfolk to blackmail us into giving the food and feed they need. Just like in Wareham."

Osric interrupted. "I suspect we will see townsfolk hung over the walls again very soon."

Alfred pulled the chair back and sat.

"Garrulf, do we think any surviving longships from Swanage will make it here?"

"If some did survive, they can't know Guthrum is in Exeter. Not yet. Though we must assume they would get news eventually."

"True. Unless Exeter was always part of the plan."

Odda said, "To bring the Cornish in on their side?"

Alfred nodded. "Let's hope King Hywel stays out of this war. If the fleet had not been destroyed and had arrived here in the River Ex along with Guthrum's men in Exeter, I think he'd have been very tempted. Do we know if Guthrum sent emissaries to Hywel when he arrived here?"

"It was all too chaotic to know, I'm afraid. I'd be surprised if he didn't though. And Hywel will be close to the border. Launceston almost certainly."

"What about the Cornish who live in Exeter? Where would their loyalty lie?"

Odda thought a moment. "Hard to say, Alfred. Many of the Cornish in Exeter are not free - such as those who were captured after the last war. We're still seen as invaders. Exeter was part of their Dumnonia before it was part of Devon. It's a question. Would the Cornish see the Danes in Exeter as worse than us? Or would they be tempted to work with the Danes in return for..."

"Vengeance?"

"Possibly."

Alfred's mind went to Bennath, looking after his own children. What would she feel if she were in Exeter? What does she feel now?

"Then," Wulfhere's voice was full of anger, "we kill them as well."

Alfred turned to the Ealdorman. "We need clear heads, Wulfhere. We need to work out what to do next."

"The Cornish might want vengeance. So do I."

"Wulfhere, once we have the Danes out of Exeter, we will not slaughter the Cornish. Am I clear?"

The Ealdorman sat sullenly silent.

"Odda," Alfred said, calming his voice again, "we should still dissuade King Hywel and the Cornish outside of Exeter from becoming involved. Let's make Exeter as secure from raids out beyond the walls as we can, then I'll want to see King Hywel."

"To say what?" Garrulf asked.

"Initially to persuade him not to be involved."

"And if he won't be persuaded?"

"Then we would go with force."

A tentative voice spoke. Eadred. "What about Ubba? We still hear that he operates around the shores of Wales with a fleet of longships of his own. Often not far from Somerset's shore."

"Or Devon's", Odda put in.

Osric said, "I've heard the same. If he landed and marched south towards Exeter with another army, that would change things again." He ticked off his fingers. "Guthrum, Odda, the Cornish, maybe surviving longships from Swanage..."

"Alright, Eadred, would you go back to Eadwulf and gather men to keep watch on the Somerset shore line. And Noth, would you go to my and your manors in Somerset, raise as many men as you can and head to the north Devon coast?"

Eadred looked affronted. "Lord Ethelnoth cannot raise men within Somerset. That is for Ealdorman Eadwulf to do. Or me, as his representative."

"Eadred, I am not asking. I am telling you what is to happen," Alfred said.

Eadred started to speak, but clearly thought better of it. He lowered his eyes and nodded.

"Alfred." Wulfhere's angry voice from the far end of the table. "I'm not hearing what we do to get to the Danes in Exeter. Only that they will blackmail us into feeding them."

"I'm aware of that. And if you have a suggestion, I'm open to it."

"Starve them. Starve all of them."

Odda stood. "My people are inside those walls. And family. I have family in there. So do most of my men here."

There was a wave of restless unhappiness from Devon's thanes listening from around them.

"We have to be ruthless," Wulfhere replied, ignoring them. "How else will we win this war? If people die, that is the Danes' fault. But the Danes will die as well. We can't be weak like we were at Wareham. Look what happened there."

Osric was now on his feet as well. "Ealdorman Wulfhere, I can be as ruthless as necessary, as you probably know, but I am also realistic. It might take weeks or months before the Danes start to go hungry in Exeter, and in the meantime, the people of Exeter will be thrown over the walls. We rely on their families, their friends for support. For warriors. For food for our own. They will not abide seeing their families sacrificed in that way. That is not a way to win a war."

"And perhaps more to the point," Odda said, "I would not permit my people to be treated that way. Just as I hope you would not permit the people of Hampshire to be treated like that."

Wulfhere sat down, muttering to himself.

It was Garrulf who spoke next. "So what do we do, Alfred? Like at Wareham, do we feed them and wait?"

"First we need to make sure that there's no outside help for them. From the Cornish or Ubba. Then we wait on developments."

"Alfred," Garrulf said, "you know I want vengeance for my daughter as well."

"I do, Garrulf. For you, for Wulfhere, for..." He thought

of Elswith and her closeness to young Oswald. "For all of us who have lost someone to the Danes. But this is a long war. Not a short one. We must use our heads and not our hearts. Look at East Anglia. Look at Northumbria and Mercia. We - you - only get vengeance if we survive as Wessex. If we win."

CHAPTER 19

"Guthrum wants to speak to you," Odda said, as Alfred emerged from his tent the following morning.

"He would."

"His messenger says he will be at the south gate in an hour."

Alfred frowned. "Alright. Say I will be there."

As Odda left, Noth appeared.

"I'll head north to Somerset later this morning, Alfred. Then take as many as I can across to the north Devon coast."

"Good. Take Helm."

"I will. But how long I can keep the men there is another matter. We have no idea how long this might go on for."

"True. While you're there, see what you can find out about Ubba. Whether he really is over in Wales and whether he might be planning on joining forces with Guthrum. There may be traders that have heard."

"I will. I'll wait and see what Guthrum has to say to you, then go."

***

"King Alfred."

Guthrum was waiting a short distance in front of the south gate. Mail-coat, sword in sheath, bare-headed, feet apart, relaxed, facing Alfred.

Alfred stopped in his approach. Two sword lengths apart. "You killed the hostages," he said, trying to contain his anger.

Guthrum frowned. "That was not my intention."

"What do you mean?"

"I gave instructions to deal with the hostages while we prepared our escape. It was misinterpreted."

"Their throats were slit and they were left to die in agony."

"As I said, that was not intended."

"Then you rode west to Exeter rather than out of Wessex. You broke your oath to your god Odin and to our Lord God through the relic of St Aldhelm."

"Are there no circumstances in which you would not break an oath?"

"Lord give me strength. No. I swore an oath to God. You swore an oath to your Odin. An oath."

"To Odin the trickster. He would have been proud."

Alfred was so furious, he could hardly control himself. He took a deep breath.

"And you know you broke an oath to our Lord God."

"On the relic of St Aldhelm? Alfred, your God is weak and relics are just bones. What should that mean to a man like me?"

"It means something to God, our Lord God. 'Vengeance is mine, says the Lord.'"

Guthrum smiled. "We will see what your God does then."

"He already has, Guthrum."

"What do you mean?" The smile was gone.

"I mean that your fleet of longships came just as you fled Wareham. And so did a storm. The fleet was destroyed on the rocks by Swanage. Absolutely destroyed. Nothing left."

"I don't believe you."

"You don't need to. I've sent Oscetel to see the evidence and then he's to be brought here."

Guthrum was silent and Alfred went on, "Our God, Guthrum, is greater than any pagan god. And our God is a vengeful God."

Alfred turned on his heel and walked away.

"What did he say?" Odda asked.

"That killing the hostages was not meant to happen."

Garrulf said, "You believe him?"

"I can't believe anything he says. It might be true, but he also seems proud that he tricked us. That Odin would have been proud."

"I hate them all."

"I know. He also doesn't believe the fleet has been destroyed. Garrulf, when Oscetel is here, take him to see Guthrum. Keep them a distance apart and keep Oscetel bound. We need to keep him as our hostage, but I want him to convince Guthrum that he has no fleet arriving. Even better if the Bishop has persuaded Oscetel that it was vengeance from God."

"Yes, Alfred."

"Now, Odda, Garrulf, have you enough warriors to keep the Danes inside Exeter?" Alfred asked.

"I hope so," Odda replied. "You're taking your men into Cornwall?"

"No. Not into Cornwall. We'll send a message to Launceston to get King Hywel to come and meet us part way from Launceston to here. That will show us which side he is on. Where do you suggest, Odda?"

"Okehampton might suit. Small village on a hill above the river north of Dartmoor. There's a church on the hill there and a few houses, not much else, but it would be the best place that's half way between here and Launceston."

"That will do. I really just want to see if he comes. If he doesn't, we'll know we have a problem. Can you organise a messenger? Hywel should meet me there in, what, three days?"

"That should work."

"Good. Where's Wulfhere?"

"With his warriors and his son."

Garrulf said, "He's not exactly the most patient of men. He won't stay."

"He's angry. I understand that."

"I'm angry," Garrulf replied. "But I'm staying."

"You know what I mean."

"I know that Wulfhere is angry and that he wants to take out that anger on someone. If it can't be the Danes, watch out it's not you. He may have lost Helm to you, but he still has Wold. And Wold is also the son of a King of Wessex."

"Would Wold let himself be used by Wulfhere?"

"It's a close run thing which of them hates you most. Wulfhere, Wold or Winifred."

"Wulfhere's not as dangerous without Eadwulf at his side."

"Eadwulf isn't going to be happy about Noth gathering men in Somerset to take across to the Devon coast."

Odda said, "Eadwulf's really not well, by all accounts. Dying, possibly. I spoke separately to Eadred. I'm told Eadwulf has been wasting away and that he's in a lot of pain."

Alfred sighed. "I may not like the man or trust him, but that's not the way any of us would choose to go."

"Be that as it may, Alfred," Garrulf said, "you'll have to choose what to do if and when he dies. In choosing an Ealdorman, I mean. Eadred, who would inherit all Eadwulf's own lands, manors and warriors anyway. Or Noth, as I think you may be planning, with much less of all of those, but who is just a bit more reliable."

"Yes. And with much more experience of war. Of life generally, in fact."

"What would Eadred do if you pass over him though?" Garrulf asked.

Odda said, "He'd be a disappointed man. Bitter, maybe, as Eadwulf has practically promised him everything, whether or not it was in his power to give. And he'd have Eadwulf's wealth and warriors behind him. He could be a dangerous enemy if you drive him into Wulfhere's camp. Be careful in your choice, Alfred."

"Noth says I'm to go with him to Somerset and then to the Devon coast," Helm said.

"Yes. You're my heir. I want you there to show how much support Noth has from me."

"I would rather be here."

"Why?"

Helm blushed. "I want to be with you. To be part of your..."

"Family? You already are, Helm."

"I know that. And I am grateful."

There was a silence, then Helm said, "There's another reason."

"Tell me."

"If there is to be a battle with Guthrum, I want to be part of it." In a rush, he went on, "He killed Oswald. And Oswald was so kind. So-"

"Guthrum says it wasn't his intention that the hostages should be killed."

"I don't believe him. And even if it wasn't, Oswald would still be here if Guthrum had not lied, if he hadn't been here at all."

"I can't disagree with that, Helm. And I'm sorry. We all feel Oswald's death."

"Wold will as well."

"They were close?"

"Not exactly. It's more that Wold looked up to Oswald, him being older."

"Would he blame me? Do you blame me?"

"No!" This was said fiercely. "No. I blame the Danes and Guthrum. But Wold, well, he already..."

Helm's voice trailed away.

"I know. It's alright. Go with Noth for me. You are family. Nothing will change that. But I need you to go with Noth now."

"Yes, Uncle Alfred. Whatever you say."

Noth came striding towards them.

Alfred said, "You've heard about what Guthrum said?"

"Yes, from Garrulf. He's a bastard liar, Alfred."

"Maybe."

"Anyway, we're ready. Helm?"

"Yes, coming, Noth."

"Good. I'll send messages when I know more, Alfred. Take care with King Hywel. Someone else you can't trust."

It was three days later that Alfred approached the village of Okehampton. He and Osric had skirted the great mass of Dartmoor with a strong force of warriors.

They had ridden through woods and forded rivers and streams, passing through some villages where they had been welcomed and others where their presence instilled fear and hatred, doors closing on them, children staring. There were still many who hankered for a Dumnonia before the Saxons had come, and these were poor people, scraping a living from the land and no doubt, Alfred thought, harbouring grudges.

If King Hywel and his Cornish warriors were in league with Guthrum, or even Ubba and a fleet of Danes from the north coast, this would be a good place for an ambush.

Through tall beech and ash woodland the track dropped away revealing a marshy valley with two rivers snaking through and, on the far side, Okehampton's wooden church on a hill with houses around it.

A scout rode back towards them.

"King Hywel is already here, Lord King."

"Thank you. With many men?"

"No. A handful."

"Good. What about the woods around?"

"We've had more scouts out ahead of us. No sign of an ambush. So far."

Alfred nodded.

Their horses picked their way across two fords and they rode up to the edge of the village. Alfred reined in. Small thatched houses and huts clustered along a track which rose again to the church. It was wooden, rather than stone, clearly built some time before and not well maintained. Moss grew on the roof and one of the walls had been roughly patched with planks.

A number of his own men were waiting alongside the track, glancing watchfully at the six or so men standing outside the church.

Alfred dismounted and a hand reached for his reins. He said, "Osric, shall we go and meet King Hywel?"

Osric nodded and signalled for a group of their warriors to follow at a short distance behind.

The men outside the church were led by a short, dark-haired man. His chin was shaved but he had a dark moustache. He was perhaps of a similar age to Alfred, standing with his feet apart and appraising the King of Wessex.

"King Alfred," he said.

"King Hywel. I hope you haven't been waiting long."

"Long enough to borrow some benches to put in the church." The accent was strong, the voice rising and falling, but his words were understandable. "Shall we talk in here?" he went on.

Hywel turned his back and walked towards the church, lifting the latch and letting himself in. His warriors stood back to allow Alfred space.

"Osric," Alfred said, "come in with me, would you?" To the scout who had spoken to them earlier, he said, "You've checked the church?"

"Yes, Lord King."

"Good. Then stay out here with our men and King Hywel's."

The man nodded, but gestured for his companions to stay alert.

Alfred paused, then walked past the Cornish warriors, aware of swords and knives hanging from belts, but none to hand. Osric was close on his heels.

The church was dark and cool. Hywel was seated on a bench, with another bench opposite him.

Alfred glanced around. There was nowhere in the church an ambush could have been set. The church was too small and bare for that.

It was Hywel who began as Alfred and Osric sat.

"You asked to meet, King Alfred."

"I did. We've not met before King Hywel."

"Saxons have never been very welcome in Cornwall. They tend to come in force rather than friendship."

"This is a meeting in friendship, I hope. You had my message promising safe passage?"

"I did. So what can I do for you, King Alfred?"

"We have Danes occupying Exeter."

"I know."

"What did their messages say to you?"

There was a pause.

"Their messages?"

"They sent you messages. Guthrum sent you messages. What did he say?"

"Why would I tell you what was in a private message?"

"Because I need to know whether you can be trusted not to interfere on the side of the Danes."

"There is not a great deal of trust between the Kingdom of Wessex and the Kingdom of Cornwall. Your warriors have ravaged my land, taken my land. This should be part of my Kingdom, not yours." Hywel gestured around at the church. "But now, when the Danes might do to Wessex what the Saxons did to Dumnonia, you want to be friends?"

"I want us to live as neighbours, Hywel. I could understand that friendship is too much to ask for."

"You are not asking for active support against the Danes?"

"No. Only that any request from the Danes to get involved should be rebuffed."

"And are you asking or are you telling me? Is this a hand of friendship, or is it really a warning?"

Alfred said nothing for a long moment.

"Can it be both?"

"No, Alfred, it can't. In which case, I will take this as a warning."

"Very well, that is your choice, not mine. A warning then, if Cornwall supports the Danes in any way - whether Guthrum in Exeter or Ubba on the north coast, my warriors will make Cornwall pay a heavy price."

Hywel stood. "We understand each other then."

"What did the message from Guthrum say?"

Hywel shook his head. "You have delivered your warning, Alfred. And I have your promise of safe passage. Goodbye, Alfred. Perhaps I should wish you good luck in fighting the Danes, but in all honesty, I can't. Cornwall has suffered too much from the Saxons."

"These are pagans, Hywel, and they would have no love at all for Cornwall if they are successful in Christian Wessex. I've prayed at Christian churches in Cornwall when I was younger, in your father's time. That could all end."

"Your version of Christianity has not stopped the Saxons from doing what they have done to Dumnonia and my people. No, Alfred, I will not interfere, but nor will I cheer you on. Now, my men are waiting for me."

Hywel turned on his heel and left.

***

A small party of horsemen had ridden out to meet them as they were approaching Exeter the following day.

The leader of the riders looked familiar from a distance.

"Ethelwulf, what's happening?" Alfred asked as they met up.

"No change within Exeter, Alfred. But Bishop Athelheah has arrived with Oscetel. And Elswith is here."

"Elswith?"

"Yes. She's upset. Well, angry. Thought you should know."

"Thank you. Where is she?"

"Round on the east side."

"Alright. I'd better go to Elswith first. And the Bishop and Oscetel?"

"Being kept out of reach of Wulfhere. He's raging. Wants Oscetel strung up. Garrulf, Odda and I have been keeping them at a distance. Not easy though."

They rode together around the outside of the walls until Ethelwulf led them off eastwards towards a hamlet of a few houses.

Elswith appeared from the door of one of them and Alfred swung down from his horse.

Walking quickly over to her he held out his arms to hug her, a smile on his face, which vanished as her chin went up and her eyes blazed at him.

"You let them take Oswald. You let them kill him."

Alfred opened his mouth to speak, to say it was the Danes who had killed his nephew, to defend himself. And then realised he couldn't.

Shoulders slumping, he closed his eyes and raised his face to the sky.

After a slow moment, his chin sunk down and he looked at Elswith.

"Yes," he said. "I did."

Elswith blinked and said nothing.

"I was wrong," Alfred went on. "And I am so sorry."

She stood back from him. "Odda is waiting for me. He has found somewhere for me to stay overnight. We can talk about this tomorrow."

"Yes, alright. Until the morning."

Elswith looked him in the eyes for a moment, then turned and walked away.

Oscetel had his hands tied behind his back, a rope leading back to Alfred's horse, where it was tied through the wooden arch at the front of the saddle and looped around the pommel.

"Walk on," Alfred called and, although the horse perked his ears up, the words were meant for the Dane walking on ahead.

Alfred's was not the only horse bearing a rider towards Exeter's walls. Ethelwulf, Osric and Radmer were all mail-coated and riding just behind him, along with Bishop Athelheah in his robes.

Across to one side were the Ealdormen of Devon, Dorset and Hampshire, well equipped, with swords and long-knives evident.

Many rows deep, warriors of all the western shires of Wessex were craning to watch.

Somewhere behind, accompanied by Wulfred, would be Elswith, while ahead of them on the town walls, the faces of Danish warriors were watching them.

Well short of the east gate, Alfred halted his horse. The rope tightened suddenly on Oscetel and jerked him backwards. Alfred felt a small surge of satisfaction at that. He hated this man.

"Guthrum!" he shouted.

From behind, he heard a wave of unrest amongst the warriors and the slow movement of horses as his three friends came close behind.

"Guthrum! Come out. Oscetel has a message for you."

There was the sound of wooden bars being lifted from behind the gate. Slowly, the gate opened. Just enough for a small group to step through.

Guthrum, clearly, was the first. Behind him came several warriors, each holding the end of a rope tied round the necks of women and boys. The warriors had knives already drawn.

There were two women, one with head held high, the other crying and holding on to one of the boys, probably no more than ten years old. Three other boys were of a similar age, all of them looking petrified with fear.

Guthrum walked towards Alfred, while the other Danes held their captives by the gate.

"Are we exchanging captives, Alfred?" he called from distance.

Alfred let him come closer, then said, "No, Guthrum. This is not an exchange. Not yet. I want you first to hear what Oscetel has to say."

Guthrum's eyes fell on Oscetel and took in the dishevelled man, his bruised face and the way he held one leg stiffly.

"Speak, Oscetel," Alfred said. "Tell King Guthrum what you have seen."

Guthrum made to move closer to Oscetel, but Alfred jerked the Dane backwards again.

"No closer, Guthrum."

Guthrum frowned but, from a distance away, called across to Oscetel in Danish.

Alfred felt a horse come alongside. "Radmer, can you hear?"

"Yes, Lord King."

Oscetel was answering Guthrum's questions now, short answers to begin with, but then a long reply, with Guthrum's face looking increasingly angry.

Beside him, Radmer was relaying what was being said.

"Oscetel is telling Guthrum about seeing the broken up

ships at the foot of the cliff. The vast amount of broken spars and planking, of sails and of bodies. That he doesn't know how any longships can have escaped the storm under those cliffs. Then Oscetel told him about the two survivors who had been brought up the cliffs. They had confirmed the fleet was blown onto the rocks and destroyed."

Finally there was two short sharp questions from Guthrum and two one word answers from Oscetel.

Radmer whispered, "Guthrum asked how many longships had got into Poole Bay and was told 'none'. Then he asked how many longships Oscetel believes had escaped. Again, 'none'."

Guthrum raised his eyes to look at Alfred.

"Now you understand, Guthrum. Your fleet was entirely destroyed. You are trapped at the far end of Wessex with no longships, with the weight of Wessex's warriors against you. More than that, I told you ours was a vengeful God, and now you know that to be true. You broke an oath to your god, Odin, and perhaps he smiles on that. But you also broke an oath before our Lord God, and he did not smile. He broke your fleet of longships. Tomorrow, Guthrum, be here tomorrow."

Alfred turned his horse and rode back through his friends, Oscetel scampering to keep up.

Alfred was woken in the deep darkness of night.

"Alfred. Alfred, wake up."

The tent door was being held open.

"Osric? What is it? The Danes?"

Alfred stood, remembering where he had put his weapons the evening before, his hand groping for them.

"No. Oscetel."

Alfred stopped his search.

"What do you mean, 'Oscetel'?

"He's dead."

"What?"

"Dead. Killed."

"Who by?"

"We don't know. We had Oscetel well back from the gate in case there was an attempt to rescue him. But a group of masked warriors broke through our guards. Oscetel's throat has been slit."

"From Exeter?"

"No."

Alfred sighed.

"No. No, of course not."

CHAPTER 20

It was mid-morning when Elswith arrived from the farmhouse that Odda had found for her to stay in overnight. Alfred was with the Council and had been telling them about the meeting with King Hywel.

Odda was saying, "Probably the best you would... Lady Elswith."

They were outside, well back from the walls of Exeter, but within sight of them. A thin sunshine broke through clouds overhead.

"Ealdorman," Elswith said. "Please go on."

"I was just saying to Alfred that an arrangement for the Cornish not to interfere is the best we could have hoped for. They were never going to be of active help, given our history."

"Alright," Alfred said. "Next. Oscetel."

There were murmurs amongst the Council and from a larger body of men around.

"Would someone like to tell me what happened?"

There was silence until finally Osric spoke. "We are no nearer to knowing who the men were who killed Oscetel."

Alfred looked at Wulfhere and his son across from him. "Wulfhere, anything to say?"

"Nothing, Alfred. Except that whoever did it has my thanks. It should have been done before."

"You know the reasons we wanted him alive, Wulfhere." The Ealdorman's son had a strange expression on his face, one Alfred could not interpret. "Wulfhard, anything to add?"

"No, Lord King."

"Very well. There's no denying that he deserved it. It's just for practical reasons I would have had him alive, and that was my instruction."

Wulfhere said, "You would have used him as a bargaining tool?"

"If need be."

"Then I'm even more glad he's dead."

"I do understand you wanting vengeance, Wulfhere."

"I'm not sure you do. Not really. And I think the Lady Elswith might agree with me."

There was a pause as his words sank in.

It was Elswith who spoke. "Ealdorman Wulfhere. There is nothing that I would not support King Alfred in. Nothing. And there should be nothing that you would not support him in. He is your King. Anointed by God as King of Wessex."

Bishop Athelheah, next to her, said, "Amen." Ripples of that ran around the men surrounding the Council.

But then there was silence.

After a time, Alfred said, "I think that brings that subject to a close. I proposed to meet with Guthrum and then come back to the Council. We will see what a night's thought about the fate of his fleet of longships has done.

"Thank you, Elswith. For supporting me in the Council."

They were in the farmhouse where she had been staying the night. It was small, cramped and dark. Alfred was sitting on a wooden bed covered with a rough woollen blanket.

213

Elswith was standing away from him, her face in deep shadow.

"Of course I supported you against Wulfhere He's a... well, we both know what he is. That doesn't stop me still being angry."

"With me?"

"Yes, with you. With the Council. With the Danes. With Guthrum."

"I made a mistake, I know. I said that yesterday."

"Yes, you did and Oswald was killed."

Alfred said nothing.

"And now you will be negotiating with Guthrum again?"

"Well, yes."

"If you even consider offering Helm as a hostage-"

"I said no to them having Helm last time-"

"Because he is your heir. Not because he is your brother's son and, like Oswald, he's a boy and I love him as if he was my son."

"Elswith, I'm so sorry. If I had known this might happen, I would never have agreed."

"Of course it might happen. They are pagans, following pagan gods. And you believed them."

"I had no choice."

"This time, Alfred, make sure there are other choices. I'm going back to our children."

"Are they...?"

"Alright? I suppose so, though with Oswald murdered, who knows?"

She cast another furious look at him.

"Elswith, please don't be angry with me. I know I'm not getting everything right. Perhaps not getting much right at all, I don't know. But... I need you to be on my side."

Elswith sighed loudly. She moved to sit on the bed by Alfred, light from a candle illuminating her eyes. "I know that. And yes, I am on your side."

Alfred made to speak, but Elswith went on, quieter now. "Am I angry? Yes, I still am. But, no, not really with you. It's

Guthrum. All the Danes. They are evil. I know you are doing everything you think you can."

He took her hand. "Sometimes it's not been good enough."

"No. Sometimes it's not. I do have faith though. Bishop Athelheah tells me that we all need faith in God and that He will not abandon us."

"Athelheah says the storm was God's work. Radmer says the Danes were stupid to sail in that weather. Perhaps we can believe both?"

"I know which I believe."

Alfred held out his arms to Elswith and, after a moment, she leaned into him, her arms around his body, his around her shoulders. Her head lay against his chest and he felt her tension ease.

"Give our children a hug from me. Tell them... I don't know what to tell them."

"I'll tell them you love them."

'Calm,' Alfred said to himself as he stalked towards Guthrum by the town gate. 'Be calm.'

It didn't work.

"Guthrum, why would I believe you didn't murder those hostages in cold blood? That's what everyone else believes."

Guthrum pursed his lips.

"I'm not sure I care what your people believe."

"You should. If you don't want you and your horses to starve in there, then you need a plan to satisfy us. To satisfy me. There are no longships coming. King Hywel is not coming. There's no sign of Ubba. He clearly has other shores to be raiding than these ones. You're trapped, Guthrum. Now I just need to decide what to do with you."

"Are you forgetting my hostages in Exeter? The townsfolk, those who were inside the gates when we closed them."

In truth, in that moment, Alfred had.

"So we feed you and in return you don't slaughter more innocents, is that it?"

"Yes, that's it."

"But what then? You are still trapped. Nobody is coming to relieve you."

"So you say."

"Yes, so I say. You have mile upon mile of Wessex to ride if you plan to escape and this time we would be ready for you. Before you reached safety, we would have hunted you down."

"Alfred, have food and horse feed here tomorrow morning, or the first of the bodies will be outside the gate."

Now it was Guthrum who turned away from Alfred and, walking back to the gate, didn't look back even as Alfred shouted, "Ours is a vengeful God, Guthrum. Don't forget that."

The following morning, with Alfred watching on, carts were wheeled to the south gate of Exeter. Grain, meat, cheese. Feed for the horses.

It was Huda who came out to oversee the carts being taken inside.

He saw Alfred watching and called across, "Not enough, Alfred. Make sure it's more tomorrow."

As the last of the carts was wheeled inside, Huda shouted again, "Or you know what will happen."

"How long are you prepared to do this?" Ethelwulf asked the following morning, as more carts arrived than the day before.

"If there is no sign of Ubba coming, then as long as it takes."

"As what takes?"

"For Guthrum to realise that he is trapped. That if he wants to go back to his 'Kingdom' of East Anglia, then he will have to do it on my terms."

"You will agree terms then?"

"Yes. But he'll have no hostages from us. And we will have hostages from him."

Odda came up to them. "What do you want me to do, Alfred?"

"Keep supplying the food and the feed. The payments will have to come largely from my funds, so speak to Forthred. Then, if it looks like we are going to be here some time, we should begin to rotate the men, some going home but ready at a moment's notice to meet at a fixed point somewhere east of here."

"So that we would catch them breaking out?"

"Yes, and let's make that more difficult."

"How?"

Ethelwulf said, "Thorn bushes. Brambles. Cut them down from elsewhere and bring them here. Make a ring around Exeter."

"Yes, and a ditch."

"That will take some time," Odda said. "It's a big area."

"If we keep feeding them, perhaps we will have time. Send your people out, Odda. Bring back anything that would stop the Danes' horses in their tracks, but keep it out of sight until we are ready."

"That's your plan, Alfred?" Wulfhere said. "Feed them and put up some puny thorn bushes."

"Do you have a better idea?"

The Council had gathered and had listened to Alfred's plan. In truth, Odda had already sent men out to gather what they could and sites had been found to store it until the time came.

"I've told you, starve them."

Odda's voice was as angry as Wulfhere's, "And I've told you that's not happening."

"Well, then, I've had enough. Eadred, with me."

The Ealdorman of Hampshire strode from the meeting, along with Wulfhard. The young Eadred shot Alfred an almost apologetic look and followed.

When they had gone, Alfred turned to Garrulf. "You have every right to be as furious as Wulfhere. What do you say?"

Garrulf frowned. "I am. But I am also more patient. We will have vengeance, I'm certain of that. But slow vengeance is still vengeance."

Two weeks later and the delivery of carts to the gate had become almost routine. At this delivery though, Guthrum himself appeared.

"King Alfred," he called across.

Alfred, with Osric and Ethelwulf close by, plus a number of warriors, began to move towards the Dane.

"Just you, Alfred. Just you and me."

Alfred said to his friends, "Wait here."

"Alfred-"

"I won't get too close, Osric."

He walked on. "King Guthrum. Isn't East Anglia seeming tempting now? Are you prepared to give up on this?"

"No, no, we're comfortable here, thank you, Alfred. Just waiting on developments."

"You mean waiting on your one hundred and twenty longships. I've told you, they're not coming. They're destroyed. Oscetel told you as well."

Guthrum frowned. "I think I should speak to Oscetel again. Perhaps exchange him for some of the worthies here. And some of the women and children."

"No."

"No?"

"Oscetel is dead."

Guthrum paused. "You took your vengeance then. You killed Oscetel, even though I told you I had nothing to do with the killing of your people."

"Someone on this side did. Not me."

"Convenient for you that I can't talk to him again and find out what he really saw in Dorset."

"Guthrum, it was my plan that he would tell you in detail what he saw. Your fleet destroyed. That's why I wanted him alive. However, some of my people clearly wanted revenge and even you can see why that is."

"Not good enough, Alfred. Not good enough." Guthrum turned to the warriors beginning to pull the carts towards the gate. "Get them inside. Come on. Get them in."

From the gate Guthrum shouted at Alfred, "There will be blood spilt over this."

Alfred, to himself, muttered, "Even more blood."

CHAPTER 21

Night was falling, a dark night with thick cloud. Men were waiting out of sight of the walls. Many had shovels. Others were finishing the preparation of the thorn and bramble barriers put together over the weeks since the Danes had taken Exeter.

"Do you think this would stop a determined break-out, Alfred?" Ethelwulf asked.

"Hard to say, but it can only make it harder. If we can get it in place before they try anything, that is."

"When do we start?"

"About now, I think. Odda, are your men ready?"

"Yes, Alfred."

"Let's do it then."

Odda whistled a long note. The whistle began to be echoed along on each side of them, disappearing into the night.

Then men were moving forwards, oaths and curses from those tripping or colliding or falling over shovels in the dark. Soon, beyond where Alfred stood, came the sounds of digging.

More oaths, and now others were bringing fences and rails covered in thorns and brambles, some with wooden stakes protruding. Anything that would slow down a rider.

Alfred stood by, occasionally asked by Ethelwulf or Odda what he thought of a particular piece of barrier.

The men worked through the night and into a slow dawn. By then, the barrier was only part constructed, but enough warriors were on show to prevent a sudden break-out, and during the day weaker sections were reinforced.

Later, as afternoon wore on, the warriors on duty were moved to the roads which had been left clear.

Finally, in the beginnings of evening, Odda said, "I think we're pretty much there. Was this how you envisaged it?"

Alfred nodded. "I think so. I'll ride around the outside, then we can have a Council before I next meet Guthrum. I think, though, he will have to admit that he is indeed trapped."

Wulfred was standing close to the gate. Warriors were watching him from high on the walls.

"King Guthrum," shouted Wulfred, looking up.

There was no response. The Danes just watched.

"King Guthrum. King Alfred wants to talk."

Again, there was no reply from the walls.

The gate remained firmly closed.

After several more attempts, Wulfred turned back from the gate and walked back to Alfred and his friends.

"Nothing," Wulfred said. "What do we do?"

Alfred thought a moment. "We carry on as we are," he said. "They'll be well able to see the ditch and the thorn fence. We keep on supplying food and feed to them - so long as they don't start leaving bodies outside the gate. Then we see if their will to stay there will break. They must realise at some point that no fleet of longships is coming."

Odda spoke. "Are we in this for the long haul, Alfred, do you think?"

"It could be. Work out a system, Odda. Enough warriors here on watch. The remainder back at home. Then switch them over."

"Yes, Alfred. Are we expecting a break-out?"

"We're ready for them if they do. Would they be mad enough to try? I don't know."

Garrulf spoke from behind them. "I hope so."

"This is impressive," Noth said.

It was three weeks later. Noth and Helm were back.

The ditch had been dug deeper. More thorn fencing was added every day, including movable sections for the roads at night.

"Any sign of them trying to break out?" Noth went on.

"None," Alfred said. "Now, tell me how you've got on."

"Just as you said, we raised warriors from your and my manors and farms."

"Did you get any resistance?"

"Not from our people."

"But from Eadwulf's?"

"He seems to have put word out that he wouldn't look kindly on those who answered my summons."

"Did it work?"

"Not really. It helped that Helm was with me, like you thought."

"Good." Alfred smiled at Helm, who looked pleased.

Alfred went on. "Eadred would have arrived back in Somerset while you were there?"

"He did. We didn't see him. He went to Eadwulf and it was after that we had word of them interfering in our raising men."

"So who is in control in Somerset now? Eadwulf or Eadred?"

"Hard to say. Eadwulf is said to be very ill, we knew that. Few people see him though."

"Alright, what happened next?"

"We took the warriors across to Devon's north coast, but to be honest, it didn't seem necessary in the end. Word from merchants arriving by sea is that Ubba is nowhere to be seen. Maybe back in Ireland even. So we stayed a while but in the end, I set up a chain of beacons to alert us of any change and sent most of the men back home."

"So Guthrum shouldn't get any support from Ubba. Good."

"What about Hywel and the Cornish?"

"Not from there either."

"He is trapped then. With all this." Noth waved his arm at the ditch and fence.

"Yes, he can't easily get out, we hope."

"Though we can't get in."

"Also true. For now, we have a stand-off."

"Negotiations?"

"Each day Wulfred goes down at the same time as the carts. He stands and waits. But nothing. They take the carts in and that's it."

Noth frowned.

"Does Guthrum have some other plan then?"

"I just wish I knew, Noth."

Garrulf said, "I need to send more of my men back to Dorset. For the harvest."

"When?"

"Soon."

Alfred and his Ealdormen, Garrulf, Odda and Ethelwulf, were together, a warm August sun on their backs.

"We all have the same issue," Ethelwulf said. "My warriors are getting restive. They know they need to be back home to deal with the harvest or there will be hunger this winter. The same must apply to your men, Odda?"

"It does."

"You're right," Alfred said. "The men from my manors have mostly had enough. We'll need to bring this to an end somehow."

"You need to get Guthrum out of there and negotiating,

Alfred," Ethelwulf said.

"I know. Alright, tomorrow morning, instead of Wulfred going down with the carts, let's try something different."

"What do you have in mind?"

"No carts. No food. No feed. Just me, a table and two stools."

Odda nodded. "That should make Guthrum think."

Alfred waited.

He sat on one of the two stools, a long stone's throw from the gate. Deliberately, he was not looking towards the gate or the walls.

On the low table in front of him stood a flagon and two cups. He took a sip of ale.

Well back from him stood his friends. Watching.

On the walls were ranks of Danes. Also watching.

Alfred took another sip.

He heard the clunk of the gate being unbarred and, from the corner of Alfred's eye, he saw a figure step through, the gate closing behind.

Still Alfred looked away, seeming more interested perhaps in the trees off to his left.

Steps approached.

Alfred said, without turning, "King Guthrum."

The figure sat.

"King Alfred."

Finally Alfred turned.

"Ale, Guthrum?"

"Thank you."

Alfred didn't move and Guthrum poured himself some ale.

"Time for you to go, Guthrum."

"Oh?"

"Yes, more than time."

"Why would that be?"

"You have no idea what is happening in the lands you

have conquered. Once you were 'King' of East Anglia, you had London and you had Ceolwulf of Mercia at your beck and call. Now," Alfred shook his head, "what, 'King' of Exeter? And with no means of escape."

Guthrum flushed but said nothing.

Alfred went on. "You have failed, Guthrum. Perhaps it's the first time for you and it has taken you too long to recognise it, but that is the position. You and that fleet of longships were going to destroy Wessex. But now you have nothing."

Silence between them.

"I can offer you a way out."

"I don't need a way out."

"No. You can stay there, as 'King' of Exeter." Alfred paused. "But not 'King' of anywhere else. And how many warriors will follow you after this?"

Guthrum frowned.

"Like I said," Alfred went on. "It's time to go."

After a long pause, Guthrum said, "Supposing we are ready to go, what will you give us?"

"My word, my oath, that you can walk out of Wessex unhindered."

"And?"

"And nothing. You have lost, Guthrum."

"You offer no payments?"

"None. And no hostages from us. You - or your men perhaps - are not to be trusted with hostages."

"And you are?"

"I am. Yes, I will have hostages of yours. You will have none of ours. You are in no position to argue, Guthrum."

"You said 'walk' out of here."

"I meant walk. You will take no horses with you. You and your men will walk north to Mercia on the Fosse Way, from Exeter all the way to the town of Bath. From there you may go where you will. On foot."

"Alfred, if you give me nothing, then my reputation will be gone."

"The only thing I am prepared to give you is your lives. And even that comes hard."

"I will need to consider. To discuss with my captains."

"Then be here tomorrow at the same time. And make sure your answer is 'yes'."

"Garrulf, this is the only way."

"So I get no vengeance for my daughter? The Danes walk out with no one to pay for what they did."

"I'm sorry. Assuming Guthrum appears with his captains as our hostages, I will give Guthrum my oath that he will not be attacked as they leave Wessex. I need you to say that you will abide by that."

"This is not right, Alfred."

"No, it's not, but it is the least worst way."

Garrulf said nothing.

"Will you abide by my oath as King of Wessex?"

Garrulf stared into Alfred's eyes.

"Yes," he said, turning to walk away.

Behind him stood Ethelwulf. He too looked unhappy.

"What is it, Ethelwulf?" Alfred asked quietly.

"I swore my own oath to you and I am an Ealdorman of Wessex now, despite my life in Mercia. But Alfred, I still have friends in Mercia. Where we are to deliver all these Danes."

"I know, Ethelwulf. Elswith has friends there as well. I'm going to send Wulfred and Helm to her to tell her what I'm doing. But what else can I do? We need to get the Danes out of Exeter before winter. When the snows come we won't be able to keep warriors in the fields surrounding the town. Even with the harvest, you've been telling me you need to send men home. Imagine the Danes camped inside the town with most of our warriors dispersed. They would raid and kill and destroy all around. We have to get them out of Wessex."

"Yes, yes, I know that."

"And Guthrum won't leave without an oath from me. So marching them to Mercia under the protection of my oath is surely the best option."

"But do you need to abide by an oath not to attack the Danes on the way? They're pagans. They happily broke oaths to us. As the Danes are marching north, they'd be at our mercy."

"You think I should break an oath before God? An anointed Christian King of Wessex."

"I... I don't know."

"I'm sorry, Ethelwulf. I really am. But a Christian King of Wessex can't do that and I don't know a better way to get Guthrum out of Wessex."

Ethelwulf's head dropped.

Alfred said, "Will you live with my decision?"

"My oath holds, as much as yours will."

"Good. Thank you. I needed to hear that first, but there is something else. I want you to send messages north to Mercia. Tell King Ceolwulf that Guthrum is on his way. Tell him that we will deliver a weary army to his border. A weakened army. Tell Ceolwulf that as soon as the Danes are beyond our border, my oath finishes. And that a Mercian army can then deal with Guthrum. If Ceolwulf's oath to Guthrum was made under duress, there should be nothing to stop him."

Ethelwulf finally smiled. "Yes. Yes, I see. We give Ceolwulf the opportunity to destroy the Danes. Of course."

"But for now, keep this to ourselves. Word must not get back to the Danes or everything is lost."

"You didn't tell Garrulf?"

"No. Not yet. If he tells one of his men and word gets out, and our warriors shout out mocking the Danes. So, no, not yet. What about Noth, Osric and Wulfred?"

"That's different."

Ethelwulf nodded. "Where shall we say to Ceolwulf that we will deposit the Danes?"

"Where the Fosse Way crosses into Mercia. Bath."

"Let's hope he takes up the challenge. King Ceolwulf is under oath to hand over the Kingdom of Mercia whenever Guthrum demands it. If he abides by his own oath, aren't we just creating a bigger problem north of Wessex?"

"I hope not."

"So we'll have hostages from them, Alfred?" Noth asked.

"We must."

Alfred was with Noth, Ethelwulf, Osric and Wulfred.

"And they'll have none from us?"

"Definitely not."

"But they're free to go, after everything they've done," Noth said. "Garrulf and Wulfhere won't like that."

Osric said, "None of us will like it, not even Guthrum and the Danes, but I think you have the only solution, Alfred. We can't leave them in Exeter over the harvest and winter."

Ethelwulf raised a hand and the others fell silent. "Alfred, I think you need to tell them what you just told me."

All eyes turned to him.

"I've asked Ethelwulf to send messages to Ceolwulf of Mercia to say that we plan to bring a weakened army of Danes across the border. And that my oath is then fulfilled, but he might choose to deal with his problem with the Danes."

Noth said, "Take battle to the Danes?"

"Exactly that."

"It would be good if he did, but I can't see it."

Alfred said, "He will never have a better opportunity to show that he is a real King of Mercia and not a puppet of the Danes."

"He would be breaking his oath."

"He would."

Osric said, "He's slimy. He wouldn't let that stop him. Though whether he is strong enough, that's another matter."

"Now, say nothing outside of this circle here. No word to anyone."

"Elswith?"

"Wulfred can tell Elswith. Wulfred?"

"Yes, Alfred."

"Go as soon as we are done here."

Wulfred nodded.

Osric said, "What about Garrulf and Odda?"

"Not yet."

"The thing is though, what if Garrulf or Wulfhere attack the Danes as they go?"

"I can't see Garrulf doing that if I specifically tell him I've given my oath that they would not be attacked."

"No, perhaps not, but the Danes would have to march through Somerset to get out of Wessex if they are not to go the long way around. And Eadwulf or Eadred in league with an angry Wulfhere? You can see there might be that danger."

"I'll need oaths from them that back up my own oath."

"Good luck with that."

"Or we get them underway quickly, before Wulfhere can react."

"That's a better idea."

"Alright. Let's try that."

Alfred approached the stools but, as he heard the bars of the gate moved, he turned back to Osric just behind him, his back to the gate and the stools.

"Tell me what's happening," he said quietly.

"It's Guthrum. He's walking towards the stools."

"Alright, let's keep talking a moment. Tell me when he is sitting down."

"He is now."

"Just a minute or so then," Alfred said.

"You're keeping him waiting on purpose?"

"He needs to understand who is in control here."

"Don't leave it too long then. He might just walk back inside."

Alfred smiled. "Probably long enough then." He turned to face the Dane.

Guthrum stared at him while Alfred walked slowly over.

"King Guthrum," he said.

"King Alfred."

"You accept the terms?"

Clearly unhappy, Guthrum said, "I accept the terms, but I have two conditions. First, I will need an oath from you as King of Wessex and sworn before your God that we can walk freely out of Wessex, with no attacks from you or any of the men of Wessex. That includes at the border or even over the border in Mercia. No deception. No tricks. Second, we must keep our weapons, in case any renegade warriors from Wessex should not abide by your oath. As you say they did when Oscetel was killed."

"Agreed. I also have a condition. I will have my choice of hostages from your army."

Guthrum nodded. "Agreed. But I also need hostages from you-"

"I told you. There will be no hostages from Wessex."

Guthrum frowned. "Then how do I know that I can trust you?"

"Because you have my oath."

Guthrum said nothing and Alfred went on, "You will go tomorrow. First light. But I will have the hostages today."

"Alright. I will send hostages out."

"Not just any of your men, Guthrum. When I've been riding around the walls, it has been clear which are the captains of yours at each gate. The hostages will be your most trusted men. I will have all of them. Two from each gate. Ten hostages."

"I can't-"

"You have no choice, Guthrum. Send them out before dusk today and, if there are any tricks, I and my men will recognise them. Also, if any of the people of Exeter are left with their throats cut, you know what will happen. The families and friends of the hostages will be wanting their own vengeance. Do we have an agreement?"

A pause.

"Yes."

Alfred turned on his stool, looking towards his captains and finding amongst them Bishop Athelheah.

"Bishop," he called. "If you would, please."

The Bishop walked purposely towards the two of them, a casket in his hands.

"The relics of St Aldhelm," Alfred said to Guthrum. "My oath for your hostages."

Shortly before dusk, the east gate was pushed open. A group of men came through.

Watching on from a distance, Alfred heard Noth counting out loud, then say, "Ten, plus Guthrum."

Alfred breathed a sigh of relief.

"Noth, Osric, Ethelwulf, with me please."

He led the way towards the gate.

Osric, behind him, was giving orders. "You, bring warriors this side. You, the other side. Knives and swords ready but not visible. I don't think we'll need them, but we can't trust these bastards."

Alfred walked on. Confident now.

This was his first victory as King, and with no battle. For that he had to thank the sinking of the fleet of Danish longships. God, fortune, fate, miscalculation, a combination of all those things.

"King Guthrum," he said.

"King Alfred."

CHAPTER 22

"I'm not happy with this, Alfred."

"I know, Garrulf."

The two of them, with all the warriors and captains of Wessex, were watching as the first of the Danes began to file out of the gate into early morning sunshine.

"Osric?" Alfred said.

"Ready, Alfred," Osric replied from his horse. "This way, men."

Osric led a troop of warriors, each of them mounted, towards the Danes, all of whom were on foot.

The Danes held spears and shields, swords in sheaths, bags on their backs. Some had heads held high, others angry or downcast and dejected.

When Osric reached them, he called out, "Follow us."

One man detached himself from the line of Danes and made his way towards Alfred.

Guthrum.

"Will you be following on, King Alfred?"

"Sometimes in front, Guthrum, sometimes behind. Don't worry, I will be keeping my oath. You should join your men."

Guthrum gave a searching look at Alfred, then walked

back to join the column winding its way out of the gate and heading along the road where the thorn barriers had been pulled aside.

From his horse, Osric was looking back at Alfred. He nodded then turned to watch the Danes.

"Noth," Alfred said, and his friend stepped towards him. "We had better let Eadwulf and Eadred know that the Danes will be marching through Somerset towards Bath, I think. Will you send one of our men with the news and say that we will be shepherding them out of Wessex?"

"What about Wulfhere?"

"Mm, we'd better let all the Ealdormen know, but perhaps those messengers will go more slowly, arriving once the Danes are out of reach?"

"Yes, Wulfhere would be very tempted to attack the column."

Ethelwulf spoke up. "My warriors will come as far as the border before I send them home, Alfred. That will mean Garrulf's and Odda's can stand down."

"Good. Your men and my own should be enough to stop the Danes doing any mischief."

"Or Eadwulf and Eadred."

They took the old Roman road eastwards. Osric led them, keeping the pace up, as he and Alfred had agreed.

By the time the sun was at its highest, some of the Danes were beginning to wilt and the line was being stretched out.

Alfred, riding off to the side of the column amongst a host of his men, called across to Osric, "Let's let them get their breath, Osric."

Slowly the Danes began bunching up, casting their weapons down and pulling bread and other food from their bags. They sat, eating, except for Guthrum, who walked over to Alfred.

"What is to happen about food, Alfred?"

"Your men have brought some out of Exeter? I hope

they've not left the townsfolk there starving."

"They have not brought enough to walk all the way to Mercia."

"Perhaps you should have thought of that before you set off for Exeter. It was no part of our agreement for us to feed your men."

"Hungry men make angry men, Alfred."

"Then perhaps your men would like to buy food along the way."

"Buy?"

"I suspect there is more than just food in the bags your men are carrying."

Guthrum said nothing.

"At Honiton," Alfred said, "gather silver, gold, relics and whatever else your men have stolen from Wessex and perhaps that will buy food along the way."

Guthrum said nothing, but turned and walked back towards his warriors.

Alfred found Odda at his side.

"What's the position with Exeter?" he asked.

"The Danes pretty much stripped the town of anything they can carry on their backs."

"I thought so. Did you hear what I said to Guthrum just now?"

"I did. Let's hope we can get back at least some of what's been stolen."

"We'll need all the horses they took into Exeter. For our men to shadow the Danes as they walk."

"I'll organise it."

"And the people of Exeter? How were they treated?"

"I have to admit I thought it would be worse. They are hungry, but it seems that by and large Guthrum kept his men under control. Not entirely, of course. But he hung two of his own men who stepped over the line."

"That surprises me."

"I think there is more to Guthrum than we have seen, Alfred."

"Let's hope so."

After Honiton, the road, such as it still was, rose into the hills. It became harder to keep his warriors off to the side of the Danes, so Alfred rode ahead with Osric, Noth and a small number of warriors, while Ethelwulf held the mass of men behind.

Even as they came out of the hills into the flatter country to the east of the Somerset marshes, Alfred kept that pattern. The Danes were causing no issues and were gradually being emptied of their treasures in return for food. The sun shone, with Alfred and his warriors riding almost at leisure as the Danes plodded along.

They were near Ilchester when a large party appeared on the road ahead of them. They were heavily armed, with helmets and mail-coats, spears clear even from a distance.

"Osric, halt the column and send a messenger back to Ethelwulf to bring warriors forward."

Alfred rode on with Noth by him, while Osric gave the orders.

As the warriors on the road drew closer, Alfred guessed who it was. He said quietly to Noth, "The Ealdorman of Somerset?"

"I think he's too unwell. Eadred, my guess."

Alfred reined in, glancing back to find the column of Danes had halted. Guthrum was at the front, watching, while Ethelwulf had yet to appear with his warriors.

"Well, if it is Eadred, shall we see what he wants?"

"I think we know what he wants."

"I mean now."

"Ah. Yes."

They waited while the horsemen approached, with Alfred recognising the young Eadred at the front, older men on either side of him.

"Eadred," Alfred called. "Your men are blocking the road there."

"Lord King," Eadred said, dismounting.

The young man walked towards Alfred, leaving his men behind him.

Alfred looked down at him. "I said, your men are blocking the road."

Eadred flushed. "I'm sorry, Lord King, but I am bringing a message from my cousin."

"I see. What is the Ealdorman's message?"

"He says..."

"Yes?"

Standing now close to Alfred's horse, Eadred spoke so that only Alfred and Noth could hear.

"He says he - he and the Ealdorman of Hampshire would have expected a Council before any decision on giving the Danes leave to go. That he, that they would have argued that the Danes be destroyed. That, well, they could still be destroyed. Now."

"I have given my oath as King of Wessex that they will be allowed to march out of our Kingdom."

"Yes, yes, I know. But the Ealdorman says that need not bind him or the Ealdorman of Hampshire. And that the Ealdorman of Hampshire will not be happy until he has avenged his son."

"I am your King. I am his King. It was my oath as King of Wessex."

"I'm sorry, but-"

"Are you, Eadred?"

Alfred heard mounted warriors arriving from behind.

Osric, now next to him, murmured, "Ethelwulf."

From the corner of his eye he saw Ethelwulf's warriors begin to circle around and then behind Eadred's warriors.

Eadred glanced left and right.

"Yes, yes, of course."

"I think it's time that I met with your cousin again, Eadred."

"Eadwulf is not well, Alfred. He is seeing no one."

"Apart from you?"

"Yes, of course, and his advisers."

"Well, I'm sure he will see me. Osric, will you continue the march north with the Danes? Eadred is going to take me to see Eadwulf. I think I will take Ethelwulf and Noth as well. Together with some of Ethelwulf's men."

"Alfred-" Eadred tried to interrupt.

Osric said, "That's King Alfred."

"Sorry, Lord King, I don't think you understand. Eadwulf is... Eadwulf is near death. He has been fading fast these last few days. Not eating or drinking."

"So the message you have given me?"

"May have been his last words to me."

"I see. And I'm sorry."

Alfred paused.

"Then we had better go right away."

CHAPTER 23

"It's been a long while since I was in Somerton," Alfred said to Noth as they rode up a hill leading towards the Ealdorman of Somerset's hall and the surrounding barns and smaller houses.

"You've not exactly been welcome here. Nor have I for that matter."

He glanced behind, where Eadred was riding with two of his companions. Behind them were Ethelwulf and a great column of the warriors of Wiltshire. Behind them again would be the Eadred's own warriors.

Alfred didn't try to keep his voice down. "I had forgotten that there's not much in Somerton apart from the hall."

"I suspect we won't be staying overnight."

Alfred smiled. "I don't suppose so."

He could make out a commotion at the door to the hall. There were guards in place, but more men were running to join them from the surrounding houses. Too few compared with Ethelwulf's men. There was no defensive wall apart from a low fence designed to keep animals from straying. If Alfred had wanted, he was thinking, he could certainly have taken the building by force.

"Eadred, ride on ahead and tell those men that we're not

here for a battle, just to speak to their Ealdorman."

Eadred and his two companions rode forwards, trying to reach the guards well before Alfred.

Noth went to follow, but Alfred said, "No, we'll let them be, I think."

He slowed his horse and turned to look back.

"Ethelwulf, would you bring, say, twenty of your men and join us? The rest can wait here."

"I'll spread them out so that Eadred's men don't find their way around us."

"Good. Thank you."

The small party rode forwards. There were now ten or so warriors by the door to the Ealdorman's hall, hands on sword hilts or holding spears.

Eadred could be seen closing the hall door behind him.

Slowly, Alfred approached.

The hall was a large one, thatched, with carved animal heads on the building's wooden frame. Smoke was easing out from high up at one end of the hall.

The warriors formed a line across the door, though no weapons had been drawn. They seemed unsure. Here, they must know, was the King and behind him a great number of Alfred's mounted warriors.

The door opened again, Eadred stepping through. The warriors made space for him and he walked towards Alfred.

"Lord King," he said. "The Ealdorman begs a short space of time to prepare and then he would welcome you into his hall."

"His words?"

"I-"

"No need to answer, Eadred. We will give your Ealdorman time to prepare. We'll wait here."

Alfred remained sitting astride his horse, Noth on his right, Ethelwulf on his left. Eadred retreated into the hall.

Time passed slowly, but Alfred waited, his horse less patient than him, shuffling under him.

Eadred reappeared, saying, "Lord King, the Ealdorman

is ready for you now."

Alfred dismounted, with Noth and Ethelwulf doing the same.

Ethelwulf turned to his men. "With us."

The warriors also now dismounted and formed up behind Alfred and his friends.

Alfred spoke. "Eadred, tell the guards to allow us through."

Eadred nodded at the guards, who moved either side of the door, still with hands to weapons.

"Good. Shall we?" Alfred said to Noth and Ethelwulf.

The hall was dark, with very little light making its way into the dim corners of the building. Only in the centre of the great space was there light from a large fire crackling in its stone surround, and from which smoke spread wide and billowed high into roof. There was a smell, more than the smoke. Unpleasant. Acrid.

All around the walls, standing by benches, were men and women in the half-light. Some with weapons, others clearly servants, all watching Alfred.

He waited, aware that his friends had followed him in, while in the doorway behind, Ethelwulf's warriors waited.

His eyes adjusting to the darkness, he could see that close to the fire there was a chair, high backed, with a figure in it, small by comparison. The flickering light from the flames fell across the man's face.

Eadred, in front of him, said, "Lord King?"

"Thank you, Eadred."

Alfred made his way across the beaten earth floor to the figure by the fire. The acrid smell was stronger here.

Where once Eadwulf, Ealdorman of Somerset, one of the great men of Wessex, had been a haughty, powerful figure, now he was shrunken. His face was thin and pinched and he was wrapped in cloaks and blankets that seemed to swallow him. He made no move to rise and, Alfred thought, perhaps he can't.

"Ealdorman Eadwulf," Alfred said, standing in front of the Ealdorman. "I am sorry to see you so unwell."

From the gloom on one side, servants appeared with chairs.

Alfred sat, his two friends on either side.

Eadwulf's voice was faint, as thin as his face. Alfred could only just hear him.

"Alfred," he said. "You find me-" He coughed, a wracking cough, spittle flying from his mouth. He sat back, breathing heavily.

A woman came to his side, wiping the Ealdorman's mouth with a cloth. He batted her away and she stood back.

Alfred waited.

"You find me more than just unwell." A pause, while he caught his breath. "I'm near death, Alfred. But-"

Another bout of coughing.

"But, I still have my wits."

"I don't doubt it, Eadwulf. And I'm sorry. You and I have never seen eye to eye, but this... This is not the way to end a life."

"No. No, it's not. But now, Alfred, will you listen to me?"

"Of course."

The fire spat beside them, sparks flying.

"You are wrong to allow Guthrum to escape."

"I had no choice. We needed them out of Exeter and we could not fight our way in."

"Of course you had a choice. As I understand it," a breath, a pause, "you still do. Fall on them, Alfred. Destroy them."

A sudden energy took hold of Eadwulf. He sat forward, his voice rasping.

"If you allow them to escape into Mercia, they will be back. You will regret not seizing this chance."

"I made an oath."

"Then break it!"

"I have sworn an oath to allow them to walk out of Wessex."

"Then let me break it for you. Or, at least, Eadred. Stand your men aside. Let Eadred lead the warriors of Somerset in destroying the danger you are leaving."

Alfred felt, rather than heard, Ethelwulf almost agreeing with Eadwulf.

Should he? Could he? Guthrum was almost at his mercy. What was his oath worth? More than the security that Eadwulf suggested.

His mind went to Bishop Athelheah and to the destroyed fleet after Guthrum had broken his oath before God. What would Athelheah say? Would he say that God would punish Alfred in the same way? And if God punished Alfred, as King of Wessex, would Wessex itself suffer?

The fire spat again and Alfred came to a decision.

"I will abide by the oath."

Eadwulf sat back. Somehow smaller again.

"Alright, Alfred. One more thing then. Somerset must be strong. Must not be weakened when I have gone. My cousin Eadred will inherit my own lands. My manors. My men. If he is also Ealdorman, he will unite the shire just as I do. You must make my cousin Ealdorman when I am gone."

Alfred waited, aware of all eyes on him, including those of the slight figure of Ealdorman Eadwulf in front of him.

He said, "Your cousin will be Ealdorman after your death."

Eadwulf made to sit forward again and speak, but more coughing started, wracking his thin body. The woman standing behind him moved in front of Eadwulf, holding his shoulders. More women gathered, the coughing going on and on.

Alfred stood. "Enough. Noth, Ethelwulf, we need to go."

He walked to the door and, looking back, saw Eadwulf being half carried towards the back of the hall and the curtain that would lead to his private rooms.

Standing by the fire, watching his cousin, Eadred was part lit by the flickering flames.

Ethelwulf laid a hand on Alfred's arm. "Time to go."

With a last look at the wretched scene of the Ealdorman, still coughing, being carried out of sight, Alfred said, "Yes, let's get back to Osric. And Guthrum."

"Was I right? Am I right?"

They were part way back to the main column heading north, Ethelwulf on one side of him, Noth on the other.

"About which?" Noth said.

"Allowing Guthrum to march his men out of Wessex without destroying them."

"They're gone from Exeter. They'll soon be gone from Wessex."

"But we've heard nothing back from Ceolwulf. If he doesn't attack them and the Danes just come back, what have we gained?"

"Time? And a dent to Guthrum's reputation that he might not recover from? Who will follow his lead now after a humiliation like this?"

Alfred nodded. "Ethelwulf? What do you think?"

Ethelwulf said nothing for a while, and the horses jogged along together.

"Ethelwulf? You don't agree."

"I'm sorry, Alfred, but I don't think you should have sworn that oath."

"It's done."

"I know."

"But now do you think I should break it? Or at least allow others to break it for me?"

"I would break it for you."

"It would still be the King of Wessex breaking an oath before God."

"Noth is right about Guthrum being humiliated, Alfred.

But won't that just spur him on to get revenge? And what about the people of Mercia, where we are shepherding them? What about them?"

"You think I've made a mistake?"

There were shouts from behind. Ethelwulf turned back to his men, one of whom came forwards. "Lords, there's a party of warriors behind us."

Alfred said, "Alright. Let's wait and see what this is."

They reined in and within a short time a group of riders came past Ethelwulf's men.

Noth said, "That's Eadred."

"So it is."

Coming to a halt in front of Alfred, Eadred dismounted. "Alfred. I..."

"What is it, Eadred?"

"It's Eadwulf. He's gone. Dead."

Alfred frowned. "I did wonder. I'm sorry, Eadred, but for Eadwulf, perhaps it is for the best."

"I know. It is. But Alfred-"

"Lord King," Ethelwulf said to him.

"Yes, sorry. Lord King, I need to know-"

"You need to know who is the next Ealdorman of Somerset."

"Eadwulf made me promise to follow you to make sure. Those were his last words to me."

"Then I will tell you. Eadred, I need a man as Ealdorman of Somerset who has battled alongside me, who I trust with my life."

Alfred glanced briefly at Noth, whose eyebrows were raised, but who then nodded.

Eadred flushed. "But you said to Eadwulf that you would appoint me."

"I said I would appoint his cousin. Noth is also Eadwulf's cousin, just as you are. Noth from now on is Ealdorman Ethelnoth of Somerset."

Eadred's mouth fell open.

This, though, was the moment. "Do you oppose me,

Eadred?"

"No. No, of course, but-"

"Then it's time that you took your own oath to me."

Alfred slid off his horse and stood in front of Eadred.

Noth and Ethelwulf also dismounted and stood either side of the young man.

Ethelwulf said, "It is customary to take your oath on one knee."

Eadred looked at each of them in turn, then got down slowly to one knee.

"I suggest," Ethelwulf said, "that you repeat my words. Take the King's hand in yours."

Eadred did so, clearly feeling hemmed in on three sides.

Then Ethelwulf intoned, each phrase copied by Eadred, though with occasional stumbles, his eyes on Alfred's, "Before the Lord God, I will be faithful and true to Alfred, King of Wessex. I will love all that he loves and shun all that he shuns, according to God's law and to the laws of Wessex. I will never, willingly or intentionally, by word or deed, work against Alfred of Wessex while I am in his service and at his command."

Alfred said, "Good. Now Eadred, I think you should deal with the funeral of Eadwulf, and tell your warriors that there is a new Ealdorman of Somerset."

Ethelwulf added, "And that you have sworn your oath to King Alfred of Wessex."

"Yes. Yes, I will."

Eadred stood.

"You may go, Eadred, but you will be called on again soon, either by me or by the Ealdorman of Somerset."

As the party from Somerton rode away, Ethelwulf said, "Will that oath hold him, do you think?"

"Time will tell, Ethelwulf."

"There is one man who has never sworn that oath, of course."

"I am well aware of that. The Ealdorman of Hampshire."

***

"How long have you been planning that, Alfred?"

"A very long time, Ethelwulf."

They had set off again, riding slowly eastwards towards the column of Danes.

"Did you know, Noth?"

"Yes. Alfred has been steadily giving me land in Somerset ever since he became King."

"I realised that, but not that you would be so... ruthless, Alfred." He smiled. "Well done. Anyway, I'm glad for you, Noth, but, Alfred, you know you'll have made more of an enemy in Eadred and his men. And he will inherit all the lands and manors that Eadwulf had already built up."

"It's a risk, I know, but I couldn't give him even more power than he already has."

Noth said, "You'll have broken the strength that the Ealdormen of Hampshire and Somerset had in the Council. That can only be a good thing."

"Yes, and now we'll need you to bring the shire of Somerset along with you, Noth."

"I already own a good deal of land in the south, as do you still, so we have a fair number of warriors that would follow us. The lands surrounding the marshes, in particular. The northern part of Somerset - from the Mendip Hills up towards Mercia - is much more difficult. Eadred and his side of the family own much of the land there and have the warriors to show for it."

Ethelwulf said, "What do you think Eadred will do then?"

"I hope he will just lick his wounds and come round to us."

"And in the meantime?"

"In the meantime, Noth, you should send out messengers with the news that Somerset has a new Ealdorman."

"I think," Ethelwulf said, "perhaps Noth should go

further than that and, as Ealdorman, call out some of Somerset's warriors to meet up with us as we march north. We will, after all, be marching into lands where Eadred has just inherited land and power. Eadred may not be prepared to just lick his wounds."

Alfred thought for a moment. "True enough," he said. "Noth, how quickly can you gather men from around here?"

"I could bring in a reasonable number fairly quickly, and the Danes march slowly. We could catch you up just using mounted warriors. You're still planning on following the Fosse Way?"

"As much as we can. It will take us over the Mercian border into Bath. That's where Guthrum will become King Ceolwulf's problem, not ours."

Ethelwulf shook his head, clearly still unhappy.

Noth said, "I'll plan to be back with you before you reach Bath."

"Good. Let's do that then. Speed, not overall numbers, is probably your priority."

"I'll try for both."

Alfred smiled. "Alright, take care."

CHAPTER 24

The column had marched over the Mendip Hills, still following what remained of the road the men of Rome had constructed. That road led them straight for the most part, but took little account of hills, with the way rising and falling constantly.

For Alfred and his men on their horses, only the steepest of the hills took their toll on their beasts. For the Danes carrying their own war gear and any remaining treasure or food, each hill must have appeared steeper than the last and progress was slow. Quarrels had broken out amongst them, particularly when it came to using treasure to bargain for food.

The column was now just five miles from Bath with the afternoon drawing to a close. Scouts had been sent out and there had been no sign of Eadred so far.

Guthrum had become increasingly testy in the past days. "Alfred," he called.

Alfred reined his horse to a halt and waited while the Dane approached, looking hungry and tired.

"King Guthrum."

"We need to break for the night. When would be in Mercia?"

Alfred considered. "It's five miles from here to Bath. Five quite hilly miles. We can camp here. I've sent men ahead to find what food can be bought. You have treasure still to bargain with?"

"Very little."

"Good. That was always part of my plan."

Guthrum stared at Alfred, then turned and stumped back to his men. "Huda," he called out, seeking out the Saxon interpreter who would do the bargaining on his men's behalf. There followed a stream of angry words that Alfred could not follow, but which made him smile.

The night was closing in when Osric brought two scouts towards Alfred and Ethelwulf.

"You have news?" Alfred asked.

"Yes, Lord King," the spokesman for the two said. "There are men camped across the road on Odd Down, the hill above Bath. Eadred and his men."

"Ah. How many?"

"Possibly one hundred."

"So we outnumber them quite easily."

"Yes," Osric answered. "However, not far from them, and still riding when our scout saw them, there's another larger group. I believe it's the Ealdorman of Hampshire."

Alfred glanced at Ethelwulf, whose face had registered shock.

"Any more information?"

"No, Alfred."

"Nothing from Noth?"

"Not so far."

Alfred paced and said, "Send out more scouts, behind and on either side as well as ahead. In the morning we'll pause here. We need Noth and more men."

Ethelwulf said, "Is this a rebellion? Are they planning on a battle?"

"Surely not. They may have as many or more men than

we have here, but not enough for a rebellion. Plus there are all the Danes here. They would surely not plan on an open rebellion and a battle with armed Danes on hand. So, not here and not now."

"Then what?"

"I imagine they want to persuade me to alter my opinion. To attack the Danes while they are at their weakest." He looked searchingly into Ethelwulf's face. "And is that still your view as well? To destroy the Danes before they can wreak more havoc in Mercia?"

"There is... there is merit in it."

"That would mean me breaking my oath. Who would ever trust my word again?"

"But in these circumstances..."

"In any circumstances, don't you think a King's oath must be binding?"

Ethelwulf frowned. "So be it. I've sworn my oath to you, and that is binding as well."

Alfred looked at enquiringly at Osric.

"You know you don't need to ask the question, Alfred."

Alfred's tent had been placed well away from the Danes, though surrounded by his own and Ethelwulf's men.

He had woken early after a restless night, with his stomach grumbling but no sign of pains.

As he ate bread and cheese for breakfast, Ethelwulf found him.

"Alfred," he said. "Noth is just arriving. He must have ridden through the night."

"Good. With many men?"

"A fair few. I'm not sure just yet. Also, he's not alone. Elswith, Wulfred and Helm are with him."

"Elswith?"

"Yes. I don't know why or how just yet. Bishop Athelheah is also with them."

Alfred nodded. "Where are they?"

"They'll be here shortly."

"The Danes?"

"No change."

"What about Eadred and Wulfhere?"

"They've joined their forces. Lying in our path."

"Noth!"

"I told you I'd catch up with you before Bath." He grinned. "And as you can see, I've brought company."

From behind Noth, Elswith stepped forwards. She looked tired, her travelling cloak dirty.

Alfred felt a rush of gratitude and stepped towards her. "My love," he said quietly, "how are you here? With Noth? And have you travelled through the night?"

"We were on our way to Exeter when Wulfred caught up with us on the road and we came north instead. We met up with Noth. I should say that we met up with the new Ealdorman Ethelnoth of Somerset. Anyway, it seemed safest to come together when he told us about Eadred. Though I have to admit, after riding through the night, I am very tired now."

Elswith smiled. Then, keeping her voice low, said, "Wulfred told us about your messages to Ceolwulf. Is he going to do it?"

"We still don't know. I have to admit I'm taking that as 'no'."

Elswith's face fell. "I hoped..."

Alfred took her hands. "So did I."

"But I understand now. That was a hope, but you had to get the Danes out of Wessex before winter. And you have."

"Nearly. But now I need to find out what's happening with Eadred and the Ealdorman of Hampshire. There's food-"

"Wulfhere? He's here?"

"Yes. He and Eadred and their warriors are blocking the way into Mercia."

"Oh."

"Look, you need food and some rest." Stepping away from Elswith, he called across, "Wulfred, would you take everyone to Osric's men and they can provide some breakfast? Helm, Bishop Athelheah, would you go with them? Then perhaps in an hour we should all meet and share what we know."

He found Elswith watching him. Then she nodded and walked after Wulfred.

They met in the open, some distance from the Danes' encampment.

Alfred stood amongst an arc of his friends. Noth and Ethelwulf, Osric and Wulfred, Helm and the Bishop of Sherborne. Elswith stood next to him.

Quietly, Alfred said to Osric, "Any sign of a Mercian army?"

"None."

Alfred nodded. By now, it was not unexpected. Louder, he said, "So, Osric, do we know any more about Eadred and Wulfhere's movements?"

"They appear well set up across the road. Mercian Bath is just down a long hill behind them on the far side of the river."

"Do we know how Wulfhere and his warriors got here so quickly?"

Wulfred answered. "Yes, Alfred. I understand my uncle was on his way to see the Ealdorman of Somerset - the previous Ealdorman, I mean."

"Why would he be doing that, I wonder?"

Osric answered, "For the same reason he is encamped with Eadred and blocking us and the Danes. He wants revenge for his son."

"Against the Danes?"

"At the least, Alfred, I would guess. I imagine he wants the combined strengths of Hampshire, Wiltshire and

Somerset, such as we have here - and your warriors, Alfred - to destroy the Danes before they reach the border."

"He knows they are only here and vulnerable because I gave my oath that they could march safely out of Wessex?"

"I imagine he knows that full well."

"Does anyone here agree with him?"

There was silence amongst his friends.

Only the Bishop spoke. "You made an oath before the Lord God, Alfred, and I need hardly remind you of what happened to the Danish fleet after Guthrum broke his oath before God. And there is more. If a man breaks an oath before God, then God will turn his face from him and he will be unable to reach Heaven but will find torment amongst the devils in Hell."

Alfred sighed. "That, Athelheah, is very hard to argue with. Very well, I think we should take our Danes northwards. We'll stop them well short of Eadred and Wulfhere and then I think a fuller Council is called for. Are we agreed?"

There were murmurs of assent, then Osric said, "I suggest that I and you lead our men at the front of the column, with the men of Wiltshire shadowing the Danes on one side and the men of Somerset the other."

"Yes, Osric. In fact, the closer the Danes are to the border, the more they may be inclined to break out, to escape. Where are the hostages?"

"At the rear, with a full guard of our men who have orders to kill rather than let any escape."

Alfred nodded. "Good, Osric. Even so, we need to watch for dangers both within and outside the column." He turned to Elswith. "I think you should-"

"If you think I'm leaving now, you need to think again."

"Alright, but, well, take care. Wulfred, take as many men as you need and look after Elswith."

***

So they began their ride northwards, Alfred and Osric leading the way, with Elswith, Helm, Bishop Athelheah and Wulfred amongst a large number of warriors just behind them.

The long column of marching Danes followed on, headed by Guthrum, while on each side of them rode the warriors of Wiltshire and Somerset, each led by Ethelwulf and Noth.

Well to the rear, amongst large numbers of Osric's men, trudged the Danish hostages.

There was little talk, no banter, just the tramping of feet and of hooves as they headed north.

They had crossed a small river, the Danes once more getting wet legs and feet. Now the road rose straight towards Odd Down, the ridge where Eadred and Wulfhere were placed and which looked down on Mercian Bath below.

"Let's leave the Danes here and ride forward with just our men, Alfred," Osric said.

"Agreed. And we'll take Noth and Ethelwulf, plus some of their men."

Alfred turned and found Elswith not far behind him. She rode forwards.

"Elswith, I-"

"If you are having a Council with Wulfhere and Eadred, I will be there, Alfred."

"Yes. Yes, alright. Wulfred, Helm, Bishop Athelheah, you too then."

They were a significant party that reached the ridge top. From there they could see the armed warriors who blocked the road that would fall steeply into Bath.

Alfred led the way, Osric and Noth on either side of him. He had asked Ethelwulf quietly to have his men guard Elswith closely and Ethelwulf was riding alongside his half-sister.

Two men rode towards them. Alfred raised his hand and everyone came to a standstill, waiting.

Wulfhere and Eadred approached slowly, Eadred a half horse's length behind.

It was Wulfhere, large and cumbersome on his horse, who spoke. "Alfred," he said. "We need to talk. Privately."

"No, Wulfhere. We'll talk openly or not at all. In fact, we will have a Council. Here and now. Call one of your men forward to take your horses."

Alfred dismounted, and all around him came the sounds of warriors doing the same.

Ealdorman Wulfhere turned and gestured behind him.

"Hey," he shouted. "Come and get our horses."

He heaved his body off the horse, landing heavily. Eadred followed, and a warrior came and took the reins, leading both horses back towards the Ealdorman's men.

Alfred said, "Good. Osric, send our men back a little."

He looked around.

As well as Osric, he had Noth as his new Ealdorman of Somerset, Ethelwulf as the Ealdorman of Wiltshire, the Bishop of Sherborne, plus Elswith, Wulfred and Helm.

"Wulfhere," he said. "Tell me why you are here? And why the Ealdorman of Hampshire is blocking our road into Bath."

"Alfred-"

"King Alfred," Osric said forcefully.

Wulfhere frowned. "King Alfred, you... we have the Danes trapped. Between us, we can destroy Guthrum and all the men who took Wareham and Exeter. We can have vengeance on the very men who killed my son. Who killed the Ealdorman of Dorset's daughter." He glanced at the Bishop. "Who killed the Abbot." And then his eyes fell on

Elswith. "And who killed Oswald."

Alfred felt Elswith's hand take his arm.

"The Danes are here because I gave my word that they would be safe on the road out of Wessex. My oath, Wulfhere. Before God."

Wulfhere opened his mouth to speak, but it was the Bishop who spoke next. "Ealdorman," he said, "we must not risk the wrath of God by breaking oaths. You know of His power from the destruction of an entire fleet of longships. We have sworn oaths before God to King Alfred and he has sworn an oath before God to this Guthrum."

There was a pause, as Alfred and no doubt his friends recalled that the Ealdorman had never yet sworn an oath to Alfred as his King.

Wulfhere went on, "Bishop, this is a matter for those on earth. A matter of vengeance and of the security of our land. You should also know that I have consulted the Bishop of Winchester. He is of the view that even an oath before God can be set aside in extreme circumstances. These are those circumstances."

"The Bishop of Winchester is wrong." He paused. "If that really is his opinion."

Wulfhere flushed. "I assure you that it is. The Bishop of Winchester and even the Archbishop and I see eye to eye on many things."

"So I have heard."

There was a silence. What did Wulfhere mean? Did the church now see Alfred's nephews as more legitimate than him to be King of Wessex?

"Enough," Alfred shouted. "Enough. I will not break my oath before God."

"Then just do not hinder me. Lend me some men and let Eadred and me lead them and our own men into dealing with the Danes. They are in no state to fight, Eadred tells me. We could end this with Guthrum dead."

"No."

"Alfred-"

"No."

There was a silence. No one spoke.

Then Wulfhere took a deep breath and said quietly, "A man who is fit to be a King must make hard choices. For the security of the Kingdom. And for vengeance for your people."

Alfred's friends shuffled their feet, but remained silent.

Wulfhere went on, one arm gesturing in the air, "From the very start I was doubtful that you had it in you to be King of Wessex."

Osric made to speak, but Alfred raised his hand to stop him.

"Go on, Wulfhere," he said evenly.

The Ealdorman raised his eyes and looked beyond Alfred to the warriors there. He seemed to come to a decision.

"So, I cannot change your mind. But I have warned you." He raised his voice and looked around Alfred's circle of friends. "I have warned all of you and I hold you all responsible. You will come to regret this. Eadred, come."

After a brief glance at Alfred, Eadred followed in his wake, Wulfhere stalking back towards his men.

When the Ealdorman was some distance off, Osric said, "I would like to deal with Wulfhere."

"That won't do, Osric. He is an Ealdorman of Wessex."

"Those words were more than disloyalty. That was a threat of rebellion."

"To what end though?" Noth said, his hand resting lightly on Helm's shoulder. "He can't surely think he could make himself King? And Helm here, well, what do you say, Helm?"

Helm's face flushed. "You know I am your man, Uncle Alfred. Not Wulfhere's."

Osric's voice dropped into the talk. "Yes, but Wold is a different matter."

Alfred said, "We need Hampshire."

Noth interrupted. "We need Hampshire's warriors. We

don't need Hampshire's Ealdorman."

"Perhaps not, but the Ealdormen of the eastern shires would not accept that one of their own could be removed. It would be a complete schism, west and east, and Wulfhere seemed to be saying that the Archbishop would side with him rather than me. It's just what the Danes would make the most of. Before we knew it, Wessex would be reduced to Wiltshire, Dorset, Devon and whatever part of Somerset we could keep hold of, given the role Eadred seems to be playing."

Wulfred spoke, "And part of Hampshire, I hope. Wulfhere is very strong in the east - from Winchester to the sea. But the west is different. They remember me there and don't much like Wulfhere."

"That may be, but we need to be united against the Danes."

Osric said, "What we heard is not unity."

"No, but nor is it a complete schism."

"Not yet."

The Danes had been brought up on to the ridge, Guthrum at the front.

"Guthrum," Alfred said. "Hold your men here."

"Why? I understood that Mercia lies just beyond this ridge. That is where we have been walking to, where our agreement ends."

Alfred hesitated. "Come with me, Guthrum."

He turned and his men parted for him as he walked through them. He glanced back. Guthrum had not moved.

"Guthrum, you are under my protection. Follow me."

The Dane slowly began to walk down the corridor of silent warriors towards Alfred.

Alfred restarted his walk, the Dane now just behind him. All eyes on either side followed them.

They reached the point where Alfred's men had stopped on the ridge. Beyond them Wulfhere and Eadred's warriors were waiting. By now they were at least not spread across the road, but had pulled back to either side.

"Who is that?" Guthrum asked.

"They are warriors of Wessex who do not want you to pass into Mercia. Your men murdered the son of the Ealdorman of Hampshire. The man you see there on the right is the Ealdorman of Hampshire."

"We are to walk through those men to arrive in Mercia."

"Yes. But I and my men will accompany you."

"To prevent your own warriors from attacking us? Your Kingdom is divided, Alfred."

"Not as much as you appear to think."

"Even so, we don't need your protection from the Ealdorman of Hampshire. We have our weapons still. We are veterans of battle after battle. And we have many more men than I see there ahead of us. If they attack us, we will fight them off without a problem."

"Do you think my warriors would stand aside if there were to be a battle here and now? Do you think I could stand aside?"

"I have your oath."

"That oath won't be tested if we accompany you past the Ealdorman and his warriors."

"Alfred, this is one humiliation too many. It will appear to my men that I believe we need your protection."

"I am not giving you a choice, Guthrum. Go back to your men and walk with them along this ridge. My men will be on either side as we walk past Ealdorman Wulfhere."

There was a look of anger and frustration from Guthrum.

"So be it."

The Dane marched back through Alfred's warriors, mostly silent still, but some muttering. Others clearly had hands on weapons and were perhaps more than happy for battle.

***

Alfred led the way.

The long line of Danes behind him was flanked by equally long lines of warriors, from Wiltshire on one side, from Somerset on the other.

Slowly they passed through the ranks of Eadred and Wulfhere's men. There was a remarkable silence apart from the sounds of the horses being walked along, but the tension was high.

As Alfred reached the far end, still a long column behind him, he found Wulfhere and Eadred waiting.

"Wulfhere," he said. "Come with us into Bath."

"No, Alfred. You are making a mistake. I will not be part of it."

"Then take your men back to Hampshire, Wulfhere. Eadred, what about you?"

"Lord King, I have to agree with the Ealdorman of Hampshire."

"Nevertheless, you have sworn an oath to me. Perhaps I should command you to come."

Eadred shuffled his feet and said nothing.

"Alright, Eadred. Go back to your manors. But I will call on you one day and I expect you to follow."

Eadred bowed his head.

Alfred began to ride onward, the road beginning to fall away ahead of him. The hills on the far side of the valley were now visible, though the town not yet. On the road, though, were more warriors.

"Wulfhere, are these your men?"

"No, Alfred. You may find we are not the only ones who wished you had made different choices. I think you will find those warriors are from King Ceolwulf of Mercia."

"Finally. Good."

"It's not an army, Alfred. I hope you didn't expect an army."

CHAPTER 25

"I am Beornoth," the Mercian warrior said to Alfred. The man sat tall in his saddle, helmeted with a mail-coat, a sword in its sheath at his belt. He was an older man, grey-bearded. "The King has ordered me to welcome you to Mercia and to lead you to him in Bath."

"You know that I have been bringing Guthrum and his men?"

"Yes, King Alfred, your messages did reach us."

"I don't see any Mercian army."

Beornoth looked away. "No."

"Then what?"

"King Ceolwulf would like you to accompany the Danes into Bath."

Ceolwulf had brought no army. There would be no ambush of the Danes.

Beornoth swung his horse around and now Alfred had a view down the hill to the town of Bath. Aquae Sulis, he remembered. From here he could see thatched roofs amongst stone walls. Perhaps that was a tower on the walls and a bridge across the river.

"Lead on, Beornoth."

The Roman road led steeply down into the town and

Alfred's horse slipped once or twice on cobble stones worn smooth from many feet and hooves.

As they arrived at the bottom of the hill, Alfred could see that the town walls of honey-coloured stone on the far side of the river were ramshackle, no longer complete as they would have been. Standing proud above them were ruined buildings and a few broken red-tiled roofs.

They rode over the bridge and to their right a stream ran down, mist hanging above it, a smell from it that Alfred could not recognise but that filled his nostrils.

The wall was broken where a gate would have stood and beyond it were more ruins, more of the beautiful stone and broken red tiles. Amongst them were houses and huts, thatched or wood-tiled. The road here was no longer cobbled but had become a stretch of mud littered with manure. It was a terrible contrast with what must have been.

Alfred stopped his horse, looking around. There was no one in sight and no smoke from fires nor smell of cooking.

Once, Alfred had copied carefully the words of a poet who had read to them in his hall. Aloud, he said, "These walls had been wondrous, until disaster broke them, the work of giants destroyed."

What else did the poem say? Something about a hot stream and a bath within a wall.

But here was the town, a broken memory of better times. Like Mercia.

"The people have fled," Beornoth said. "When rumour came of the Danes being brought here. The land all around is empty."

"Is there still a bath and hot water from the ground?"

"Hot water still comes from a spring, but, as you can see, where there had been baths, they are mostly collapsed. Bathing has not been a priority."

"I see."

"King Ceolwulf will see you in his hall," Beornoth said. "I suggest you hold the Danes on this side of the bridge."

Osric, by his side, wheeled and signalled a halt.

"Osric, Noth, Ethelwulf, Wulfred, come with me please."

Elswith rode forwards. "I need to see this Ceolwulf as well, Alfred."

"Of course."

King Ceolwulf looked a nervous man. He was standing with his back to a table within the hall. His hands fiddled in front of him and his eyes darted from face to face.

"King Ceolwulf," Alfred said, "We have brought Guthrum and his men."

"Where is he?"

"The column is waiting. Behind us."

"Can we... can we talk, Alfred? You and I."

"Ceolwulf, these are my friends. You can talk in front of them. Ealdorman Ethelnoth of Somerset-"

"Not Eadwulf?"

"Eadwulf is dead."

"Then Eadred?"

"Is not the new Ealdorman."

"Ah."

"This is Osric, captain of my warriors. Wulfred, nephew to the Ealdorman of Hampshire. Bishop Athelheah. My nephew, Helm." He paused. "You will remember my wife Elswith from her days in Mercia. And her brother Ethelwulf, my Ealdorman of Wiltshire."

Ceolwulf looked from one to the other. No doubt he knew just how close Elswith and Ethelwulf had been to Alfred's sister Edith and his brother-in-law King Burgred while they were growing up in Mercia. And those two had fled Mercia under pressure from Guthrum and had been replaced by Ceolwulf.

"Yes, yes, I remember them."

Alfred felt, rather than saw, the enmity of Ethelwulf and Elswith to this man who had pledged himself to Guthrum in exchange for the Kingship of Mercia.

"Let's talk then, Ceolwulf."

The King gestured to benches around the table, while he made for the chair at one end.

Alfred sat, Elswith next to him, his friends on either side.

Ceolwulf said, "These are two of my Ealdormen, Beornoth, you have met. And Ferth with young Ethelred."

Like Beornoth, Ferth was an older man, while Ethelred was a boy, perhaps twelve or thirteen. He seemed excited. Eyes shining as he and Alfred looked at each other.

"Ethelred," Alfred said to him. "My brother's name."

"Yes, Lord King," the boy replied.

Ceolwulf broke in, though speaking quietly. "Alfred, I'm not sure this has been wise, bringing Guthrum here."

"Why do you say that? I sent you a message. Several messages. You could have had a Mercian army ready to ambush them. I swore an oath not to and that bound my Ealdormen and my warriors, but it didn't bind you. So far as I can see, you are his man, Ceolwulf."

"I had no choice, Alfred. He has my family hostage. Somewhere in East Anglia. But if he had not come back from Wessex..."

"Then you would have remained King? At least until another Dane picked up where Guthrum had left off."

Ceolwulf frowned.

"And no choice? I think we all have choices, Ceolwulf. And this was mine. To get Guthrum and his warriors out of Wessex. After that it was your choice."

Ceolwulf chewed his lip, thinking. "Does he have his whole army here?"

"He does. I swore to him that they could walk out of Wessex and that is what he has done. My oath ends here. Your oath to Guthrum, you had let it be known, was made under duress. I have delivered footsore and hungry Danes to you. What do you propose to do?"

"Do?"

"I told you. You could have had an army waiting for them."

"What? No. There is no army."

Alfred glanced at Beornoth and Ferth. They were stony faced, while the boy Ethelred looked as though he would burst with frustration. Ferth put a hand on Ethelred's arm.

"Then..."

"Then I should meet Guthrum again."

"To see if you are still a King in Mercia?"

There was a sudden flare of anger. "If you had destroyed Guthrum, I would be."

"If you had brought an army, you would be." Alfred stood.

Elswith was staring at Ceolwulf. Alfred saw hatred there.

Alfred said, "Osric, with me."

Elswith said, "Where are you going?"

"To speak to Guthrum. And to bring him here."

Beornoth rose.

"No, Beornoth. You and everyone else can wait here. We will not be long."

Osric followed him out of the heavy oak door to where warriors were waiting with their horses.

"Alfred." Ethelwulf was behind him.

"Ethelwulf."

"The Danes will have free rein over Mercia if we release them here. Ceolwulf is their man. What about the people of Mercia?"

"Wessex is not strong enough to defend Mercia from the Danes, Ethelwulf. Not yet, at least. I'm sorry, Ethelwulf."

His friend frowned and Alfred took the reins of his horse, a warrior helping to lift him on.

Alfred said, "I will do my best. Though I know it won't be good enough."

"Where are my captains?" Guthrum said.

"The hostages are safe. They are with my men at the rear of the column."

Alfred had ridden the short distance back over the

bridge outside the town.

"I want them freed."

Still on his horse, Alfred said, "In due course, Guthrum."

"That was your oath, Alfred. They would be released when we had marched out of Wessex. We are now in Mercia."

There was anger in Guthrum's voice.

"And I will abide by that. Soon."

"We will not be humiliated, Alfred. I will not be humiliated."

"Guthrum, come with me."

"What? Where?"

"To see Ceolwulf."

"My captains-"

"Are safe. Follow me, Guthrum."

Alfred turned his horse. He glanced back and found Guthrum following, a look of fury on his face.

Alfred's horse made short work of the mud on the way to the hall.

Guthrum, meanwhile was failing to find a dry-shod route. Mud was plastering up his leggings and trousers. His boots were caked. At one point he nearly slipped and fell.

Alfred dismounted by the door, with Guthrum some way behind.

"Alfred," Guthrum said. "You will regret this."

"Guthrum, if you come into Wessex uninvited again, if you invade my Kingdom, you will receive more than a humiliation."

"We will see, Alfred. We will see."

There were raised voices from inside the hall.

Ethelwulf and Ceolwulf.

No great surprise, Alfred thought as he pulled the door open and stepped through.

Standing in front of his chair, hand raised and pointing, Ceolwulf was shouting. "This is my Kingdom, Ealdorman.

You are in my Kingdom of Mercia. If you don't like it, you can get yourself back to your new home in Wessex."

"Ceolwulf-"

"King Ceolwulf."

"King by the actions of Guthrum and the-"

Ethelwulf stopped. He had seen Alfred. Taking a deep breath, he sat down on the bench.

Alfred said levelly, "And here is Guthrum for you, Ceolwulf."

Now there was silence around the table.

Guthrum stepped to one side of Alfred, saying nothing, looking around the table until his eyes fell on Ceolwulf.

The Mercian King seemed to shrink into himself.

"So," Guthrum said, "King Ceolwulf, I have returned. And I am here with my men to establish that the oath you swore to me still holds. If it does, then you and I can come to a suitable arrangement. One that favours us both. Two Kings in Mercia. And perhaps your family can be returned. If the oath does not hold..."

"It does." This had come out in a rush. "It does, King Guthrum."

"Good. Then, Alfred, it is time to release my men under your oath and for you to leave."

"What will you do, Guthrum? When will you leave for East Anglia?"

Guthrum thought for a moment. "I will send some of my captains back to East Anglia on my behalf. But I... I will find some suitable place to stay in Mercia. I imagine that King Ceolwulf can make my men's stay comfortable. They are hungry, Ceolwulf. And tired."

"There is no food here," Ceolwulf said. "The townsfolk have fled. They've taken their supplies and animals."

Guthrum bit back. "Then we will go somewhere with food, which you will supply. I think, Ceolwulf, we will even over-winter in Mercia. Alfred, my men? It's time they were released. The warriors and my captains you have held as hostages. You swore an oath before your God. The God you say destroyed an entire fleet of longships when I broke an oath. So release my men or I will think that your God is not who you say he is."

Alfred felt the rising anger of his friends. He turned to them.

"Come outside," he said.

For a moment, none of them moved. Elswith, standing by her brother and normally so calm, had rarely looked as angry.

He made for the door, aware of movement behind him.

Outside, a planked walkway led away from the hall. He followed it, watching his step.

"Let's get out of earshot," he said.

The walkway turned a corner and he found himself in a larger open area with drier ground surrounded by thatched wooden houses, doors shut, windows shuttered.

"This will do."

He waited while Elswith, Ethelwulf, Noth, Osric and Wulfred formed a small group by him.

"Ethelwulf, speak first."

Ethelwulf was silent a moment. "I don't know what to say, Alfred. I want this man crushed, and all the Danes."

"We all do, but how?"

"I don't know. I suppose there is no choice now. Ceolwulf has not done it for us. So I suppose we have to leave it at that."

Alfred said, "Osric?"

"The Danes are out of Wessex while Mercia is in no different a position to what it was before. This is a victory, Alfred. Believe that."

Wulfred spoke. "It is, Alfred. It is."

"Noth?"

Noth frowned. "I'm with Osric and Wulfred. We've done what we needed to. You've done what you needed to. You've won. Release the Danes. And let's go home."

"Elswith?"

She was silent.

"Elswith?" he repeated.

She turned away, but then faced Alfred again.

"I will never forgive them. Never forget what they did. To Oswald. To the others. I wanted justice, Alfred. Vengeance, if you like." Her eyes dropped. "But you've given us what Osric calls a 'victory'. And I know I have to be able to accept that." She looked into his eyes again. "Yes, take me home, Alfred."

CHAPTER 26

Winter and summer had passed. A new winter was on them.

Midwinter's day - Yule - was gone. It had been the solstice, a feast day every year since first the Angles and the Saxons had come to this land, and even before that.

They had celebrated Christmas Day itself in Chippenham's stone church with prayer led by Bishop Athelheah, with fasting and then with gifts to servants and to those who worked in Alfred's fields.

But now it was twelve days since Yule. There would be prayers for Twelfth Night in the church and afterwards a feast. There would be singing and dance and poetry. There would be ale and mead and food. So much food.

Alfred lay in his bed, Elswith tucked into him on one side, little Gifu on the other.

There was something to celebrate. Not just the end of the quiet fasting period of Christmas, but looking forward to another winter ending. A second winter ending with no Danes inside Wessex.

Early dawn light was finding its way through the rafters in their room off the great hall. He could just make out Ethelflaed in her small bed, breathing deeply. How could she be nearly nine years old? And Edward would be six. Where had the years gone?

"Edward, stop it." Elswith had turned her eyes on Edward. They were sitting at the table eating breakfast and Edward had flicked a piece of bread at his older sister. "Ethelflaed, don't-"

Too late, she had retaliated, with a piece of crust hitting Edward in face. Edward looked shocked, then raised a fist with another piece ready to fly.

Alfred laid a hand on his son's arm. "Edward, it's time you realised that Ethelflaed is bigger than you, stronger than you and, really, not someone to throw bread at."

Elswith said, "Stop it, both of you. You're embarrassing yourselves in front of guests."

Edward said, "Uncle Ethelwulf's not a guest. I think he's an uncle and he's family."

"And Noth?"

"He's almost family. And Helm definitely is."

Ethelwulf and Noth were grinning at each other. Helm, no longer a boy, smiled to himself and went on eating.

Noth said, "So you can embarrass yourself in front of family, can you?"

Ethelflaed leaned across her brother and said to Noth, "He's just embarrassed that a girl can beat him at anything."

Edward grabbed at his sister but Alfred was too quick for him, spinning him off the bench and away.

"Enough," he said. "Edward, calm down. Save your energy for the feast."

Edward was off and running. "Bet I can beat you to the river, Ethelflaed."

She slipped from her place at the table. As Edward ran through the doorway out into the frosty air, Ethelflaed was not far behind.

Their shouting at each other began to fade.

Elswith said, "I'm sorry."

271

"For what?" Noth said. "That was great fun."

"Where's Osric, Alfred?" Ethelwulf asked.

"He'll be patrolling with the warriors."

Elswith said, "He's been twitchy these last few days."

"He doesn't like us being so close to Mercia. To Guthrum. I have to admit I'll be happier when we've gone south and we can leave Osric and Cuthred to watch the border."

"It's our last day, Alfred. Our last night here. Our home, it feels like. Enjoy it."

"I will. I enjoyed Yule and Christmas. It's a shame Athelheah has gone, but I suppose Twelfth Night is not for him."

"Why do you think the Archbishop didn't come?"

"I don't know. His reply was a little vague."

"Nor the Bishop of Winchester."

"Yes, it's a little worrying, I must admit. He's too close to Ealdorman Wulfhere for my liking."

She looked beyond Alfred. "That's Bennath looking for me. I'd better see what she wants."

Alfred watched Elswith go to the door, where Bennath waited, and followed her out.

Beside him, Helm asked, "Do we know if Guthrum is still in Cirencester?"

"So far as we know. No change at all. He holds one part of Mercia still, plus East Anglia. Ceolwulf has his part of Mercia on sufferance. Meanwhile the Danes have been settling. Farming, would you believe."

"Is that why we're safe?"

"Safe, Helm? Well, I don't know. We wouldn't be here except that Elswith..."

He trailed off as Elswith reappeared chatting in the doorway with Bennath. The Cornishwoman was holding Gifu at her shoulder.

Alfred heard a quiet murmur from Ethelwulf to Noth. "I know Osric would rather there wasn't a Cornish servant with access to all our plans."

There was an equally quiet reply. "Alfred trusts her."
"At least we're going tomorrow."
"Good."

That night, Chippenham's great hall was more crowded than Alfred had seen it in many a year. A great fire in the centre was roaring and spitting with new wood piled on, iron pots suspended above with more of the night's meal cooking.

The crush of men, women and children celebrating Twelfth Night just added to the heat.

Alfred looked on as pockets of his people danced or joined in with a poet reciting tales from their past, or just drank and ate.

Children ran, chasing each other, screeching and shouting. Dogs scouted for some of the fallen food from tables that were filled with happy faces. The fasting of the last twelve days was over and this was a proper feast.

His friends and family were squeezed into the top table - Elswith, Helm and the children on one side, with Gifu perched on Bennath's lap. The children were squealing and giggling with each other, Helm the object of their games, Elswith trying to defend him.

On the other side were Noth, Ethelwulf, Wulfred and Osric. Noth and Ethelwulf were loud, having been enjoying some serious drinking. Beyond them Wulfred and Osric were quieter. Talking seriously of something.

Alfred stood and stepped back from his chair.

"Elswith," he said, laying a hand on her shoulder and raising his voice so that she could hear above the din. "Just going for air."

She nodded and turned back to help Helm out with her children.

Alfred threaded his way amongst men and women in high spirits, the mead and ale flowing well. He was feeling distinctly sober amongst them, having drunk far less so as not to start his stomach pains off.

He pushed open the heavy door and stepped through, closing it behind him. Cold air enveloped him, his breath steaming in front of him, and he shivered. Why had he not brought a cloak?

Out here the sounds of feasting were muffled.

The night was dark. There were stars above but no moon.

He stepped away from the doorway, finding the frozen path to the gate with his feet. He looked around. No one was in sight. Everyone would be in the feast apart from the handful of warriors at the town gates.

There was silence, broken momentarily by a roar from within the hall, which fell away into laughter.

Yet here they were, so close to the border with Mercia. So close to Guthrum and the Danes. One more day and they would be gone.

The door to the hall opened behind him, light and noise spilling out. The distinctive silhouette of Noth stood there.

"What are you doing outside? Come on, it's Twelfth Night."

Noth set off towards him, grabbed an arm and swung him back towards the door.

Alfred found himself propelled inside, and the music, singing and dancing drove away any thoughts of where they were.

Then Ethelflaed was there, his daughter pulling him towards where the singer with his lyre was playing.

He smiled, his concerns gone, and looked across to see Elswith grinning. Next to her, Edward was standing on the bench, arms up and shouting something at him. And there was Bennath, wearing a cloak, heading into the dim recesses behind with Gifu. A cloak. Why-

"Dance with me!" an excited Ethelflaed said.

He looked down. Her arms were reaching out to him.

"Dance with you?" he said to her. He took her hands and began to spin his daughter around him. "Dance with you!"

Those closest shouted and called out, making space as the two of them whirled around, faster and faster.

He finally slowed down as dizziness took hold.

But then young Edward was there.

"Now me!"

He took his son's hands and felt Ethelflaed clasping his leg as well. Grinning, he spun them both. All around, his people were cheering them on. Again and again the three of them spun and laughed and shouted.

He brought his children to a halt, half falling, to find Elswith and Noth by him, holding him up, all of them laughing.

He felt just so happy at the moment. At their home in Chippenham, celebrating Twelfth Night.

No thought, for that moment, of Guthrum and the Danes so very close by.

HISTORICAL NOTES

This book, like Book One, is a novel, rather than a history. It is an 'imagining' of the continuing story of one of the great leaders of history.

Again I have used the work of historians and archaeologists as the basis of the novel, but there are enormous gaps in our knowledge of the period. Most of what we do know comes from the 'Anglo-Saxon Chronicle' and Bishop Asser's 'Life' of Alfred. Both were probably written at the behest of, or at least with the knowledge of, Alfred himself and are very much open to interpretation in different ways by historians.

Where that is the case, I have tended for the main events to use the work of Richard Abels (Professor Emeritus of History at the US Naval Academy, a specialist in Anglo-Saxon history and author of 'Alfred the Great'). For example, some historians write that a Danish fleet actually landed at Wareham, while Richard Abels believes they did not and that is the structure of this novel.

Where there is no reliable historical detail I have had to use research and story-telling to recreate what might have happened. There is, for instance, no record of what happened to Oswald, Oscetel and Anwend. They simply are no longer mentioned in the sources and so where there is no evidence at all, a novelist's imaginings come into play.

I also had the choice of using names of the period or modern equivalents to aid readability. I chose the latter, eg Alfred for Aelfred, Elswith for Ealhswith and Winifred for Wulfthryth. I have occasionally used nicknames rather than full names, given that many of the names of those involved were either identical or so similar that a novel would be very hard to follow, such as Noth for Ethelnoth, Helm for Ethelhelm and Wold for Ethelwold. For place names I have used the modern equivalent, such as Chippenham for Cippanhamme and Southampton for the nearby Hamwic. There is also a complication over dates because the start of a year was not fixed at January at this point. I have taken the years to be those that seem most likely.

As regards the individuals in the novel and their characters I have viewed Asser's 'Life' of Alfred as likely to have been largely correct, but exaggerating Alfred's character and role. That is how I have written Alfred.

Most of the other characters in the novel were real people and here I am indebted to David Sturdy's book, also 'Alfred the Great'. David Sturdy was the Archivist at University College, Oxford amongst many roles as a historian. He examined in detail the charters of the period and recreated brief life stories and family relationships of the main figures in the novel. These include Ethelnoth, Oswald, Osric and Wulfred. His detailed studies also allowed him to name Wulfhere as Ealdorman of Hampshire and not Ealdorman of Wiltshire which other historians have said.

On all these points I ask for leniency from historians. If there are mistakes and misinterpretations on my part, blame me and not the historians and archaeologists.

The men and women of this period were only different to us as a result of the society they lived in. They would have suffered or benefited from the same traits to be found in our times: loyalty and treachery, friendship and enmity, trust and jealousy, good and bad judgement, and many more.

There was certainly intrigue, which one historian, Justin Pollard (author of another 'Alfred the Great'), sees as an attempted coup.

All of the above references, and many more, can be found in my bibliography online at https://mikecarden.co.uk/alfred-of-wessex-bibliography/.

Finally, I believe that ambition, dissatisfaction and family ties are most likely to have caused the intrigue around Alfred and his family even in the face of invasion. I have therefore woven these themes together as the background to the novel.

But it is still a novel. An imagining. And I hope you enjoy it.

THE MAIN CHARACTERS

ALFRED AND HIS FAMILY
Alfred: King of Wessex
Elswith: Alfred's wife
Ethelflaed, Edward and Gifu (Ethelgifu): their children
Oswald: Alfred's nephew, illegitimate son of Alfred's brother
Winifred: Alfred's sister-in-law, sister of the Ealdorman of Hampshire
Helm: nickname for Ethelhelm, Alfred's nephew, older son of Winifred
Wold: nickname for Ethelwold, Alfred's nephew, younger son of Winifred

ALFRED'S INNER CIRCLE
Noth: nickname for Ethelnoth, related to the Ealdorman of Somerset, and married to Ealhburh
Ethelwulf: Elswith's half-brother, Ealdorman of Wiltshire, and married to Leofe
Osric: Alfred's cousin, captain of the King's warriors, and married to Mildthryth
Wulfred: nephew of the Ealdorman of Hampshire and married to Hild

Cuthred: a captain of Alfred's household warriors
Forthred: Alfred's secretary
Radmer: a Frisian in charge of Wessex's longships
Bennath: nurse to Alfred and Elswith's children

THE EALDORMEN OF WESSEX
The Ealdorman of Wiltshire: see Ethelwulf above
The Ealdorman of Devon: Odda
The Ealdorman of Dorset: Garrulf, with his daughter Gunhild
The Ealdorman of Somerset: Eadwulf, with his cousin Eadred
The Ealdorman of Hampshire: Wulfhere, with his sons Wulfstan and Wulfhard

THE BISHOPS
The Archbishop of Canterbury: Eahlstan
The Bishop of Sherborne: Athelheah

THE DANES
Guthrum: 'King' of East Anglia
Fellow Kings Oscetel and Anwend
Huda: Anglo-Saxon interpreter
Halfdan: 'King' of Northumbria
Ubba: Halfdan's brother

MERCIA
Ceolwulf, King of Mercia
Beornoth, Ealdorman
Ferth, Ealdorman
Ethelred

CORNWALL
Hywel, King of Cornwall

THANK YOU

I hope you have enjoyed reading
Alfred of Wessex. Book Two: Vengeance.

The story will continue in the third book of the
Alfred of Wessex series.

'Alfred' has been a long time in the writing. If you would
like to know more about the history, the research or the
writing of the book, please go to my website at:
https://mikecarden.co.uk/alfred-of-wessex/.

You can also find me on Facebook at:
https://www.facebook.com/Mike-Carden-
113936563786042.

On the website, on Facebook and Amazon you will find
my other books - quirky cycling tours of England, of
Scotland and of the Lake District. I hope you enjoy them
as well!

Finally, if you would be able to review 'Alfred' on either
Amazon or Goodreads, I would appreciate it very much.
Thank you.

Best wishes

Michael Carden

Meantime, Book Three is in progress.

Also by the Author

The Full English

Pedalling through England, Mid-Life Crisis and Truly Rampant Man-Flu

Covering 650 miles of England and twelve counties, the author struggles heroically with Mid-life Crisis, Man-Flu and also with Scott, a bike with a serious attitude problem. Cycling from the Dorset coast to Northumbria via Glastonbury, Ludlow, the Peak District, and the Yorkshire Dales, he indulges his passion for the history of England through its castles, abbeys and ancient towns.

'Mike's relaxed and chatty style is never less than entertaining, making The Full English the sort of book that can put a smile on your face even when it is cold, grey Winter outside.' *Dorset County Magazine*

'An easily read book, humorous, well written and full of the eccentricities of the English.' *Arrivée Magazine*

An 'articulate and witty account of one fortysomething man's quest to ride from one end of England to the other…' *London Cyclist magazine*

'Warm, well observed, unpretentious and very funny, this is the kind of cycle tour we can all imagine ourselves taking, though hopefully without the Man-flu.' *Adventure Travel Magazine*

A Bit Scott-ish

Pedalling through Scotland in search of Adventure, Nature and Lemon Drizzle Cake

A Bit Scott-ish is the tale of a journey through Scotland, meeting locals and fellow travellers, delving into Scotland's tumultuous history, surviving storm and wind, and discovering how hopeless it is possible to be at Nature. And at finding the way.

"This is an easy to read, charming and very funny book taking in some of the most breath-taking sights of Scotland." *The Local History Magazine*

A Lake District Grand Tour

Pedalling through Lakeland: The Challenge, The History, The Wildlife, The Scones

In 'A Lake District Grand Tour', Mike visits all the lakes of Lakeland, pokes into its most distant corners, and cycles over every mountain pass (well, he attempts to).
Along the way he tells the story of Lakeland. He sees where poets wrote and climbers climbed, he tells of 'oond trailin' and fell-racing, and he hunts for golden eagles and elusive ring ouzels.

'For the armchair adventurer, cycling the Lakes with Mike is an enlightening experience.' *The North West Evening Mail*

Printed in Great Britain
by Amazon

37590886R00162